THE PRIMARY TARGET

The Primary Target

Published by The Conrad Press Limited in the United Kingdom 2022

Tel: +44(0)1227 472 874
www.theconradpress.com
info@theconradpress.com

ISBN 978-1-911546-90-0

Typesetting and Cover Design by: Charlotte Mouncey, www.bookstyle.co.uk

The Conrad Press logo was designed by Maria Priestley.

Printed and bound in Great Britain by Clays Ltd, Elcograf S.p.A.

THE PRIMARY TARGET

JOSHUA DENYER

This is dedicated to you, Mum,
for everything you've done

1

The man parked his Ford Mondeo in the furthest space away from the entrance, in the open car park. He always occupied the same space. It had become a routine and he took comfort in knowing that he could always exit the car park without needing to queue. He sat in his seat for a minute, leaning forward, his wrists gently resting on the worn steering wheel.

He was wearing brown leather gloves, which slightly muted the noise of him drumming his fingers on the dashboard. He stared forward at a bush, not blinking. He knew he had been awake around thirty-six hours. He didn't sleep much anymore. He would lie in the darkness listening to the sounds of the outside world throughout the night. His mind wouldn't shut off. It was whirling, more than ever in the past few days.

He left his engine idling, the emerging exhaust fumes visible from his wing mirror. A, keyring his wife had bought him, was hanging from the ignition, gently swinging from side to side. He turned his engine off and pulled the key out. He then opened the storage box near his handbrake and pulled out a paper cutting. He folded it in half and using his right hand, stowed it in his left breast pocket.

He opened his car door and swivelled ninety degrees in his seat. Placing one hand on the backrest of the chair and the other on the car door handle, he heaved himself out. His body wasn't as youthful as many years before, but in the past week he felt a new spring in his step and a reason to live. He knew his wife would be so pleased.

His hair had aged to a pure white colour, which was combed back across his head. It was wavy in parts and anything he tried wouldn't hold it down. Every day he tried but without success. His eyes were a dark green, which looked younger today than they had for many years before. He was tall and fairly built from his younger days when he was athletic. He needed to get his body working again now. His nose was slightly crooked, and his mouth had changed over the years into sneer whenever he moved it.

Planting both feet on the floor, he subconsciously touched his left knee, which he had injured twenty years previously. His wife had said his knee would only get worse with age. Now she was proven right. He straightened up and rubbed his eyes in the morning light and began to look around the car park; it was empty. It seemed it always was. He preferred it that way. He wanted to spend time alone with his wife.

He pulled his long, black, thin coat down behind him and closed his door, locking it afterwards. The exterior was dusty and the tyres were smudged with dried mud and oil. The sun shone brightly, reflecting its heat off the car roof, which was slowly losing colour from lack of attention and age. The car only did two different journeys a week; to his place of work and to see his wife. He began to walk towards the entrance.

The scenery around him was beautiful. Fresh flowers were growing each side of the pathway and across the perimeters to the chain-link fence. The wild colours of yellow, purple and red flowers were growing proud in the natural sunlight and the shrubberies and privets were maintained daily. He felt pleased to know his wife was surrounded by beautiful views.

He took a wheezy breath and again touched his left knee. He had a limp and this came with a pain that worsened with every passing year. His right hand touched a days' worth of stubble darkening his cheek. He started to walk forward slowly. The birds were beginning to tweet in the background serenely. They were gliding in and out of the rays of sunlight.

He was staring ahead and saw no-one looking back. It was quiet and peaceful. He could stay here indefinitely, but not now. Not now he felt he had a purpose. As he climbed the hill, feeling the small pebble stones moving beneath him, he thought about what he knew now and his heart thumped with triumph and anger.

As he reached the top of the small hill, he used his left hand to rub his left knee. The hill was always the worst part of the visit. He stood still for a moment, breathing shallow, trying to keep his heart rate normal. He stood up slowly and brushed his white hair backwards. The sides of his hair by his ears were still a slight grey. He didn't want to think he was getting old; he couldn't afford to be now.

He moved forward along the path, eyes focusing ahead and he saw his wife. He could feel himself smiling. She always made him happy. He knew she would be smiling back. As he reached her, the smile turned to sorrow. He stood at the end of her resting place and stared hard at her gravestone. It was a solid, flat granite stone, chiselled with words and dates. The surroundings were calm and peaceful, yet all he felt was pain and revulsion.

He walked to the side of her grave and slowly knelt down on his right knee. He could feel his leg shaking as he lowered himself down. His grey trousers sunk slightly into the grass beneath him. He placed his right hand on the ground above where his wife had been laid to rest twenty years ago. Behind him, the sun was rising high into the sky and noises were emerging around him. He could hear the muffled sounds of car engines and the chatter of people. The day was beginning.

The church in front of him, stood tall and proud and a small cross was visible at the head of the building. The church was grey and isolated in the acreage surrounding it. The large oak front door was closed and he could make out a glass stand, with paper pinned inside. He imagined the vicar or priest or whatever he was called changing the old papers for new ones every week.

The image changed to his wife Linda standing there in front of him. He imagined her brown hair hanging just beneath her shoulders, her green eyes inviting and sincere. Her smile was beaming from ear to ear even after all the tragedies they had suffered. She was in her favourite dress; a light blue summer garment, which hung off the shoulders and finished just above the knees. She had worn the dress on their eighteenth wedding anniversary. A year before she was taken from him.

He cleared the image from his mind and now focused on what needed to be done. His life had changed course suddenly all those years before. He was never able to lead a normal life again. As he looked down at his wife he thought about the things he now knew, and he took a deep breath, thinking about time wasted, valuable, precious time. How could he have missed it all this time?

He recollected the night where he stood talking to Ben, asking him the questions he needed to know, the questions, which would change both their lives. Ben told him fortuitously about his childhood adventure and why he was moved to another village. He had been talking about it as if it were nothing. Ben divulged everything quickly. He seemed more than happy to help him, once he had been offered rewards in return. He would keep Ben close as he knew he had to find out everything. He was sure there was more to find out wasn't there? There was plenty of time for conversations now.

He stared at her gravestone, which had remained in good condition over the past two decades and he read the words aloud to remind himself he still had a voice; he still had a purpose. "Linda Howsy" he said. He swallowed hard and felt a tear surface and run down his wrinkled cheek and off onto the floor as he continued, "Aged 39, loving wife and best friend, closed eyes, heart not beating, but a living love".

He rose, using his arms to thrust himself upwards quickly. He brushed down his right knee and again rubbed his left knee. He stood still for the last time that morning and stared at the ground. He reached into his pocket and pulled out the paper cutting. He unfolded it carefully, as it was browning at the edges. The paper was from twenty years ago and it covered a long story of the night his wife was killed. There was a picture of himself, looking care-free and much younger alongside his wife in her blue dress. The caption underneath the photograph read 'Linda and Roy Howsy on their eighteenth wedding anniversary.'

Further on, it explained how the man who killed his wife had died moments later; Roy felt it saved him a job. Roy placed the photograph back in his pocket, as he heard footsteps behind him; the caretaker. The caretaker was smiling as he carried out his daily duties; care free and visibly content. Roy looked at his wife one more time and spoke clearly and purposefully, 'their time will come.' He bit his lip and turned his back against the climbing sun, heading for home.

2

Stephen Farley stood in his kitchen drinking black coffee in a white mug. The news was playing quietly on the television in the background, but he wasn't listening. He was of medium height and solidly built. His job as a mechanical engineer for a building company had worked his upper body throughout the years. He had short, light hair, which parted perfectly on one side. He had high cheek bones below his dark brown eyes.

He sipped the final part of his coffee, tilting his cup, watching the sludge in the bottom flow towards him. Placing the cup on the work surface, he looked out the window to the back garden, which was covered in concrete, littered with plant pots, which surrounded the outskirts. Erect in the centre of the garden was a bird feed, with nuts hanging in a netted bag. Stephen squinted at the side door to make sure it was fully shut, and he then twisted slightly to try and see the back gate, which led towards a public alley way. You could use this as a shortcut towards some shops. The gate was hidden from view from the back garden.

'I'm leaving in a minute, Stace,' Stephen shouted from the kitchen as he switched the television off at the mains. Stephen liked perfection and liked appliances to be turned off, when not in use. He was sure it was a form of OCD, which he felt he had inherited from his late mother. He walked into the hallway and arrived at the bottom of the stairs, picking up his keys from the mantelpiece on the way.

As he reached the base of the stairs, he tilted his neck back and saw Stacey standing at the top. She was wearing a black top and a black skirt. The skirt was tight against her legs and smooth over her curves. Stephen looked at her and fell in love all over again. She had long blonde hair, which hung to her shoulder blades and piercing blue eyes, which made her look athletic, just above dimples and defined cheekbones.

She was smiling at him, a mixture of mischief, confidence and shyness on her face. 'I'm leaving as well now,' she said throwing her handbag over her shoulder, descending the cream carpeted stairs. 'Had your coffee yet?' she said as she wrapped her arms around him from the second from bottom stair. Stephen smiled back at her and kissed her gently on the lips. Her lips felt soft and he could smell soap on her skin.

They had met one night in a bar. Two more doubles and twenty minutes later, he approached her and it began. He always remembered looking into her eyes and felt as if she could see straight through him. They were piercing. If he compared her then to now, she had only gotten more beautiful. Ten years on they were happy as ever. The only thing Stephen would have changed was that his mum was there to see it all. She had died a year after the wedding. Pictures of his mother hung on the wall leading to the stairs, above the mantelpiece.

'Of course I have. I can't start the day without it,' Stephen replied holding her waist, pulling her closer. 'How many clients you meeting today?' he said, lost in her eyes. She was a successful lawyer in the centre of town. She dealt with family disputes. Her reputation had grown wildly across town, yet she remained modest.

'Only two today,' she said releasing Stephen, skipping the remaining step into the lounge. She picked up her briefcase, which rest against the sofa. The lounge was decorated in photos of the two of them, hung on painted walls of pale grey and a purple feature wall. The corner sofa was covered by a soft purple throw and cushions, which rest at each corner. The fireplace stood proudly at the head of the room. 'I have to travel to the office first to pick some things up. Is it the usual busy day for you?'

Stephen reached under the stairs and grabbed his shoes. He worked just outside of town. He had the ability to do, what his boss said was key; 'to think outside the box.' He was intelligent, yet modest. He could remember the finest details. He was always reading and his passion lay in fixing things. At home he was always playing with things of a mechanical description. 'Probably. I won't be home too late tonight, so fancy me cooking my speciality?'

'That would be lovely.'

'Promise to eat it?'

'Promise,' she said as she walked towards him and leant up on her tiptoes, kissing him on the lips. She arrived at the front door and shook her feet into her heels. She folded her smart, thin, beige coat across her arm and turned back to Stephen. 'See you tonight' she said as she walked out the front door.

He smiled for a second and then went back into the kitchen to grab his lunch. His rubber shoes made no noise against the stone kitchen flooring as he exited the room and the front door. The front garden was large and wide. Dead centre of the garden was a pathway made up of an assortment of differently shaped rocks. He walked down the pathway to his old grey car, which was parked on the road.

The street was quiet, and Stephen was the only one outside. Stephen looked left and right and at the houses opposite. He remembered the year they had been built. Some detached, some semi, all coloured in light brown brickwork. Stephen continued walking down the path. He could hear the bustle in the distance from town. It was nothing compared to London.

The sun was shining above him and the temperature was humid. He got in the car and opened the windows. It was early, yet the inside of the car was hot and uncomfortable. He began to drive out of the little cul-de-sac, which was empty and quiet. He pulled part of his top away from his lower back and then fiddled with his collar. He was wearing a grey polo top, which he always wore to work. The polo was tight around his large arms.

He turned down the next road and switched on the radio. Stephen was a calm, caring, family man. His mother had raised him to be polite and loving and unselfish. The sun grew higher in the sky and the heat grew more fiercely above him. He scratched his short beard and drummed his fingers on the wheel. The roads were still empty and he hummed along to the radio.

The first car he saw was a dark people carrier. It drove past him slowly but Stephen was unable to see the driver due to the gleam of the sun. He kept his eyes ahead and then eased into town. He drove past betting shops, mini supermarkets and restaurants. Some not open yet, even though the walkways were busy with people going about their day.

He arrived at work and pulled up tight against the kerb. He stepped out of the car and walked into the garage, placing his lunch on the side. The phone rang in the next room. 'Morning, Dave,' he said as he walked past his manager and into the office. He picked up the phone and started work.

3

'How can I help you?' was what Roy heard as he dialled a well-known number. He had been sitting in his armchair at home, drinking scotch for over two hours. The front room was dark as the drapes were pulled across tight. Sunlight was creeping through at the edges. The room was small and un-kept and smelt stale. He was sitting there in his dark woollen jumper, his left arm resting across his lap, his right hand palm against his head.

Roy stared straight ahead at the mantelpiece, where in the middle was a single photo inside a dusty, discoloured metal frame. It was of Linda who was wearing a white dress holding a bouquet of flowers. The photo still had colour having rarely been subjected to direct sunlight. Roy had been thinking about this phone call all morning. How could he say what he needed to? The person he was calling was someone who you didn't want to call often. 'It's about the job I have for you,' Roy said closing one eye, concentrating, listening for a reply.

'I'm listening' was all he got in reply.

Roy swivelled backwards in his chair so his back was tight against the back rest. He knew the man whose services he required. Well enough he thought. More than what he wanted to really, until now. He knew money would be needed. It could wipe him clean. He knew that. He knew it would be worth it.

The money he had couldn't bring back the possession he craved the most. He ran through the plan in his head over again, trying to think of all the minor details.

Roy was suddenly restless. He slid forward until he was sitting on the edge of the worn chair. He lifted himself off the chair, standing still for a moment to allow his knee to adjust to his body weight. He paced forwards to the other side of the room, looking at the picture of his wife. 'I need you to carry out what we discussed' he said, not blinking, not breaking the stare on his wife. Roy was quiet again for a beat and continued, 'I need you to do it soon.'

Roy just listened. He could hear his contact breathing down the phone, thinking, weighing up the confirmation. He would surely carry out the job? His contact said, 'the price has changed. It's now £50000 for the job. And you have my word it will be done when needed.' Roy's eyes closed slightly into a mini squint, as if trying to read a small print of text. His mind began to work hard. It was a game of chess, except for the wrong move meant more than losing.

He turned his back on his wife and tilted his neck side to side, a little crack audible and deafening in the silence. The £50000 would be worth it. It was the best investment he could have imagined. But was it too easy? He changed the plan. '£50000 is acceptable. But I have a change of my own.'

'I'm listening,' his contact said for the second time.

'I want you to kill someone else.' His contact didn't reply. Roy could feel his heart racing and his chest thumping. Adrenaline was kicking in. He had made his penultimate move and needed his opponent to make theirs. If they were happy to change the target, he felt the upper hand.

'Who?'

Roy picked up his scotch and emptied the glass, taking two large gulps. It seemed to breathe life into his voice and breathe life into his plan. He placed the glass down onto the wooden table, hearing the little thud as he stood upright again. He repeated the new instruction in his mind. He took another look at his wife and spoke clearly now, 'I need you to kill Stacey Farley.'

'Ok,' his contact said and the line went dead.

Roy smiled and placed his own phone on the table. *Checkmate* he thought.

4

Stephen threw his sports gear into a small gym bag. He picked up a pair of shoes by the laces heading for the front door. It was around five in the afternoon. It didn't happen often but he and Stacey had rowed earlier in the day. They had gone to work and the argument continued as soon as they walked back through the front door. Stephen usually changed at home, but not today; he knew he had to leave the house.

'Why don't you grow up?' shouted Stacey from the top of the stairs. She descended the stairs holding onto the bannister, angry and annoyed. Stephen had been on his phone, not listening to Stacey talking. Then a disagreement broke out, followed by an argument. Stacey was frustrated that they had fallen out over such a petty subject. But neither was happy to let it drop.

'I've told you, I'm sorry. It's so ridiculous, we're arguing over something so small.'

'But you do it all the time. *All* the time.'

'You see me on my phone and you *still* decide to ask me things, expecting me to answer you within a second.'

'No, I expect you to use some manners.'

Stephen didn't respond and walked into the kitchen and grabbed a glass and run the cold water tap. He let the water run slowly, watching it wash away down the shiny sink. The noise of the water running away was lost to Stephen as he stood with his left hand against the work top and his right hand clutching the glass.

Once his cup was full, he turned the tap off and walked into the already open side door to the back garden. He took a sip and walked past the bird feed, listening to the sounds of cars and birds and lawnmowers surrounding him. Stephen could feel his calmness emerging, yet he still felt frustrated.

He walked over to the side gate, which was locked at the top and threw the remainder of his water on the grass. He turned around and walked past the newly planted flower pots and into the house. Placing the glass next to the purple plates from the morning, he walked into the hall way. Stacey was sitting on the bottom stair, her laptop rested on her knees, the light reflecting off her face.

'Look, I'm sorry,' Stephen said six feet away. 'I know I do it and I know I've said I'll stop. Sorry.' Stacey didn't reply. 'I'm going to the gym' he said as he walked away, picking up his gear and he left the house. The breeze shut the door behind him and the slam echoed across the street. He paced towards his car and threw his belongings onto the back seat. He felt guilty now.

He jumped into his seat and started the engine and began driving out of the cul-de-sac away from his house. He turned the radio on and opened his window slightly, just as he passed a stationary BMW, with blacked out windows, parked tight against the kerb.

5

The man in the stationary BMW was Roy's contact. His name was Xavier. He was of Spanish descent and he worked as a labourer. His main job was as a hitman. He sat in his car, looking out of each side mirror and rear view mirror for three seconds at a time. He saw Stephen's car and he kept his eyes firmly focused on the number plate. Xavier could see him dropping the window slightly as he drove straight past him on his way to the gym; like clockwork.

Xavier sat still for a further five minutes, now concentrating on his rear view mirror. He began to flicker between this view and the one in front of him of the small alley, which he knew led to houses and a row of shops. In all of the stake outs he had carried out over the past three weeks, he had rarely seen anyone use this shortcut.

Xavier had no hair and was cleanly shaven. His eyes were brown and they were sunken into his wrinkled face. His skin was olive, but for the scars on the back of his head, which were white and pink. They were the scars he obtained from years before. From a time he would never repeat. The scars were inflamed and itchy. They had healed naturally, but he knew he should have had medical attention. Impossible, it was a weakness he couldn't afford to reveal.

He stepped out of his car onto the road in his quiet and

untraceable, rubber boots. He walked towards the alley, one hand in his pocket gripping a piece of thin, metal wire. The wire was next to a pair of leather gloves, which he was ready to manoeuvre on when the next stage was clear. He pulled the collar up on his black jumper, so that his neck was fully covered.

Xavier had been scouting the property for three weeks, ever since his previous conversation with Roy. He knew Roy well enough. He remembered the night Roy called, sounding desperate and angry and his voice wrathful. He met him that evening outside an abandoned industrial estate curious. The expectations become clear soon enough.

Xavier had been given limited details for the job. It was strange that Roy wanted someone dead but couldn't provide an address. It was as if he didn't know the target. Xavier didn't ask questions. He preferred to carry out the dirty work, pleading ignorance to the reason. Xavier knew he was able to obtain the information through a system, which he shared with no-one.

Roy offered £25000 for the job, all upfront. Xavier didn't even name a price. He took it willingly, but his mind wondered; could he ask for more? Who else offered a service like this? There was no other market for this. He had done all the work and had made the necessary enquiries. He had spent time watching and waiting for hours on end. He asked.

He had been told to kill Stephen Farley immediately. He was told to ensure his death was non-suspicious. But Xavier had his own set of rules. He felt as if Roy wanted to play a game. Like a game of chess. Xavier knew he couldn't kill the man called Stephen Farley straight away. He needed to prepare. He wasn't prepared to fail. He agreed to Roy's demands.

The plan changed significantly. Roy had played a move he

hadn't foreseen. Roy wanted the wife dead, not Stephen. Xavier didn't ask why. Xavier agreed knowing the change wouldn't matter too much. He knew just as much about the wife as he did the husband. He had the upper hand.

He had spent the next twenty one days, watching the Farleys every day. He had noted every detail; times they left each morning, times they came home, activities they did on certain days. He had it all stored. He decided the day to strike was when Stephen went to the gym, leaving his poor wife at home.

Xavier had managed to access the back gate the week previous, whilst the Farley's were at work. He had peered into the house and saw the outlay. He would go in via the side door. No question. To go in the front door was suicide. How would he know if a neighbour was watching? He could tip toe and unlock the gate from the outside; easy enough.

Xavier walked into the alley way. Trees and bushes overhung from gardens, creating a shadow on the cracked path. He kept walking forwards and passed no-one. It was deserted as it had been every day at this time for the past three weeks. He turned a slight corner and saw the gate ahead of him. When he reached the gate, he checked behind him once more. Empty. He placed his leather gloves on and pulled himself to the top of the gate and looked over. Empty.

Stage one was complete. He reached over and felt slowly and gently for the lock. He found the lock and unbolted the gate. It slid across, metal rubbing against metal and it clicked as it reached the furthest point it could go. Xavier felt the gate move slightly, as the force of which it was being held was gone.

Xavier walked through the gate slowly. As the gate curved, it squeaked at the hinges. Xavier knew he had to lift the gate to stop the creaking growing louder. He opened it enough and side stepped through, keeping his eyes firmly on the house. He pushed the gate back, his hand wrapped around the metal lock to prevent any unnecessary sound. He bolted the lock slightly so that it wouldn't bang, but so that his exit would be quick and seamless.

He walked towards the house. His rubber boots glided across the concrete floor. He stepped past the pots spaced feet away from one another. He placed his right hand into his pocket and felt for the metal wire occupying his pocket. He arrived at the side door and checked his surroundings once more. He knocked on the door, standing to one side and waited.

Stage two was complete.

6

Just as Xavier had knocked on the side door, Stephen's next door neighbour Shirley was watching the street out of her sitting room window. She had been waiting for her steam kettle to boil and was dusting her glass, television stand, when she heard a door slam outside. She peered through the white netted curtains and looked out the window. She saw her neighbour called Stephen marching away from this house. She only ever used pleasantries with the man and didn't know him well. However, she could tell from his face, that he didn't look happy.

Shirley loved to gossip, and regularly did so. Her kettle whizzed and smoked in the kitchen. She watched Stephen throw something into the back of his car and drive away out of the cul-de-sac. She moved back into her hallway, which was all coloured in pink, and through to the kitchen. She poured herself a tea and reminded herself to tell Betty as soon as she finished her first cup. Shirley wasn't aware; she wouldn't even make it that far.

7

Stacey was upstairs changing into her evening wear. She was upset about the argument, and Stephen leaving. Was he sorry? Silly question, she thought as she knew he was. They never argued, but when they did, they really did. She was sat on a wooden stool slowly taking her make off. Their bedroom was similar to other rooms in the house. Three of the walls were painted a light pebble grey. There was a matching grey feature wall, consisting of different patterns and elegant trees.

The room was bright and the curtains were pinned back against the wall, by a grey curled rope. The final remnants of the day's sun were desperately trying to shine into the room. By the window was a single photo of Stephen and herself on their wedding day. They were both smiling at something to the side of them, oblivious to the photographer taking a photo.

Stacey threw the final make up wipe into the white bin, placed beside the dressing table and pulled her hair back into an untidy bob and stood up. Behind her was a queen size bed with the covers pulled down showing off the bed sheet and leaving the pillows solitary at the head of the bed. She pulled her cotton top down, tucking it into her waistband, and picked up the photo of the pair of them.

She slid into her slippers and walked out onto the landing and down the stairs. Midway down the stairs, she heard a knock at the door. *Stephen,* she thought and her heart skipped a beat. She missed the final step and came to the front door. She yanked the door open, seeing no-one on the other side. She looked left and right and couldn't see his car. The side door, she thought. Why would Stephen come in this way? Maybe he had forgotten his keys? She walked towards the kitchen, still holding the photo.

She moved towards the kitchen and placed the photograph down next to a glass, alone and isolated on the work surface. Brushing the single pieces of stray hair away from her face and smiling, she reached to open the door, ready to forgive and forget and to apologise for being childish. As she twisted the door handle and dragged the door open; her face was stricken with fear.

8

Xavier saw a beautiful lady open the door. She was wearing a plain top and large pyjama bottoms. She looked youthful and he stared into her blue eyes as he quickly assessed the situation. He had said to himself, *door open, twist her round, wire round her neck, squeeze.* It didn't turn out as planned.

He pushed himself in through the door and into the kitchen quickly and with his left hand, he reached out, wrapping his fingers round Stacey's throat. Her eyes were wide open, confused and filled with terror. He pushed inwards and with his right hand, swung the door shut. The door was swinging on its curve and automatic mechanism connected with the door frame, shutting it tight.

As she moved her free arm, Xavier saw a glass falling off the work surface followed by a photo frame. Xavier saw the glass fall as it smashed into a dozen pieces beside their feet. Xavier remained still, gripping Stacey's throat tighter to keep her quiet. He looked down briefly at the damaged photo and saw the woman before him, but in a white dress.

'Are you alone?' he said quietly, slowly pushing her into the centre of the house and away from any doors. He knew he had to be quick and he didn't want to tread glass into other rooms. His adrenaline was kicking through and his lower back was secreting sweat. He kept his eyes firmly on hers, unable to change his gaze. He listened for any noises in the background. His mind was thinking of his escape.

She quickly nodded left to right repeatedly. Xavier could see her panicking. Xavier kept his fingers firm against her throat as he began to reach for the wire in his pocket. His hand stopped moving towards his pocket when he felt Stacey shake her body and let out a scream. A terrifying high pitch scream echoed around the room and no doubt to the outside world. He knew he had to be quick.

He pushed her forward into the living room, his rubber boots not audible over the sound of Stacey hitting the floor, knees first. Xavier stepped over her slippers, which had come off during her fall, and as he stood over her, as she screamed again louder than before; deafening. This time it was too far.

Xavier pushed her head down to the floor and grabbed the nearest thing he could see. He had to stop her screaming. If someone next door heard then there may be problems. Screaming was construed as a sign of distress and trepidation, clear and distinct, for the world to hear. Xavier grabbed the iron rod, resting next to the fire place and pushed himself up and away from Stacey.

He looked down at her once more, staring into her blue eyes, just as his arm came crashing down through the air. The unforgiving iron rod connected with the side of Stacey's cranium, just above the ear. She collapsed from her partly seated position into a motionless ball on the floor. Xavier could see blood weeping from her cut, the blood spreading and running down her top and onto the cream carpet.

He gripped the iron rod harder and brought it down violently once more. He had more time with this blow to ensure his aim and power was in sync. The rod connected with the same part of her head, as a small splatter of blood landed on the sofa and Stacey remained static on the floor. Xavier stood up straight, remorselessly and listened for any sounds again.

Without kneeling on the front room floor, he then squatted next to Stacey, whose hair was drenched in claret red, and felt for a pulse. No pulse. He stayed in this position for another minute. No pulse. He placed the rod gently onto the floor. The rod left a small trace of blood on the carpet along with matted hair and bone.

Xavier walked through to the kitchen, checking behind him as he walked for any prints or blood marks. Nothing. He used his left hand, which hadn't used to check for Stacey's pulse, and pulled the door open, sneaking through it faster and purposefully. He now needed to be quick.

Xavier moved hurriedly through the garden and reached the gate. He unlocked it and stepped through, checking ahead of him as before. He pulled the gate back and reached over, pulling the bolt across for the last time. He moved away from the gate and took the gloves off, ensuring they were inside and out and placed them into his pocket. His scars were itching and dry.

He came to the end of the alley and cars were driving past from both directions. He waited until there was a big enough gap in the traffic and he moved, jumping into the driver's seat. He sat still for a moment and looked at each of his mirrors in turn. Quick enough. Stage 3 was complete.

He had been sat still for less than five minutes, when out of his wing mirror, he saw a grey car approaching from behind. Much earlier than expected he thought. It skated past him, approaching the close. Xavier knew it was Stephen. He wasn't sure why he was back early. Had someone called him? He was sure he hadn't been seen. He was sure it had been an almost perfect execution. However, Xavier had the smallest doubt. Xavier watched the car turn into the close and closed his eyes, trying to push doubt out of his mind. He did know one thing for sure; he wouldn't want to be Stephen Farley tonight.

9

Shirley was standing in her hallway dialling the police. She had just been about to call Betty, when she heard a shrill cry from next door. She looked out the window and saw no one. The cry sounded as if she had been in the same room as the scream. She put down her small, flowery, china cup and walked to the hallway.

The operator connected her with the police and she briefly told them what she had heard. They were going to send someone round straight away. They were used to domestics she thought. They probably got it regularly. Maybe it was nothing, but she felt she'd done the right thing by calling. She remained next to phone for a few minutes, listening for further screams. When everything remained quiet she made sure the phone was on charge and slowly moved back into the living room.

She walked to the window once more and saw Stephen's grey car stationary at end of the front garden. Her mouth twitched and her story to Betty blossomed instantly. She walked back to the phone, picking up her tea on the way and dialled Betty's number. Betty answered and before she got chance to say anything other than hello, Shirley said, 'I think my neighbour is attacking his wife.'

10

Stephen was on his way back to the house, mad at himself for leaving when he did. He was calm and still in his work gear. He had driven round a roundabout twice, looking at the different signs, contemplating the route he should go. But he knew the one place where he needed to go; home. He would give the gym a miss tonight. Tonight was a valid excuse. He normally came up with much weaker excuses than this one.

He drove through the town, which was busy with people ending their days, tie knots pulled lose, tired eyes and the frustration of rush hour. The heat was starting to abscond, as the sun settled in the distance, the orange glow lighting up the skyline.

Stephen thought of his wife and smiled. He imagined her sitting at home, pacified, wine in hand, feet underneath her and the television on. He also imagined her sitting there waiting for another apology. Stephen's mouth opened and he laughed. He thought of memories and he knew tomorrow they would laugh at this argument.

He passed mini-supermarkets accompanied with special offer signs followed by charity shops with large, crumpled white bags beneath the window followed by betting shops with smokers leant against the eroded brickwork, holding a small piece of white paper whilst puffing away leaving a cloud of white smoke visible in the evening air. Stephen drove on and thought of his mother. She would have had said, "I'll come over there and bump your heads together" or something to that effect. Stacey's mother would have said the opposite; Stephen would have been wrong whatever the story.

Stephen kept his speed constant and clicked a small button by his window, which was followed by a grind as his windows begun to close. The sun setting seemed to suck the humidity with it and the cold night air was slowly seeping into the atmosphere. He placed one hand on the other and listened to the faint noise of the radio playing. He couldn't make out the song, but he hummed along.

He came to his road and turned slowly into the close, parking solid against the kerb. Switching his engine off and listening to the noises under the bonnet starting to cool the engine down, he exited his seat and walked round the back of the car towards the front door. Everything was quiet around him, other than the sound of cars in the distance.

The sun was fading slowly still and was lost to eye in the horizon. He rubbed his hands together, the hard skin on his palm rubbing against one another and he then twisted his set of keys in the air, until he was just holding his silver door key.

He placed his key smoothly into the metal lock and walked through the solid front door.

11

Stephen rested his keys down on the radiator next to the front door. 'Stacey,' he shouted. No answer. It was silent. The only noise he could make out was the whirring of the fridge freezer. Stephen thought Stacey may be out for a walk. Just behind the houses were a sports park and children's gymnasium. It was Stacey's main source of relaxation. Usually, she had with Stephen by her side.

'Stacey,' he shouted for the second time. After no reply, Stephen decided he would go to the park. He left the door ajar and walked into the house. As he reached the kitchen, he heard a small crack beneath him; glass. Stephen saw shattered glass in a dozen pieces, spread out across the flooring surface. Amongst the debris, broken in one corner was a picture of Stacey and himself on their wedding day. The argument wasn't that bad was it?

'Stacey,' he shouted again, urgency in his voice. Before he entered the hallway, he held onto the work top and lifted his leg up towards him, turning his foot so he could brush the glass off from his sole. He stroked the glass from his foot, gently so as not to cut himself. He looked back at the windows for cracks to try and locate the source of the broken glass.

His eyes rested onto the work surface and he noticed the glass he had used a short time ago, was no longer there. He tiptoed on the spot and peered into the white washing up bowl, which was empty, but for a folded yellow cloth. He shook his head and couldn't believe she had smashed a glass and their wedding photo. She would have had to have purposefully gone upstairs to get it.

He tiptoed twice around the fragments of glass, making a mental note to sweep it up once he had spoken to Stacey. In the hallway, he stopped still, his heels falling like a dead weight back to the ground as his whole body went tense. Looking straight ahead into the lounge, he could see a lifeless body on the floor with blonde hair surrounded by a pool of blood.

12

Stephen had watched countless fictional crime programmes in the past. He enjoyed a "who dunnit" type of investigation. The one thing he always found comical was the reaction of the innocent bystander who finds the body. There was shortage of breath, panic and fear all in a set order. Ninety-nine percent of the perpetrators were known to the victim. The crime was usually committed for monetary gain.

This was different.

Stephen ran forward, taking large strides as he leant down beside his wife. She was rigid and cold. Her eyes were shut. Her mouth was slightly lopsided with partially dried blood around her lips, a trail visible onto the floor. He looked down at her and could feel his chest heaving and he began to panic. He looked over each shoulder, desperate for help, desperate for someone to walk in and wake him.

He placed two fingers onto her neck anxiously waiting and begging to feel a pulse. Fear was setting in as he looked down at her body hopelessly and forlorn. To his left, he saw the iron rod from the fire place covered in blood and blonde hair. He picked up the rod and looked at it, dropping it suddenly, when he realised what it had done and where it would leave him; destitute and vulnerable. 'Stacey,' he said, 'I'm sorry.'

He picked up his wife from underneath her neck with his

left arm and cradled her close with his right arm, pushing her tight against his chest. Stephen began to cry earnestly into her hair, feeling tears running down each cheek as he pulled her closer. He could feel his top becoming wet, no doubt his wife's blood. 'I'm sorry,' he said again as tears fell to the ground, 'I didn't mean to hurt you.'

His crying became louder and louder and confusion crept into his head. Who had done this? Why had this happened? Why did he leave her alone? All questions he didn't have the answers to yet. He pulled her away slightly from his chest and looked down at her again.

The side of her head was bruising. He presumed this was where the rod had hit her. Blood had stopped pouring from the wound. Her heart had ceased beating, not knowing that by pumping blood around her body it was only thrusting the blood out of her wound, until there was no blood left. She was limp and lifeless and he pulled her closer again.

Out of the corner of his eye, Stephen saw a shadow cast in the door frame and he looked into a man's face filled with horror, just as the new arrival raised his right hand.

Officer David Michael was due to finish his shift in thirty minutes. He had promised his wife dinner. A promise he had the best intention of keeping. It had been a relatively quiet day. Being asked to move three homeless people from a supermarket car park was the most exciting part of his day. He thought it was easy money though nowadays. Times had changed over the years. He was always telling his wife you couldn't do half the things you used to be able to.

He was a short squat man, with jet black hair and rosy cheeks. His face was small and his features looked disproportionate compared to his body. He was wearing black trousers and a black short sleeved shirt, which was underneath a padded vest. He had small arms and small legs, which carried a slightly large abdomen.

He had worked in this part of town for five years. It was twenty miles away from his home, which was a general rule of thumb for this police force. You couldn't work within a certain radius of where you lived. He used to hold onto covering this part of town like it was the be all and end all. It was usually quiet and therefore he could work on his own and he preferred that as he could manage his own day and didn't have to make small talk with anyone.

Officer Michael was sat in his car in the same neighbourhood where the Farley's lived. This town offered two benefits. Firstly, it was closer to home. Secondly, it was notoriously known for being tranquil and undisturbed. He could sit here for hours some days and watch the world go by. Today turned out to be different.

He was cruising alone, having grabbed a late light snack and a fizzy drink to enjoy on his ride home. His wife wouldn't know. The restaurant he'd promised to take her to was expensive and the portions were small. They went on special occasions and he would always leave hungry, although he told his wife he couldn't eat another bite.

As he sat at the junction, his radio bleeped requesting him to check in with HQ and confirm his location. Frustrated, he explained his whereabouts and asked what was required of him. He was told there was a potential domestic violence case, reported by a woman, this was then followed by the address. A typical police call out, officer Michael thought, but not in this part of town.

Officer Michael confirmed he would visit the address and would keep everyone up to date. He drove along the town, passing the final remaining cars of people returning home, all going to enjoy dinner in the comfort of their own home. Lucky for you, he thought. It was still light outside and he was relaxed but alert on the job. He called himself a veteran and that entitled him to relaxation once in a while.

He reached the designated address. It had involved weaving through a number of roads. It was in the heart of town and he could just make out the sounds of the cars passing through the ring roads. He imagined it was a waste of time. He hoped it was. Or he would be going home to a domestic case of his own.

He slowed down, taking his foot off the accelerator allowing the car to just glide along with the road. The address was beautiful from the outside; two storeys and it looked almost brand new. Officer Michael raised his head to look at the very top of the house and he could make out black tiles on the roof, leading down towards guttering followed by two double windows.

The front door was light and looked solid and the house attached to this one was identical. He imagined the inside layout was also the same. He looked at the pathway and then drove past until he reached the end of the cul-de-sac, where he performed a U-turn, so he was then facing the way he had come in. The tyres gritted on the tarmac as he spun around and he wound his windows up on both sides.

He parked the car up behind a grey car and heaved the handbrake. He released his seat belt and fiddled with his belt. He stepped into the street, it was a little cold as the evening was arriving. He pulled his jacket around him and felt for his badge along with his baton and stun gun, which was out of sight.

He took a slow look around as he ascended the pathway to the house in question. To his right, he could see a curtain move slightly and then go immediately still. Probably, the person who called it in, he thought. He was around eight feet away from the door, when he saw it was agape and he could make out the faint noise of someone crying.

14

Xavier was still sitting in his car. His heart rate hadn't changed in the past hour. He saw himself as a professional now, and to show any sign of weakness was immature and unacceptable. He pictured the £50000 sitting in front of him. Cash, he had been told. He would ensure it was untraceable and ready for laundering.

Xavier leant over to his glovebox, flicked the handle up and watched it roll open. He took out his phone and looked at the screen. It was an old device, which only allowed you to make calls and texts and had no camera or internet. He had no missed calls or messages. He closed the glovebox and threw the phone down into the cup holder by his gear stick.

He rubbed the wounds on his head, alternating between scratching hard with his nails to massaging the long-standing injury. He would give it a few more minutes and he would call the police. He had planned to sit where he was for another hour waiting for Stephen, but Stephen arrived early. Thank you, Stephen Farley, he thought.

He didn't need to call the police.

As he looked in his rear-view mirror, he could make out a white car, painted with yellow and blue squares moving towards him; a police car. He sat back in his car and pulled his phone up to his ear, inconspicuous and unthreatening. Xavier could make out a short man with a squashed face driving behind the wheel. Xavier thought he looked un-urgent and lethargic and as if his shift finished hours ago. Xavier had dealt with people like that his whole life.

Xavier slid gently down the seat as he watched the car approach from behind him. He threw his phone into the cup holder once more and powered his car up. The ignition clicked at the first attempt and he didn't touch the brake. He watched the police car turn into the close fifty metres from where he was positioned. Checking his right-wing mirror, he pulled away from the kerb and into dusk.

15

'HANDS IN THE AIR,' Stephen heard the man shouting at him. He looked at the small police officer stood in front of him, holding out a little gun, which was square at the end and lit up on one side. Stephen didn't move. It was all a big misunderstanding and he knew the police officer would understand that.

Stephen laid his wife down gently onto the floor, holding her limp head with his left hand. His eyes were fixed on the gash visible above Stacey's ear. He pushed himself up off the floor with his right hand and faced the officer, dazed and confused. Stephen looked down at his top, which was soaked in blood, covering every inch of his torso. His arms were plastered in blood, matted with his forearm hair. 'My wife' he said, 'we need to get some help.'

'HANDS IN THE AIR,' the officer shouted again, this time more loudly and demanding. Stephen raised his hands in the air and saw his fingertips were bright red and crusty in between the creases of his knuckles. He looked down at his wife and something clicked inside his head. He felt himself beginning to shake and felt his teeth grit, crunching against each other.

He watched as the police officer unclipped a small radio attached to his breast and placed it in between his ear and his left shoulder. He began talking into the radio keeping his right arm level at Stephen. He pointed the little gun, which Stephen didn't know if it was real. 'We need to get her help,' Stephen said. He got no reply. He was confused. 'You've got it wrong,' he continued, anger rising from within.

Stephen breathed out. There was nothing he could do. He needed answers, but he needed to clear this mess up first. Surely someone else would understand? 'Put your hands in front of you facing down,' the police officer said, 'keep them still and keep looking at me.' The small radio chattered for a second and Stephen heard a voice on the other end.

The police officer approached him slowly, the gun arm still erect. Stephen knew he could overpower him comfortably, he kept his gaze firmly on the officers, whose eyes were buried deep inside his eye sockets, above blotchy skin. He held out his hands together and prepared to move quickly.

The officer stepped close; five foot, four foot, three foot, but Stephen didn't attack. The officer took one wrist and firmly linked a hand cuff tight against his skin. Stephen heard the click of the mechanism as the officer repeated the exercise with the other wrist. The officer relaxed as he spoke once more into the radio, 'Romeo 1765, checking in for progress please,' he said quietly. He then turned to Stephen and said 'what's your name?'

'Stephen Farley'. The radio transmitter sparked into life and the response was muffled, but Stephen could just make out the words, 'CB and JO are on their way, two minutes from your location.' He fell to his knees. He could feel the police officer move quickly behind him, shuffling backwards, probably pulling his stun gun up swiftly too. He twisted to look at his lifeless wife, staring at her blonde hair, still seeing her beauty beyond the pool of dried blood encircling her. He leant forward and touched her cheek with the outside of his hand. 'Don't touch anything,' the police officer said behind him.

Stephen ignored the orders and kept his hand there. He didn't like the feel of her cold skin. He quickly withdrew his hand. He wanted to remember the warmth of her skin and the warmth of her touch. He felt his eyes well up and he started to shake violently, as the tears began to stream out of his sullen eyes, onto his cheek bones.

Moments later, Stephen heard two pairs of footsteps growing closer. He used his shoulder to wipe his eyes, just to make out another male officer and a female officer. They were both much larger than the officer who had cuffed Stephen. They looked much fitter and stronger and formidable. 'My wife,' he said, tilting his head and neck to point at his wife, 'you need to help me!'

The male officer who had just entered the room took a long look at Stephen and then turned to look at Stacey next to him. 'Help me,' Stephen shouted. The officer moved forward into the room and stood five foot in front of him, as Stephen craned his neck to look up into the eyes of the man who he knew would help him.

The new officer said to Stephen, 'we will help you' as he took a step closer, 'Stephen Farley, you are under arrest on suspicion of murder.'

16

Roy was sat in his same old familiar chair. He had been sitting there patiently for three hours. His shift at work had finished four hours ago. He had been given news that he would have a new assistant arriving anytime within the next 6 weeks, but she was yet to arrive. Work wasn't work to him anymore. Roy did it for the power kick and the reputation he gained. However, today was different.

He had dealt with his problem. He had sorted out the person, whom he had kept close. A person he needed to remain alone and isolated. Then it was a case of Roy having to leave as soon as he could. He needed to be home, with his phone by his side, waiting.

Roy was holding the same scotch glass he always used. He had a small drop left, which he was swirling round the outskirts of the cup, rotating the glass clockwise. The drapes were pulled tight and the room was dark and cold. As soon as he had the news, he would move to the kitchen and eat his usual meal, consisting of tinned food.

Roy didn't live the high life anymore, since his life changed and his wife was taken away from him; cold and sudden. He finished his glass and picked up the scotch bottle, resting on the edge of the side table. He took the top off, hearing a small pop as the air escaped, his phone vibrated violently next to him. He looked at the un-saved number flashing in front of him and picked up the phone resting it in his palm.

He put the bottle down and stood up, slowly and stiffly and clicked the little green button on his handset. 'News?' he said trying to keep the composure in his voice.

'It's been delivered,' he heard a cold voice reply in return. Roy smiled, satisfied. 'The police arrived before I left.'

'*You* didn't call the police?'

'Didn't need to.'

'You weren't seen? You sound quite calm about this.' Roy said, listening down the phone urging a response.

'No. The bitch screamed and someone called it in. I was gone by the time they made the call. I was just in time to see the husband return.'

'He came back? When? Why?'

Xavier took a moment to reply, 'calm down. He came back early. Probably didn't go to the gym. Forgot something or, couldn't be bothered. I couldn't care less.'

'How did you do it?' Roy asked excitedly.

'An iron rod. One blow was enough, but two was better.'

'No break in signs either?' Roy asked, sounding relieved.

'Roy, it's done' Xavier said back angrily and callous. 'I want the rest of my money. Tonight.'

'Yes, yes of course. Tonight. The usual place. I'll leave now,' Roy said pushing the scotch glass to one side, as if it never happened.

The line was quiet for what seemed like minutes, until Xavier did something that Roy had never ever heard him do before; ask a question of his own. 'What did this Stephen do to you?'

Roy tensed up and, in an unfriendly manner, he replied, 'more than you could ever imagine.'

17

Benjamin Durant didn't understand the can of worms he had opened three weeks ago. He was sitting alone on a cold floor and he could smell damp in the air. He could hear the constant noises of shouting and pounding against walls. It had become a daily occurrence, which he adjusted to after so many years.

He could hear footsteps in the corridor outside his room, which would grow louder and louder and then more distant. The echo would alternate every few minutes. It sounded like a soldier, parading to and fro. The room was cold but as the footsteps gained momentum, Ben felt warmer, as if there were hope.

Ben closed his eyes and arrived at Green Park tube station. He walked through the park leading to Buckingham palace, holding his mother's hand, the sun shining down. It was his first real adventure outside of his home village. He stood and watched the guards through the gates. He remembered the red coats and furry hats, which were held on underneath their chins.

Ben was just short of being six foot and had dark brown hair. His face was youthful, but for the small skin pigmentation on his chin. His eyes were brown and prominent, and his ears were small. His arms and legs were like short bean poles, which had no muscle. He was strong willed and believed in patience. "Good things came to those who wait", his mother had told him.

Ben had been sitting in this room for six hours. He had all the time in the world to spend here. He sat staring ahead at the white wall in front of him. The room was no more than ten foot by ten foot and each wall in turn were covered in graffiti, messages and stains. He pulled his top down and waited.

Originally, he didn't understand why he had been treated so well. He felt like the star. However, he knew he shouldn't celebrate because if anyone else knew what he had done, he wouldn't be so popular. He'd likely be dead. To be seen helping someone in power was dangerous and stupid and something he intended to keep close to his chest.

Ben enjoyed the power trip. He'd never had any real friends of his own. His mother was his only friend; until she ruined it all. They had lived in a small village until she moved them many, many miles away. It was too far for Ben to keep in contact with anyone; a new school, new surroundings, a new life. It was their little secret, she had said.

Ben had secrets that he wouldn't share. Who would believe him? Roy had promised him great things for all the information he could share. Ben felt privileged. He felt different. He felt wanted. Something he had never truly felt. His mother said she loved him. She made it clear about the sacrifices she had made for him. *Lies,* he thought. She had to go.

Today though, Ben felt different. He was under punishment for something he didn't understand. He had been in two separate prisons for a total of over ten years; imprisoned for murdering his mother. Life was his sentence. He couldn't confess to why he did it. Only one person would find out why he had done it and he thought he would never meet this person, until now. It had been the only item on his agenda for ten years. Ben closed his tired eyes and fell asleep into a deep dream.

His mother was called Charity. She had raised him single handed and he never knew his father. His mother would always speak of him, but, for Ben to mention him, was forbidden. Still, his mother could do no wrong in his eyes. She was his guardian angel. She was religious. Sunday service was compulsory and to pray before dinner was the norm.

She worshipped God until the day she died. Ben remembered the day she died. She had been ill for months. She called it a condition. She had never consulted a doctor, nor been diagnosed. Doctors couldn't help her, she would say. Only God would save her and repay her for her work. She had been lying in bed talking to Ben. She went quiet for a few seconds, which then turned into minutes. Ben remembered looking into her eyes, seeing a frail woman in front of him, whom he could not save. Then everything changed.

She told him things about why he lived as he did. About why his life suddenly changed so much. Why had she kept it secret? Was she trying to protect him? No, to protect herself. Ben screamed at her. She didn't fight back. She was too weak. She smiled and read off some verse in the bible. She would need to pay for her sins.

He picked up a pillow and smothered her. He pushed the pillow hard into her face, feeling her small, thin arms, merely gripping onto his, the veins bulging through her skin as she used every essence of energy to fight back. Until her wrists slackened, as her palms fell open on top of the bed cover. He took the pillow away and her eyes were shut.

His next memory was being inside a cell, enclosed in a small room for twenty hours of the day. The first week consisted of a broken arm, a fractured rib and a wound with a sharpened toothbrush to his upper leg. It was his prison welcome. It got easier with time, but no-one trusted him. Stay out of their way Ben and they will stay out of yours, he thought.

He was moved to another prison after three years, due to now being a 'low-risk.' He preferred the new prison; it was more open, and this presented Ben with a higher level of freedom. There was work available and it was poorly managed by bent and corrupt guards. But overall, it allowed Ben to remain anonymous and isolated from everyone else. Ben was self-sufficient. It was a fresh start and he relished it.

Until just over three weeks ago at 9am, Ben had been classed as having a partial mental illness. Ben felt different. He was a lone wolf, raised by a lying mother who showed him God and how to fend for himself and himself alone. The voices in his head were normal now. The voices were part of the sentence he pronounced on himself when he raised the pillow to his mother.

He had been at a weekly meeting with a councillor and several other inmates. It was a meeting where the inmates had time to talk freely and be honest about wrong doings. It was an amnesty and everyone took it for what it was; a get out of jail free card. Everyone spoke about their misdemeanours before prison; the drugs, the trafficking, the soliciting, the laundering. Ben kept quiet. Nothing was secret forever.

It came to his turn and he was sat on a plastic chair in the circle. If the circle was compared to a clock face, Ben was sat at number five. He usually kept quiet, but today it was a new guard and that meant he was more interested in making sure the door was secure than listening to the convicts talk. Ben told them about his mother. But he changed the story, not slightly, but completely. He told them his mother had asked to be killed, sticking to his original plea in court. He told tales of her deteriorating health and how she prayed for the pain to end. The room didn't ask him anything else about that night.

He remembered the rest of the conversation well. They asked him about his time growing up. *Psychological evaluation*, he thought, typical. They asked him about his village and the relationship he had with his mother. Ben began talking. 'I was raised in a quiet village. Nothing happened there. My mum moved us on one day to another village, hours away. Ben stopped for a moment, rehearsing his story. 'We never went back. A lot of people left.'

'Why did you leave?' Ben was asked.

'My mum didn't like it anymore,' Ben said. 'A lady died there. Most of the villagers lived there for the vanity, loving their top village awards. Rubbish,' Ben spat. 'But after the woman's death, it wasn't seen as a rosy location as before. We should have stayed, so when she asked to die, I helped her.' Ben looked at the room when he finished and saw most people looking at him confused.

However, the councillor hosting the meeting didn't look taken aback and she asked more questions, but Ben switched off, playing with his name tag and scratching his arms, leaving red lines across his skin. The lady moved onto other people in the circle and Ben remained uninterested and unmoved. What did it matter? Wasn't going to shave off any of your sentence, he thought.

Ben then went back to his bunk, updating his third diary, since he had joined the prison. Ben always wrote his full name on the inside cover. When he'd finished, he began reading back over his own writing, reliving his story to the councillor, when a prison guard arrived at his cell door. He explained that the warden wanted to see him straight away. It was to discuss something that had happened earlier today, to which Ben could be of some assistance.

Ben walked through the corridors, aided by a guard, whose arms were covered in tattoos across defined muscles and a tall frame. They reached the warden's office and Ben walked in alone and unarmed. The door closed behind him and sitting at a desk ten feet away, was an older man with white wavy hair and green menacing eyes.

18

'Sit down, Ben,' Roy said. Ben walked forwards to a chair in front of a large wooden desk, which was covered in trays all loaded with paper next to a light, which you could move to shine in different positions. The window behind Roy showed the orange glow of the sun. The light engulfing the room highlighted scratches on the desk.

'What?' Ben replied as he held onto the arm rests, gently lowering himself down. Ben had never had much one to one contact with the warden, other than seeing him walking around the prison, limping as he went. He was usually quiet and hidden in his office. *Bad temper* he had heard the other inmates say.

'There's something you can help me with, Ben,' Roy said. Roy rubbed his left knee and continued. 'I was speaking with the councillor today who told me an interesting part of your formative years.' Ben watched closely, as Roy stared ahead. Ben thought he could sense anger behind his old eyes. Roy gripped the table before him and continued once more, 'you told her the reason you helped kill your mother was because she took you away from your home? Correct?'

'Yes,' said Ben freely admitting his crime.' But why does it concern you?'

'Something else you said concerns me,' Roy replied, his eyes narrowing and fixated onto Bens. Ben felt as though heat was being radiated from Roy and he struggled to return his gaze. 'You left because a lady died, yes?'

'Yes?'

'How did she die?'

'I can't remember,' Ben said.

'Then remember!,' Roy replied, raising his voice to sound authoritative and intimidating, but quiet enough not to alert the guard outside, who Roy could see through the clouded glass window.

Ben sat back, thinking about why he was here and decided to ask, 'what's it worth?'

Ben saw Roy push his wheeled chair back, holding onto the desk as he fully stood. Roy walked around the desk and brushed past Ben. Ben saw something large bouncing in Roy's pocket. He watched as the warden circled the room, arriving back at his original starting position. 'It is worth everything to you. Freedom,' Roy lied.

'You've been truthful, Ben. You can make amends for what you've done. You can be free of that burden. Tell me how this lady died and I will give you optimism for the future.'

Ben looked up into the green eyes as he fiddled with his sleeve. There was something about the lady in question that Roy wanted to know. Did Roy know the full truth already? Impossible, Ben thought. He decided he would only tell part of the story, but not all of it. The temptation of optimism was something he had grown to dream of.

Ben sighed for Roy's benefit and repeated the changed story once again, 'mum was very religious. She raised me as a single child. I never went without anything. We lived in a village that was quiet and dull, but it was home and all I knew.

'Then one day, my mum came home and said something terrible had happened in our village.' Ben continued averting his eyes to a large scratch on the wooden table before him, 'She said four or five people from the church were moving and so were we.'

'Why?'

'She handed her notice in, left her job, left the flat and we were gone. Days later, she said our village had a bad reputation due to the death of this lady. It seemed a steep reason to move, but she said everyone was doing it and she had a good job elsewhere.'

Ben looked up at again at Roy, who was breathing slowly, his chest moving in and out every few seconds. Ben could sense there were more questions to follow. Ben watched as Roy glanced at the clock hanging on the wall and Roy placed both palms on the table, 'how did the lady die?'

Ben took a second longer than he should have as he tried to rehearse the answer in his head, 'a man killed her,' Ben said.

'How?'

'A motor accident, my mum told me,' Ben said. Ben looked again at Roy, whom he could sense looked angry.

'What else do you know?' Roy said standing upright again.

'I don't know anything else. Mum didn't tell me much other than the man who killed the lady died at the scene too.' Ben knew the truthful answer was to say, *by the time I found this out, it was too late. I was inside.*

Ben saw Roy clench his jaw. 'How long have you known this?'

'Since we moved, why?'

Roy turned to look out the window behind him. He sighed, keeping his ears on alert for movement behind him. He had reached a dead end. All this time in trying to make amends for Linda's death in any desperate way a husband could and he had nothing. 'Anything else Ben, before I let you go?'

Ben's mind clunked, confused yet excited as he couldn't understand why Roy was so interested in this story. What did this woman have to do with anything? Did she have a link to Ben's past? Ben felt he had no other choice but to reveal a slice of the secret he had carried for so long for the benefit of the greater good and to meet his own agenda.

Ben crossed legs, his trouser sliding up his shin bone as he looked at Roy's back. 'There was *something* my mum told me,' Ben said as Roy turned around quickly, 'this man who killed that woman. He had a son.'

19

Over three months later, Stephen was sat in a cell of his own, staring a blank wall. He felt empty. He wanted revenge, but he knew he'd never meet Stacey's killer or find out why she was killed. It had eaten away at him for three months straight. He had snapped inside. He wasn't the same man.

His hair was longer and hung over one side. The sides of his hair stuck out as if he had just got out of bed. He had a black beard, which had grown wild and uneven. He hadn't shaved once since that fateful night. His eyes looked darker and the hope he had once held inside had slowly been diminished with every passing day. His high cheek bones still stood out prominently on his skinny face.

He had been inside for two days. His life had changed dramatically over the past three months. He had been moved around constantly whilst his case progressed from court hearings, the final verdict and to now. Not a day had passed where he hadn't relived that evening.

Stephen was led out his front door after being detained, cold and blood soaked. He had been spoken to, by a female officer, about his right to remain silent. Stephen remained quiet and dazed. He had seen the crime programmes. He remembered being pushed down and underneath the roof of the car.

Then he was inside a bright room, sat at a metal table. The

room was about ten by ten foot and all that occupied the room was a camera in the top corner facing the table and a device, which looked like an old radio cassette player. Exactly like the ones he had seen on the television.

Stephen stared up at the ceiling, the bright light illuminating the room, giving it an unfriendly and unwanted feel. Two people entered the room in suits. Both looked smart and ready for business. They looked intelligent. Maybe they would believe him? They questioned him for two hours and the smallest things came back to haunt him.

The detectives said a glass was found on the floor, which Stephen guessed was the glass he had drunk from that very day. Subjective evidence, but it could mean he threw the glass in an angry frenzy. He knew he didn't, but would they?

The detectives said a photo of the Stephen and Stacey was found smashed on the kitchen floor. They accused Stephen of smashing it along with the glass. They said he didn't like the idea of marriage anymore. The things they said, the lies.

The detectives said a neighbour reported the disturbance. The *bitch* from the next door, Stephen thought. The neighbour said, she heard a scream and when she looked out the window, Stephen's car was parked right outside. Could they prove he was there when she died?

The detectives said Officer Michael saw Stephen kneeling down by his wife, a bloody weapon next to him, as he said sorry several times to her. He was happy to testify what he saw and was sickened by Stephen's actions. All the evidence pointed at Stephen. There was no escape.

Stephen thought about the looks the two detectives gave him. Some random police appointed lawyer sat in the room and offered nothing. They scribbled notes on a ring-binder note pad. The detectives looked inquisitively at him. Surely they could see he was no monster?

'Where is my wife? Stephen said aloud. Stephen was now sitting in a much smaller room, which was cold and dark and noisy. The room had a single, thick metal door, which had a slide compartment at eye level for the patrol officers to pass food over. He had seen it all on the fictional programmes.

He was being held in custody. He was wearing an off white top, with grey bottoms. He had rubber shoes on with no laces. He sat with his knees up underneath his chin, tears falling down his face. He rested his head back and woke up the next day, sitting in front of the same detectives. They were both in different suits and both cleanly shaven.

They asked Stephen more questions about the night. They asked if anyone could confirm his location between certain hours. Could he explain the screaming? Was there an argument? He couldn't provide anything, but try to plead his innocence. He was returned back to his cell.

A month later, Stephen was stood in a large room, with oak benches and oak bannisters with lights in the ceiling spaced four feet apart. To his left were ten people sitting in two rows of five. Some dressed casually, some dressed in suits. They were looking directly opposite at the other side of the room.

To Stephen's right was another stand, which was at a higher level. To his rear were many people sitting down, all dressed in dark suits and dark dresses. Some people he didn't recognise, some he did; Stacey's parents. Stacey's mother, Marina, was crying and her husband, Clifford just staring straight ahead, trying to fight back to the inevitable tears.

Straight in front of him, was a small woman, dressed in long red and black garments, with a white wig on her head. *The judge,* he thought. The trial seemed to be over after five minutes. Stephen couldn't bring the energy to fight. Death was better than this.

Stephen's mind whirled in and out of focus, staring at the jury to his left. They were flitting between their paperwork resting on their knees, to the lady, whom Stephen knew to be his neighbour, talking on the witness stand. Don't let me get out of here Shirley, Stephen thought.

'A minimum of twenty six years,' rang out across the court room and Stephen was led down a dark tunnel to be transferred somewhere else unknown to him. He had no belongings. He had nothing but the clothes on his back, and even these belonged to someone else entirely.

He was moved to a temporary prison for seven weeks, whilst he waited for his final destination to be cleared, higher up the chain by someone else, he imagined. The temporary holding prison was dark and intimidating. Prisoners were all waiting to go somewhere else depending on their risk category. Most were kept separated and the guards were consistently patrolling the corridors and the doors were permanently locked. Stephen spent twenty hours a day inside his cell.

He had no energy and no longer cried. He tried to remain alert. A light had gone out in his head. His kindness had gone. He became angry every minute of the day. He was innocent. He never found out what happened to Stacey after he was led away. He had something in him, he never knew he had; a temper. He started to work out how to relieve the tension; press up's, sit up's and cardio.

He would never have hurt anyone. Now he had nothing but the ambition of hurting someone. Like someone had hurt him. Why though? The same question, he had asked himself for weeks. He stared at the same wall for seven weeks straight and nothing came to him.

Was it related to Stacey's job? She dealt with custody cases. That could be part of it. An angry parent who had it in for her, bent on revenge. Doubtful. The detectives would have surely gone down this route too, but they found nothing at all that led them to believe that Stacey's death was work related. Stephen arrived back at square one every time and started all over, time and time again.

Stephen was moved to a prison for his risk category. He had been told by previous guards upon his final departure, that the new prison was even worse and was heavily guarded. He was told he wouldn't survive it. He was too weak. He'd never make it.

A month later, Stephen heard his cell door open mechanically as he stepped out into the chamber surrounded by people in orange jumpsuits. He was home.

20

Ben Durant sat in Roy's office, on a plastic chair, with his elbows and wrists supported by the arm rests. He was looking at the wooden desk, which had less paperwork than on his previous visit, but this made the scratches more evident in the morning brightness. Ben sat with his legs uncrossed and his feet twitching.

Ben now had to attend fortnightly meetings with Roy, after advice from the counsellor. The counsellor suggested it was good for Ben to talk to someone. Roy had apparently offered his personal services. Ben didn't doubt why. Roy was so interested in the story Ben had told him about months before. A story, which involved a man, Ben was desperate to meet too.

He had heard about Stephen entering the prison two days ago. It was just another inmate, another murderer, who had pleaded his innocence but was found guilty. It was just someone else who would be brought back down to earth in no time at all. Not such a big man.

He had seen Stephen with his own eyes yesterday and he felt a sense of satisfaction and excitement, mixed with revulsion and frustration. He saw him walking idly through the prison corridor looking around, people staring at him from every angle. Ben saw him turn around and walk past two guards and back towards his cell.

Ben heard the office door open and he quickly looked over his left shoulder to see Roy limping into the cool room. Roy's feet were alternating unevenly, drowning out the noise of the whirring air conditioner. Roy stepped past Ben and the wooden desk, his fingers sliding across the surface.

'I wasn't too long, was, I Ben?' Roy said, sitting in his firm chair. Ben kept his eyes focused on Roy's green eyes, trying not to blink or show fear. Truth was, Ben was now a little intimidated and scared. He felt he was now hanging off the arm of the most powerful man in the prison. The story would no longer remain in the past, but seemingly very much in the present and the future. Ben knew, however, that he controlled the true extent to which the story would be told.

'No,' Ben replied, still looking into Roy's eyes. Ben broke the gaze and looked at the window, where the blinds were pulled slightly across on one side to cover the sun light, yet it still crept through. 'Can I go now?'

'Why leave, Ben?' Roy replied, a smiling curling out the corner of his mouth. 'You've done something wonderful, Ben.'

'That new guy, Stephen, he's the one I told you about?'

'All in good time, Ben,' Roy said. 'We're going to be working together. We need to trust each other.'

Ben felt distrustful of Roy, and Ben guessed Roy probably felt the same. But Ben didn't need him to fully trust him. Ben only had one interest now. 'What will you do for me?'

'I will not reveal our little secret. The inmates can't know you've helped me, can they? How would that go down? Not well, I wouldn't have thought.' Ben's mind pondered on the questions as Roy continued, 'tell me about your mother?'

'My mother?' Ben said 'No.'

'Yes, Ben. Or I'll tell everyone what you've done in the past few weeks. We need to trust each other, Ben.'

Ben looked ahead and tried to think. Why did his mother matter? 'No,' he said.

Roy's smile became a snarl, 'tell me Ben, or trust me, it will all end for you quicker than you could ever imagine. I have power and I have the ability to send you away, believe me.'

'This is all under a pure amnesty?' Ben replied.

'Of course, Ben, trust.'

Ben relayed the story of his mother's death, all the way to end '...she was ready to die. But she didn't want to die. She said some harsh things to me' Ben lied wiping the sweat from his brow, 'so I killed her. I don't regret it. God would understand.'

'So you did do it? Roy asked calmly, 'you belong inside these four walls.'

'I'm here, and I accept my punishment. I have behaved since day one and I patiently await my prize. Good things come to those who wait.'

'What do you wait for?'

Ben smiled, 'for God to repay me.' Ben saw Roy roll his eyes and place his hands behind his head. Ben looked back at him and seized the moment. For the second time, Ben asked 'that new guy, he's the one I told you about?'

'The very same guy,' Roy said.

Ben looked down into his lap and his heart thumped with glee. The plan had worked, for both of them it seemed. 'What now?'

'Now he must settle into prison. An eye for an eye is what they call it. I will make him work so he can forgive himself and you will get to know him for me. I want to hear everything he does. Anything he is planning. I want to know when he breathes Ben.'

'What did he do?' Ben said.

'Killed his wife,' Roy replied matter-of-factly.

Ben sensed there was a lot more to this than maybe he was aware of. He didn't know what Roy's plan was, but did he really need to care? He had his own game plan and he felt he was winning. 'What did he do to you?'

'Nothing, Ben. It's all coincidental. He was free and now he's finished, Ben, thanks to you. People change, and he obviously has,' Roy said. Roy stood up from his chair and Ben saw him rub his left knee. Roy opened his front draw and pulled something black from within, placing it into his pocket. Ben couldn't make out what it was.

Roy circled round the desk until he was now behind Ben again. Ben could sense Roy's presence but he didn't dare turn round. He didn't want to show any fear. He had to ask Roy a question and he swallowed hard and gripped the arms rests as he asked, 'he didn't murder his wife did he?'

It was sudden and abrupt, but Ben felt an arm wrap around his neck with ferocious anger and power erupt from behind him. He could hear Roy breathing in his ear as a harsh metal object was thrust into his neck and pain rushed to his head. Roy had him pinned and Ben couldn't help but stay still because when he moved, the pain worsened.

'If you *ever* ask that question again, Ben, you will be killed. There are people in here who would be happy to kill you, you worthless piece of shit,' said Roy tightening his grip.

'I won't,' Ben said spluttering.

'Stephen Farley killed his wife in anger. This has been proven.

He has a temper problem and he is in here to be punished for his actions. It is purely coincidence Ben that he is in here.'

'Yes, I know, sorry,' said Ben, feeling his head become dazed and short of air

'Now, you will do what you are told. You will get to know Stephen Farley and keep eyes on him until the time is right. Until I decide the time is right. Yes?'

'Yes,' Ben said barely breathing.

'Find out everything. Anything he does, I want to know. Anything he plans on doing, I want to know' Roy said and Ben felt the metal object thrust further into his neck.

'Any mention and I mean *any* mention of today and you will remain in solitary for so long, you'll forget what day light looks like. Scrap that,' Roy continued, 'you will die, Ben. Understand?'

Ben nodded quickly, feeling the metal rub up and down his skin. Ben felt Roy let go of him and he collapsed forward onto the desk, gasping and puffing, his heart rate soaring above normal. Out of the corner of his eye, Ben saw Roy walk past him and he heard a thump, which he imagined to be Roy placing the object back into the draw.

'Gently, Ben, that's it. Slowly in, slowly out,' Roy said and Ben kept breathing. Ben looked ahead at the green eyes belonging to deranged man before him. Ben rubbed his neck with both hands as if strangling himself when Roy spoke again 'leave Ben. We are done here. Guard,' Roy shouted and the door opened seconds later. 'Ben is finished here. Please escort him back to his quarters.'

The guard entered the room and stood three foot behind Ben's chair. Ben stood up slowly keeping his eyes on Roy who continued to smile back at him. 'I hope you feel better tomorrow, Ben,' Roy said as Ben was grabbed by the arm and led out the room. 'Ben,' Roy shouted as Ben turned around slowly and angrily. 'A new life starts today for you.'

As the door shut behind them, all that was audible was the air conditioner above him. Roy sat back in his chair and cradled his fingers in front of him, 'a new life starts for me too.'

Lilian Martin was young with silky black hair and her eyes were wide and blue. She was tall and elegant and well built. Her blouse was tight against her chest and she felt uncomfortable in her close fit trousers. She had been working at the prison for two weeks. The reason given for her move was due to relocation from London and she was playing the act well.

She had tried to work closely with the warden, but she found him very forlorn and private. She was sat at a desk, as one of the guards roughly shepherded Ben out of the room. Afterwards, all she could hear were the sounds of pattering against a computer keyboard, coming from across the room. She stared at Roy's office door and after another minute, she withdrew her notepad and began jotting down her initial judgement on the prison.

21

Stephen left his cell and looked down over the metal railing to the bottom level, fifteen feet below him. He was wearing unlaced rubber shoes, with small air holes inches apart. He wore thick white socks, which were pulled up just above his bony ankles. A light coloured orange top was tucked into his elasticated, loose waistband.

The air was hot and bright sunlight beamed from above, shining through the only part of the transparent ceiling. Stephen stroked his dark beard subconsciously, pulling at the hairs every few strokes. It was the first time he had ever had a beard. It was the first time he had been somewhere like this too. He looked left and right slowly, watching other orange jumpsuits descend the metal stairs in orderly fashion, whilst some just stood outside their cells talking to neighbours.

Along the corridor, a guard was standing at a designated post, wearing navy blue, single pleat trousers, with a crisp white shirt and no tie. Stephen was feet away from one, but the guard paid him no attention. Stephen breathed out heavily, his bottom lip shaking as he did so. He could hear the noises of feet upon metal along with the murmurs of male voices.

He turned left towards the stairs and walked past five people in a huddle. They were all tall and slim and didn't even take their eyes off each other as Stephen brushed past them. One had a tattoo across his neck. Stephen looked around again. The corridor ran for around fifty metres with around thirty doors on each side. He saw another guard outside an open cell standing alert and focused.

The walls were made from large, heavy bricks, all painted white, which Stephen imagined years ago would have been bright and fresh, making the room look vast. Now the walls were covered in black marks and the main coat was wearing thin. Stephen pictured the prison years before. He looked at a cell door, a few metres from the staircase he intended to take.

The door was large and powerful. The door was controlled centrally. Stephen imagined the clunking and churning of the gears as the door moved. Stephen made a mental note to read up on it somehow, if he ever got that far. He saw a small bald man, with a light shade of stubble underneath his ears to the middle of his chin, sitting on their cell bed reading a book.

The air grew cooler as Stephen arrived at the bottom level. He saw people talking ahead, and he could still hear noises from above. He would need to adjust to the changes quickly. He walked towards a guard stood next to plastic table and a few trays. *Food*, Stephen thought. This is how I'm going to eat for the rest of my life.

The guard saw him coming and turned his hands fractionally so they were in front of his body. Stephen made eye contact and felt the guard must have been over six foot and around forty years old. He looked experienced and equipped to deal with trouble, his hand movement had shown he was ready for combat, maybe even expectant.

'How do you get outside?' Stephen said.

Stephen saw the guard nod towards the length of the corridor, 'just follow the others.'

'Thanks,' Stephen replied. He followed others down the corridor, some on their own and some in groups. The corridor was wide and unfurnished and the solid brick wall gave it an unforgiving look. Stephen saw offices further along, which were covered in metal bars and a cloudy type of glass. Stephen didn't dare try to see what was inside.

He passed a man being escorted somewhere by a guard. The man was red in the face and very skinny. He looked angry and on edge. The man kept walking forward, his head down as if to raise it would be a catastrophe. Stephen saw the man enter a room with the guard and was lost to sight. The corridor became a bottle neck as orange suits fell into a single line and exited ahead.

Stephen kept walking, staying to the outskirts of the hallway, which was littered with guards. Stephen could see a thickset man in front of him, with a big chest and big arms. Stephen deviated from his previous course until he arrived at the bottle neck.

Stephen made it outside and looked ahead, his right hand resting over his forehead to block the orange sun above. The vast space in front of him amazed him. It was the size of two cricket fields and was circular. In the middle of the field, were a gathering of men standing wearing white vests. He could see two large towers standing tall opposite him.

Stephen stepped across the worn grass and sand. He imagined years ago, grass grew here, green and proud, but it had now been replaced with sand and destitution and misery. To his right, he saw prisoners laughing and jumping on each other, whilst some were talking, heads bent close together.

He arrived near one of the towers, partially blocking the sun behind it. The tower was positioned outside the prison beyond the fence. It was around fifty feet in height and twenty feet wide. It was built from solid concrete and was smooth across its width. He followed the soaring tower until he reached the top, where he could make out two guards looking straight down.

A guard moved slightly and Stephen saw something black and long, held across their waist; a gun? Something you'd see in a movie; a high power rifle sniper capable of killing from any position, unforgiving and deadly. Positioned on top of the tower were a large light facing the prison. Stephen guessed it was in case anyone tried to escape. Impossible, Stephen thought.

Across the yard, Stephen saw a small building with benches on the outside. He walked towards the building and placed his hands in his pocket, trying to look inconspicuous. He knew, from the programmes he had watched, that no one was envious of a newcomer. The newbies were described as the new fish in the tank.

Stephen reached the building and saw a small signpost. The building was surrounded by its own fence, which had spiralled, barbed wire, attached at the very top. The signpost explained the building was a workshop. It described the work available and the benefits of undertaking work and additional responsibility. Stephen nodded and turned away. He made a mental note to enquire about the workshop, once he had finished meeting his councillor.

Stephen came as close as he wanted to be, from the men working out in the centre of the field. They were lifting weights and pulling themselves up and down from stationary equipment. A giant of a man was lifting large dumbbells in each arm, flexing them up and down. Others were jogging on the spot and some were sitting on the floor doing sit ups. Stephen wondered if these were the popular prisoners.

Stephen circled around the powerlifters still keeping a good distance and walked towards one part a guard had told him about, upon entering the prison; the church. Stephen wasn't religious. He'd never even been to church, but he'd never murdered his wife either. He took his hands from his pocket until he reached the large wooden doors.

The church was old and rusting in parts. A semi sized cross was visible on the roof and below the entrance the sun was blocked from view. He pushed the door open and walked into the church. The church was empty, but for a man who was in a white robe, sitting on a bench, towards the back of the room.

'Good day,' the pastoral said aloud as the door closed. 'The next service begins in a few hours. Or do you seek just to pray?'

'I wanted to come and see the church,' Stephen replied. 'Is it bad if I admit I've never been inside a church before?'

'You are in one now, so it need not matter,' the pastoral said. He began to walk towards Stephen, with his hand outstretched, 'my name is Bernard.'

'Stephen.'

'It's a pleasure to meet you. I have worked in this chapel for twenty five years. I have found my saviour here. I wouldn't be anywhere else. I was about to pray, Stephen, if you wish to pray for forgiveness?'

'I haven't anything to be sorry for, Bernard.'

'Is this your first day?'

'My second here, but I was in another place for a while.'

'We get moved depending on risk. Here is not such a high risk prison. Your sentence is?'

'Minimum of twenty six years,' Stephen said lowering his head. 'I didn't do it.'

'If I had a month knocked off my sentence for every time I heard that Stephen, my word, I'd have been out of here twenty years ago. The biggest regret I have, is not adjusting to this life earlier. I spent my first year thinking, I'll be out of here in a few years, no problem. The life sentence part was something I kept forgetting, sadly.'

'I'm not doing life in here,' Stephen said.

'I don't think we really get a choice, do you?' Bernard replied.

'I will give it a good go.'

'Be careful. Don't go pulling up trees as you may find yourself in more trouble. Folks in here don't take too kindly to others playing a sob story. I'm just telling you how it is.'

Stephen looked at the inside décor of the church. It was very plain and all that occupied the room was a table and several benches. There was no paint anywhere on the walls and the floor was pure concrete. It looked almost brand new and as if it hadn't had many visitors. Stephen could feel Bernard still looking at him.

Stephen nodded, 'It's obvious why I'm angry all the time. I was never angry. Now I've changed, Bernard, and I have nothing. No family, no friends. Sorry, I don't even know you and I'm venting out.'

'I'm here to talk, Stephen.'

'My wife was killed. I honestly don't know why. I came home and she was gone. She was my only key to happiness. They say I did it and I had no-one to support me. Now I have to sit here, unable to prove my innocence.'

'O but you can.'

'How'? Stephen replied.

'Being here shows you are sorry.'

'Bernard, I need to go.'

'Don't stay away too long. Come tomorrow evening. Believe me.'

Stephen nodded and turned walking out the door, leaving Bernard standing in the church alone. He thought about what Bernard had said; he had found his saviour and had a life sentence. What had Bernard done? Stephen never asked. Tomorrow night, should he go? Sleep on it, Stephen thought as he walked away from the church and round the corner to the fence.

He reached the wired fence. You could just about squeeze your hand through one of the bounded joints. Pointless, unless you had bolt cutters, Stephen thought. Above the fence was barbed wire, similar to what he had seen earlier. Stephen looked over his left shoulder and saw the yard look quieter than ten minutes before. Were less people working out?

He turned a little more until he was fully looking at the prison. He noticed a big clock for the first time, bound on the front of the highest part of the structure. He had plenty of time till his councillor session. He would just look through the fence and across the fields beyond, wishing his life would go back three months. Freedom.

Stephen turned back and held onto the metal fence and rested his forehead against it. The steel was cold against his skin and he could feel the sun shining down upon his back. Then Stephen was surrounded by a large shadow and he came face to face with the largest man he'd ever seen.

22

The man was easily six foot eight. Stephen had seen him working out earlier. He was completely bald, and his head was sweaty. His arms up close were the size of Stephen's thigh and he wasn't small. The guy's ears were massacred. Bits of skin were missing on both, but on his left ear, hanging midway down was dried, dead skin.

His eyes were buried deep and looked as if he was constantly squinting. He moved forward another foot and Stephen could see two other people standing behind him, grinning excitedly. The man's mouth was open and Stephen could see a few teeth below his upper lip.

'Fish,' the man said. Stephen thought the syllable seemed to have used a lot of his mental energy. The man made another step closer. His arms were covered in tattoos and Stephen couldn't see a single piece of white flesh below the graffiti. Stephen remained quiet as the man raised his hands. They were the size of gorillas, with sausages for fingers. His fingertips were black and dirty.

'My name is Honda' he said sneering. Stephen didn't reply, but checked left to right. He had no escape. He breathed out slowly and calmly and moved his hands in front of his body and stared into Honda's eyes. 'This is your welcome party.'

Stephen heard a noise outside the fence and looked as a guard appeared from behind the church, slowly strolling around the prison. He looked in their direction, 'any problem?'

Stephen looked back at Honda and he knew that if he said yes, he wouldn't have this problem now, but it was inevitable he would have more trouble in the future. Stephen kept looking at Honda, who stood there large and bulky, smiling back, not even looking at the guard, 'boys,' the guard shouted again.

'No trouble,' Stephen said averting his attention to the guard. 'All fine.' The guard nodded and Stephen turned back to face Honda. The guard walked the way he came from and Stephen made his first mistake; he watched the guard. Stephen didn't have chance to react. The noises around the prison were drowned from his mind as he saw Honda running at him.

Stephen tried to sidestep him, but Honda's frame were so vast, that Honda's swinging right arm caught Stephen on the side of the temple. Stephen felt one of his knees buckle under the blow and his eyes went black momentarily. He had never been in a fist fight before. He had been to defence classes when younger, but he never put it into practice. Stephen raised himself and turned to see Honda standing feet away. Honda aimed a straight right jab towards Stephen's face.

Stephen stepped back as the blow missed, but as Honda's arm came down, it connected with Stephen's sternum, which seemed to explode. Stephen felt his mouth move as he yelled aloud in pain. Stephen gritted his teeth and threw a hard right hand of his own, which connected with Honda's face. Stephen repeated the feat with his left hand and he felt as if he had done more damage to his hands, than Honda's face. Honda didn't raise his hands to defend himself.

Stephen saw the two men that accompanied Honda move

round further. They didn't involve themselves. They didn't need to. Honda responded with his own right hand, which caught Stephen straight below the eye. Stephen couldn't stay on his feet and he fell backwards, lying on a small patch of grass, feeling the sand rub beneath him as the heat pounded down above them.

Honda threw a hard punch downwards at Stephen, who rolled over and scissor kicked Honda's legs, feeling his shins connect with Honda's fatty muscle. Honda fell onto one knee, as Stephen twisted himself upright and moved sideways. Stephen aimed the sole of his foot into Honda's head, above his ear. Stephen put his foot back down and felt the immediate ache in his foot.

As Honda tried to raise himself, Stephen attempted to kick Honda again, but Honda caught the boot in one hand and, Stephen felt him squeeze hard. Stephen was hopping on one foot, uneasy and unbalanced. He threw a right hand over his knee, which didn't connect properly, hitting Honda's ear as Honda threw Stephen's leg into the air, knocking him backwards.

Stephen was lying on his back and the sun disappeared as Honda's face came into view as he landed another hard right of his own, but this time to Stephen's stomach. Stephen tasted vomit in his mouth and his legs jolted as he was left with no air. Honda's left hand caught Stephen across the jaw. Stephen wrapped his hands over his head and pushed his legs up trying to kick out. As he kicked both legs at once, all he saw was Honda's right, clenched fist, falling down in a smooth curve and he closed his eyes and felt no more pain.

Stephen kicked his legs again as he woke up. His mouth was dry and his lips were stuck together. He lay still, trying to listen for Honda but nothing came. There was just silence. Stephen moved his fingers gently, trying to bring back life into his arms and he heard a small clunk of metal on metal. He moved his wrist and heard the clunk again.

He opened his eyes slowly, feeling mucus and oil in the corner of his eye. The room was bright. Was he dead or dreaming? Stephen was lying in a white bed, with the sheets pulled up to his waist. There was another cotton sheet, folded over above his feet. Stephen tried to raise himself in the bed, but couldn't. He looked to his right as he heard another clunk, to see his wrist handcuffed to the bed post. Alive.

To his left, was someone in blue overalls, holding a clipboard in one hand and writing with the other. She didn't acknowledge Stephen and kept her gaze firmly on the paper in front of her. Stephen peered around the room, which was slightly bigger than his own cell. Every inch was bare and painted white.

Not far from where he lay, were two other people sleeping under a white sheet. Stephen could see that their right hands were handcuffed to the bed. Next to the lady scribbling notes was a metal stand with a water bag hanging from above it, connected by plastic wires leading straight into Stephen's arm. There were a few shelves on the wall, all supporting medical equipment such as tissues and latex gloves.

'What happened to me?' Stephen asked the nurse. She didn't reply immediately but instead finished making her notes. She placed the clipboard back into a tray and clicked her pen, as she slid it into her breast pocket.

'You've been unconscious for twenty-four hours. You picked

the wrong person to fight, by the looks of it,' she replied as she looked into his face, her eyes moving slowly from Stephen's eyes to his nose to his mouth.

'I didn't even know him.'

The nurse walked away. She opened the wooden door and turned to face Stephen once more, 'you have someone waiting to see you,' she said as she bustled through the door and Stephen was left in silence.

23

Stephen kept looking at the door. He was massaging a lump on his temple. How had he arrived in hospital? Had Honda got bored and told a guard? Did someone see the fight and then report it? Or did someone intervene?

Stephen lay there thinking about these questions, when his mind flew back months ago. He closed his eyes and saw Stacey lying motionless on the floor, blood seeping around her. He looked down and saw he was holding the bloody iron rod. He dropped it quickly and stepped back three feet, screaming out loud, sweating and shouting as the walls closed inwards and darkness surrounded him.

Stephen's eyes opened as he heard the door open. He was sweating and his eyes were wide open with panic and shock. In walked another large man in an orange jumpsuit; not Honda. The new man was smiling. He had a short, black beard with a tattoo on his neck. He was almost as tall as Honda but he was slim and lean, 'you must be Stephen?' he said.

'Who are you?' Stephen replied.

'I'm the reason you're here and not in a morgue. My name is Keith.'

Stephen looked at the man quizzically, unsure as to whether believe him. Stephen looked at Keith's serious, freckled face. Keith looked like he wasn't here to play games. 'I saw you this morning, outside a cell, huddled in a circle. *You* saved me?'

Keith just nodded back as he walked forward and began to laugh, 'not nice in here is it, Stephen? You feel completely unwanted and useless to the world. Well guess what? We are.'

Keith stopped talking and turned to face the two other prisoners, who had awoken and were beginning to sit upright, 'either of you two going to listen to this?' He asked them, harshly. They both shook their heads quickly from side to side. Keith turned back to Stephen satisfied.

'I've been in a hospital bed here before,' Keith continued, 'years ago. Similar guy to Honda did it. And guess what? I've seen it almost happen to every new piece of meat that enters these four walls.'

Stephen stared up at Keith, his breathing low. 'How did you stop it?'

Keith leant forward and began to whisper, 'me and my friends, we're called the shifters, Tony, Laurence, Peter, Karl and I. We came in for the same reason and always stick together. We saw Honda walking across the yard, following you, with his two goons. You looked at him working out didn't you?' Keith continued knowing the answer, 'Honda doesn't like that. We saw him pounding your face in, and we intervened. We do Honda some favours from time to time to keep him happy, and most importantly, sane. Then minutes later, the guards turned up.'

'What happened to Honda? Stephen asked trying to raise himself in the bed, hearing the cuff clink against the bed.

'Solitary. He will be there for a few days to a week, I'd imagine. The warden wasn't happy. Doesn't want a new inmate killed within his first week. Two weeks is acceptable though,'

Keith said and for the first time in months, Stephen felt himself smile. 'Stephen, did you murder your wife?' Keith said.

'No.' Stephen said, looking into Keith's brown eyes.

'Ok. Nurse tells me you're out of here today. Your blood pressure and heart rate are normal again. You're quite fit for an engineer, just your mind that's gone eh?'

'How did you know I was an engineer?'

'Small world, Steve,' Keith said as he raised himself, 'As soon as we heard the court case and the trial, we did our research on you. We do for everyone. You don't need to know how,' Keith said in reaction to Stephen's astonished face.

Stephen looked down at his cuffed hand and clenched his fist, seeing the white appear on his knuckles, 'I didn't do it. I'm not going to keep pleading.'

Keith bypassed Stephen's comment and continued, 'To be honest, we felt for you. We saw a man finish his trial, looking over thirty years older than before. So, we asked ourselves, would an innocent man be that drained if they were guilty?

Stephen relaxed his fist, 'you believed me?'

'*We* will reserve judgement on that, but until we decide, no-one else will hurt you in here.'

'Why?'

'Because you've taken your beating, and boy, I mean a beating. And now I'm involved,' Keith said, as he sat on the bed, looking at Stephen. 'My shifters and I are generally well respected in here. We do things, shall we say, for people who need it. To offend you, would offend us, until we make our judgement call.'

'Thank you, I guess?' Stephen said, trying to smile again. The pain of his mouth curving into a smile felt strange to him now, but fresh and as if a weight had been lifted.

'Damn right thank you. We're your get out of jail card for the moment. But now you owe us.'

'How?'

'I'll come back here when you're ready to come out and play. Say an hour from now? Soon enough you'll find out.'

Keith got up and exited the door, leaving Stephen to wonder if he was walking straight into another trap.

One hour later, Stephen was in another medical room with his shirt unbuttoned and a stethoscope pressed tight against his bruised, tender chest. There were two guards in the room watching him, whilst the same nurse from before made untidy notes. 'You're free to go,' she said to him, as she nodded at one of the guards and left the room.

The larger of the two guards moved forward and grabbed Stephen around the elbow and led him out of the door. Stephen could feel the guard's fingers' firmly holding his arm. Through the door, Stephen saw several other rooms. Some doors were open, some were shut. Everything was painted white.

Then there was an office space, which had a computer behind the desk, along with medical books and a filing cabinet. The same nurse was sitting on the chair, reading something Stephen couldn't make out. The guard led him straight past her and towards the end of the corridor. Stephen could hear louder noises growing as they approached a large metal door.

They reached the door and the guard moved forward and typed a code into a little keypad. The door jumped into life and made a noise, as if letting off steam. There was a loud crunch and the door opened. They walked through and Stephen heard the door crunch behind him. They repeated the exercise at the next door, which wasn't as loud and clunky.

Stephen knew they were in the prison's main building, when the guards released his arm and walked away. Stephen was stood alone, noises echoing around him. He tried to recollect if he'd been here before. 'Welcome back,' Stephen heard behind him. He turned around quickly, startled and saw Keith leaning against a wall, with one leg up bent to support his weight and someone he hadn't met before.

Behind him was a window bonded by metal bars. Keith was fiddling with something in his hands, 'I never did formally introduce myself did I?' Keith said. Keith pushed himself off the wall and held out his right hand.

'Where are we?' Stephen said shaking Keith's hand.

'Firstly, Steve, don't mind if I call you Steve, do you?' Keith said, continuing his sentence before Stephen replied, 'this is Tony. Tony, meet Stephen.' The other man walked forward with his hand outstretched. The man was tall like Keith, but was clean shaven and had no visible tattoos. His arms were thin and his eyes looked old and worn. He had dark hair and dark eyes.

'Keith's told you about us, briefly. I'm a shifter too. You don't look to good after your little disagreement with Honda. Look at your reflection,' Tony said, nodding towards the barricaded window.

Stephen looked at the window and saw someone different standing there. His hair was longer than ever before. His eyes were slightly wrinkled and his beard long. His face was red and purple in patches. Honda had done a good job on him. 'I look terrible. Keith, how did you get into the nurses bit?'

'You'd never believe me, Steve,' Keith said, 'let's show you around the prison shall we?' They all walked through an open doorway and into a room littered with books, a wooden table and benches. 'This is the library. Good for doing any research you want. New papers delivered every three days. You've got to be quick though.'

Stephen looked around the vast room. It was large and the shelves were covered in mounds of soft back books, which filled the majority of the room. Stephen thought there were enough books to last a sentence. He could see dust on one of the bottom shelves and a small line through the middle, as if someone had dragged their finger across the shelf. There were flat lights fixed to the ceiling and the room felt humid.

'We know more about you, than you do,' Tony said.

Stephen smiled for the third time that day. 'I can read here whenever?'

Keith said. 'You can read what you like. We don't read. We shifters come here to talk. There's never a guard in here. Books don't interest them. Let's move.'

They left the library through a thick wooden door. Ahead of them were other inmates. 'Our mates are in the workshop now, you can see that later,' Tony said.

There were two doors opposite each other in the corridor. Stephen followed Keith into the left sided room, which he knew the purpose of, as soon as he entered, 'this is the contraband room isn't it?' Stephen whispered. Keith nodded back at Stephen and then to the shelves at the back of the room.

Stephen looked at the shelves and saw food and drinks in plastic containers. Keith and Tony left the room and Stephen walked quicker to catch up, his chest still aching from Honda's attack. 'That was the contraband room, yes,' Tony said. 'Behind that fence is everything they've confiscated in the past twenty four hours. It's taken out the back and leaves on a lorry that delivers stuff here. Like a swap job.'

'Why'd you show me that?' Stephen said

'Because you'll be here a long time,' Keith said, not averting his eyes off the room opposite. Keith stuck his head in the room and waved his hand. Stephen then saw a man who he thought must have been sixty, folding up clothes. All the other noises were drowned out by the deafening sounds of washing machine drums in the background. 'That's the laundry room. Every Wednesday, you take your stuff there and wash it. That was Malcolm. He runs the place. Runs the operation actually and even folds the clothes.'

Stephen saw Malcolm hanging a shirt up, before he threw a pair of orange trousers into a plastic basket, perched beside him. They walked round the next corner and Stephen knew they were in the middle of the prison now. The sound of talking, walking and running engulfed him and he was surrounded by other inmates.

'We were at the back of the prison. The laundry room, contraband room and library are the quietest rooms in this lovely place,' Tony said. In front of them, were several people walking. Some had their sleeves rolled up and some had their trousers legs rolled up to their knees.

'Where are we now?'

'We call it the atrium. This is the hub. Look around more, you may remember it.' Stephen concentrated and then he remembered; it was where he asked the guard how to get outside. His cell was seconds away. 'We go right here. You went left yesterday. The only thing you'll see when you go that way is the yard,' Keith said.

The corridor was quieter than the previous day. The early bustle must have finished and everyone was where they wanted to be. Stephen saw cameras in the topmost corner of the room, pointing downwards. He kept walking. Tony placed his hand gently onto Stephen's tender shoulder and pointed with this left hand, 'down here is the kitchen, which you'll know and the TV centre. It's a big fight to see who has control of the buttons. Usually one guy wins, Honda.' Stephen directed his look to Tony, who smiled from the corner of his mouth. 'Big Honda won't be in there today. The people who are will probably let you choose the channel to say thank you.'

'Outside,' Keith said

They paced the same way Stephen had the previous morning, passing the doors with metal bars. Not as many guards were littered around, but Stephen could still see a couple, leaning against a brick wall talking and laughing. Stephen reached the bottle neck and entered the yard. It wasn't as humid as before, but the sun still shone down, accompanied by a small breeze, which carried sand through the air.

Stephen kept his head down and followed Keith who was already pacing forwards, his hands tucked into his pockets, head lowered. Stephen could see the gathering of men, working out in the centre of the yard. A lot of them had full orange scrubs on today, few wearing white vests revealing their inked arms.

They avoided the towers and steered left, walking past the workshop until they reached a small pathway behind some bushes, where there was a glasshouse, which was large and lengthy and surrounded by plants. 'This is the garden lab,' Keith said, as he walked up to the gate, metres away from the entrance to the conservatory, 'here is where the *stuff* goes down.'

'The *real* stuff,' Tony said as Keith opened the gate, which creaked slightly. Keith held the gate for them both, as they walked through. Stephen saw two men working in the small perimeter between the glasshouse and the low fences. They were digging with small trowels, throwing the mud into a single pile between them.

Keith entered the open glasshouse and Stephen saw him undo the second button on his top. Stephen also moved into the room and understood why. The room was uncomfortably humid. There were no windows. 'A greenhouse?' Stephen said.

'Not just any greenhouse, Steve. It's the magic greenhouse,' Keith replied. 'Everything happens in here. All the unaccounted contraband, all the secrets we never wish to reveal, all in here, once place.'

'Why are you telling me this?' Stephen said.

Stephen saw Keith smiling at Tony. Then Tony looked at Stephen and spoke in lower tone, just loud enough for the three of them to hear, 'we're telling you out of courtesy. You could say its trust we're showing you. But if you open your mouth, we'd know where to look. And trust me, the injuries Honda gave you, would be nothing,' Tony finished.

'Tony's right,' Keith said, 'There's always someone who's done worse than you. But most importantly, you did something brave, you fought back. So even after the beating you took yesterday, being in your first week, well, we want to look after you.'

Stephen looked at them, trying to work out if this was a joke. He wiped his sleeve across his brow and with the other hand, he rubbed the back of his neck, massaging it gently, skipping over the tender parts. Stephen walked outside and looked at the two men still working. They were in white vests, which were discoloured.

'These two,' Keith said behind Stephen 'are James and Lee. They work here. In return they receive tokens for extra food and treats. They're good guys.'

'What exactly do you shifters do?' Stephen asked as he walked past the shrubberies and freshly planted flowers, pulling open the gate again, moving out into the yard.

'What do we do?' Keith said.

'Why do you call yourselves the shifters?

Keith pointed at a bench twenty yards away and the three of them left for that direction. As they reached the bench, Keith moved his hand as a gesture for Stephen to sit down. Stephen did so and Tony and Keith sat either side of him. Keith kept his legs uncrossed and sat back against the wooden bench. Tony crossed his legs and looked into the distance. 'We've been in here a long time, Steve. Between us we've served over a hundred years. Came in here at twenty two, Tony was twenty four.'

'Just,' Tony said

'We shifters all knew each other on the outside. We were all in the same trade. The name shifter came from a lawyer once who was trying to pin something on us. Nothing was proven and the case was forgotten, but the name stuck. The nickname spread.'

'What did it mean? The term shifter,' Stephen said.

Stephen saw Keith swivel slightly on his bench and look sideways at Stephen. 'We were bad really,' Keith said as Tony remained silent, continuing to look around the open field. 'We originally started off conning people. Then we got in with the wrong people. Next we were importing and exporting drugs,

95

then armed robbery. Not a simple transition, but we enjoyed it, got a kick from it. Then it all changed.'

'You don't need to tell me.'

'We know everything about you and you don't seem too bad,' Tony said, speaking for the first time in minutes.

'We went to rob a jewellery store,' Keith continued, 'it was the big heist. We had done so much work on the case, we thought we were clever and had worked it all out. We grabbed the jewels but we couldn't get out the door. The door locked centrally. We didn't see *that* minor detail. We panicked. The owner wouldn't open the door, so we attacked him. We tried to knock sense into him and then it got worse. Like all the pent-up anger from years of being evil caught up with us. We beat him to death.' Stephen remained silent.

'None of us know who landed the killer blow,' Tony said.

'We were sentenced to life for attempted armed robbery and murder. Our shifter nickname still stuck. Back to what you asked us. The label shifters, was because we were clever. We got away with dozens of crimes and never got caught. We were known by everyone, but they couldn't ever finger us. Now we've brought it in here with us. The power never leaves you.'

They all remained silent for a moment and listened to the breeze whirling behind them. Stephen didn't want to speak. He was grateful to Keith because he had saved his life, but he had committed a brutal murder, which was probably what everyone thought Stephen had done. He turned back to look at Keith, 'so what do you do in here?'

Keith sat still for a minute, a small smile on his face, his eyes unblinking. 'You could say, we support the running of this prison, but that's for another day.' Keith rose on the bench and

Tony followed. They began to walk away and Stephen placed both hands on the wooden bench and heaved himself up. His torso ached with pain as new bruising began to appear.

'One more place we want to show you, come on,' Keith said, waving his arm in the air in Stephen's direction. Stephen followed the two shifters.

'Keith, what are the guards like?' Stephen said.

'The guards?' Keith replied laughing as Tony smiled ear to ear. 'Bent as they come. They don't follow the rules. Good and bad. Good, that they don't always pay attention, bad because if someone gets caught, they take the law into their own hands. We don't talk to the guards and they don't talk to us.'

'I spoke to one yesterday,' Stephen said, 'about getting outside.'

'Well, don't,' Keith replied abruptly. 'Others see that, they have a reason to play with you. Stay out of trouble. Come on. Let's get to our final stop.' The three of them walked in silence, Stephen pulling his top down at his back as Keith re-buttoned the top of his jacket. They walked for another minute, when they reached the workshop.

Stephen smiled and looked at the two shifters who were also smiling. They'd done their research, Stephen thought. 'Inside here is the stress-relieving place of the prison. You can let the day fly and do something you enjoy. You can work here every day and you get tokens, like everywhere else.'

Keith pushed the tall gate open and shut it behind Tony, who walked through last. The sun was lowering in the distance and the orange ember illuminated the skyline, unfazed by the blowing wind. There were three people sitting on a bench outside, all leaning forward, talking with their hands clasped in front of them.

They all looked up when Keith approached and Tony followed, 'these are the other shifters, Laurence, Peter and Karl. Go and look inside,' Tony said.

Stephen walked towards the large door in front of him. He was about to enter before he turned around to look at Keith. 'Keith,' Stephen said as Keith smiled back, 'why are you doing all this for me?'

Keith leant both hands on the table in front of him, still staring into Stephen's eyes. The other four shifters all turned around too, as if Stephen were the main event at a show, 'we don't think you really did kill your wife.'

24

Stephen entered the workshop smiling. Keith's last sentence was ringing in his head; *we don't think you really did kill your wife*. Stephen saw nine people sitting on benches, eight in pairs along with one man sitting on his own at the back of the room closest to Stephen. There was a guard at the front of the room, who had his feet on the desk. As Stephen entered, he jumped onto his feet.

A few of the in mates turned around, but Stephen didn't make eye contact with them. He looked ahead, unsure whether to take a seat or whether to go to the guard. The guard made his decision for him, 'sign in here,' he said, ushering Stephen forward. He was an older man, with a bushy moustache and a large waistline. He had hair on his head, which was combed over one side.

The room was bright and around a dozen bright halogen lights hung from above them. The walls had three long shelves screwed into them on each side. On the shelves were oiling cans, wooden ornaments and old scrap metal. The workshop was painted a variety of colours including red, blue and yellow. The inmates around him were looking down at their work, elbows on the edge of the table, backs arched.

As Stephen approached, the guard smiled. He looked relaxed as if he wanted an easy life and no trouble. Stephen could abide to that. Stephen smiled back trying to be unobvious and signed his name on the paperwork. Stephen didn't say anything, Keith said not to and he trusted him.

'To the right, behind you, is the tool cabinet along with things that need fixing. Oli will let you in there and you sign for what you take out.' Stephen nodded and turned around to find "Oli". Finding Oli was easy as a man with red hair, was stood leaning up against the metal wired fence, which led to the tool cabinet. His face was covered in freckles and his eye brows were so light, they were unidentifiable from afar.

Stephen approached the man he presumed was Oli, who used his right shoulder to push himself off the fence to stand erect in front of Stephen. 'I'm Oliver,' the man said, 'Oli is fine with me.'

Stephen nodded, 'I'm Stephen. Can I get some tools?' Stephen said moving his head backwards in the guard's direction.

'Let's have a look,' Oliver said unlocking the padlock and swinging the door open. Oliver was barely smiling, but Stephen could see his brown teeth.

Stephen followed Oliver and looked at the tools before him. It reminded him of his old job. He was sure they'd have replaced him. Bad for business, Stephen thought. In front of Stephen were hammers and saws and different sized drills, all with rubber power cables, wrapped around the handles. To his right were screws, nails and hinges, some of which were rusted brown and others gleaming silver.

He looked around the little boxes and saw more cardboard boxes on the floor. He wasn't sure whether to take a handful or just some. Could he keep coming back and forth? Or was Oliver the only way to get in? To his left where Oliver stood were slabs of wood and screwdrivers of different sizes, which were the same pale yellow colour. 'Fancy some electrical equipment? We got some lights here, which we need to fix for the library.'

'Ok,' Stephen said. He picked up a small lamp along with two screwdrivers.

'You need to sign those two out,' Oliver said nodding at the screwdrivers. Oliver held them and wrote down the codes, which were a mixture of numbers and letters. He nodded back at Stephen, 'good to go.'

Stephen walked into the main body of the workshop. He looked at a desk at the back of the room, which was occupied by one man, who was fiddling about with an electrical fan. As Stephen approached, he recognised him from his first few days, but couldn't say where. The table legs were screwed into the ground by four heavy duty screws. The floor was made of grey concrete, etched with scrapes and scratches.

The man sitting at the desk was bald and Stephen could make out wrinkles and small scars on his face. Stephen stopped in front of the desk, holding the lamp in one hand and screw-drivers in the other, 'Can I sit here, please?'

The man slowly lifted his head and Stephen knew it was the man who he had seen reading a book. His stubble seemed to have grown into a small beard. His eyes were an endearing brown and his facial features were small, exept for a small bump midway across the bridge of his nose. His face looked calm as he stared upwards at Stephen. 'Go for it,' he said softly.

'Thanks,' Stephen said as he placed the equipment on the table, watching the screwdriver spin a small circle. Stephen walked around the desk and pulled the heavy chair backwards, hearing the metal grind on the floor beneath it. The man continued to fiddle with the fan rotors, holding his tongue in between his teeth.

The silence was broken when the man spoke, 'first day in here?'

'In the workshop, yes, I like doing handy bits.'

'I like handy bits, but this isn't my first day, far from it. Ten years of being in here or something,' the man said still keeping his eyes focused on the fan. 'I'm Lance by the way.'

'Stephen,' Stephen said. Lance didn't blink and kept staring forwards.

'I knew you'd find me eventually. Glad we met here rather than in our cell.'

'Our cell,' Stephen said with raised eyebrows.

'They've moved you, didn't want you being alone, so you're with me. You're not the first, nor will you be the last.'

'You're not far from where I was before?'

'Seconds away,' Lance said

Stephen began to unscrew a panel at the back of his lamp, where he guessed the electrical wires were. He felt awkward as he twisted the small screw counter clockwise, until it dropped onto the desk with a little ping.

'What you in for?' Lance said

Stephen didn't want to sound like everyone else, but he had no other answer than the truth, 'they think I killed my wife. I didn't.'

'Don't we all say that?'

'No, it's true.'

Stephen waited for a response, but Lance sat quietly working on his fan. He pushed a button and the little rotors spun, slowly and smoothly, 'nearly fixed this now. Just a bit more oil and it will be good as new. Where was I? O, I can't say whether you did it or not, but if Keith is helping you out, then that's only good.'

'How did you know about Keith?'

'He told me you were headed here,' Lance said. 'What happened with Honda yesterday, reminded him of when he had the same fate as you.'

'He told me about it, briefly.'

'I've never known the full details, but I know someone helped him back then and he was passing on the deed. But another thing, Keith saw use in you.'

'Use in me because of a fight, where I got beaten senseless?'

'Yes, because you got beaten senseless, but because you fought back.' Lance placed his screwdriver and the fan onto the desk and swivelled slightly in his chair to look directly at Stephen. Lance moved his head closer and Stephen looked into his dark eyes, 'people come in here and some don't leave. The shifters heard about your trial. They knew you'd come here, but they didn't see someone not fighting for something. You showed guts and you're willing to fight.'

'I am,' Stephen said.

'There you go. So, when they saw you fight back, they thought, well someone who says they were falsely imprisoned but is still willing to fight and not give up or become exasperated or finished or whatever you want to call it, can only be good for them. And yesterday, even against one of the biggest guys in here, you gave it a go.'

Stephen looked at Lance and looked away, gritting his teeth, feeling his anger rising. 'I didn't do it, Lance. My heart told me to fight back. I need answers and I doubt I'll get them. Maybe, for a second I thought, fighting back will make me feel better, but it didn't.'

'Well, it's helped you though, hasn't it?' Lance said smiling as he picked up his fan again. 'Work on your light, before the old man at the front tells you off.'

Stephen began to unscrew the other half of the plastic door. He could feel his anger slowly sinking away. He knew he would have moments like this, but he had to keep calm. Honda was one person, but there were a hundred people in here. 'Helped how, sorry?'

'Stupid question, it's helped you because you now have five people, probably five of the most intelligent people I've met, keeping a little eye out for you.' Stephen looked at Lance confused, so Lance continued, 'the shifters came in here basically together and they've stuck together. Always have, always will. Keith told you why they're in here?'

'Yes,' Stephen replied.

'But what he won't tell you is the best part. They had more money, than they knew what to do with on the outside. They were teenagers when it began. They were so clever. They ran operations across counties. The police had nothing on them. I reckon they got bored and slack on the fateful job. Killing the guy was probably to get a buzz back,' Lance said and Stephen noticed he wasn't smiling anymore. 'I came in here at thirty. They had already done ten years each. I came in a boy really. I thought I could do things in the prison, like I did on the outside. Keith put me straight.'

'How?'

'He saved my life. I was going to kill myself. I'd be sneaking wires out of here for weeks, attaching them together each day. I was going to do it, but he stopped me. He helped me like he's helped you. Now I help him.'

'With what?'

'Another day,' Lance said. 'Keith has asked me to look after you in here. It's a close knit prison and you'll see that. Only three or four groups I'd say and a large one is more or less run by Keith. I've been waiting here for you.'

'Thank you, I don't know what to say.'

'Nothing now, let's get out of here. I've been here hours. Thought you'd be quicker than this.' They pushed their chairs back and picked up their tools. The guard was sat back in his chair reading a magazine. Oliver was sitting down at his desk and heard Stephen and Lance's chair move, so he stood up ready to open the tool shed fence.

Lance nodded at Oliver, who looked down at his clipboard and ticked the returning items off the list. Stephen repeated the exercise. They both walked out of the workshop and into the natural daylight. The sun was now almost completely hidden and the wind was stronger than before. Stephen pulled down his top and fiddled with his cuffs, as his eyes adjusted.

'Keith said you've had an overview?' Lance said.

'He's showed me around.'

'So, down the road, about a mile from here is the maximum security prison. That's where the real bad offenders go. Avoid that place, not many people make it out.' Lance began to walk towards the entrance of the prison, his hands in his pockets, a slight swagger as he walked. 'They're completely different down there to the ones here.'

'Who?' Stephen replied.

'The guards. They'll do anything for a kick. Make the ones here look tame.'

Stephen looked around seeing inmates sitting on the sand and leaning against the fences talking. The tower was visible from every angle and someone was visible at the top. 'What are the guards like here?'

'It's up for debate. Keith doesn't trust them. They will do anything to line their pockets. Other than that, they don't really care. I know it seems comical, but they don't. Old Clive, back there,' Lance said, nodding his head towards the direction of the workshop, 'He's been in there for years. He basically gets paid to catch up on his magazines and to take a break from his wife.'

Stephen laughed whilst holding his stomach, which still ached, 'do you get on with the guards?'

Lance stopped walking for a moment, waiting for Stephen to catch up with him, 'We all avoid each other. However, they are not afraid to fight us.' Stephen looked at Lance quizzically, so Lance continued, 'I've seen two riots, shall we say in my time here. Every time, the guards have basically overpowered us. They don't outnumber us. We only have our hands, but they have weapons and back-ups.'

'From outside?' Stephen said.

'Yes and from the inside. As soon as the warden hears of a riot, he clicks a button and the max security facility sends down fifty armed guards, with armoured vests and automatic weapons. You wouldn't mess with them. Also, remember some inmates don't want to fight. You know the saying happy life and all.'

Stephen followed Lance who was leisurely walking back and

seemed in no hurry. 'You ever been down to the max facility?'

'Never, don't aim to either unless the right cause occurs.'

'The right cause?' Stephen said.

'Another time. There is one guard you want to avoid. Most of the other guards do and that's the warden. His name is Roy. I've never seen him smile. You see him on the odd occasion down in the atrium. He goes to offices, but his main office is two floors up. I told you earlier about the shifters that they were intelligent and always did homework.'

'Like they did me.'

'Exactly, well, they were never able to dig anything up about this Roy. Articles they looked at, access to computers, nothing. So therefore, they don't trust him. As I said earlier, the other guards only speak to him when they need to. They enter from the front of the building, get searched and go to work, that's it.'

'You ever met him?'

'A few times, but I've never spoken to him. Anyway, he's nothing for you to worry about. Let's go check out our new bunk.'

As they approached the entrance back into the prison, inmates were filtering through the door overseen by a camera and several guards. These guards were completely different to Clive; they were well built and dressed smart, all holding their trouser belts.

'Thank you for explaining all of this to me,' Stephen said.

'Keith did for me and I'm passing it on. Now I've paid my dues. So what do you need to do now?'

'See my therapist. Apparently it's a weekly meeting in a room with other inmates. But I guess I'll find out. I was told I had to attend.'

'Best to Stephen, it's an easy couple of hours.'

'Keith said I owe him now?'

'You do. But he will tell you how soon enough I'm sure.'

They walked back towards the cells, feeling the humidity inside the prison. Stephen could also make out the smell of cooked food. He hadn't eaten properly yet, not that it was something he was excited about. Stephen felt Lance nudge him softly in the side of his ribs, forgetting his pain from yesterday.

'That's the warden,' Lance said nodding forwards to a man with white wavy hair, walking towards them clenching something long and black in his right hand.

25

Roy sat in his office reading the short, yet detailed report the nurse had brought him minutes before. The report was rolled up inside a shiny plastic wallet. Roy felt a mixture of amusement and anger. He was pleased with how Stephen had been introduced to prison life. But Roy was also worried and anxious. He had waited so long for this moment. It must be he who would carry out the necessary deed, not some overweight, steroid using anybody.

Five minutes previous, Roy had been reading the letter of resignation from one of his youngest guards. The letter said he was traumatised after the abuse he had been subject to, by the two thugs, Roger and Phil. Roy was sure there was more to it than the guard was letting on. He had no way of proving it anymore, but Roger and Phil went to solitary.

Roy placed both letters into his draw, amongst other pieces of paper and stationary. He leant back in his chair, thinking of what was next for his little puppet Ben? Roy had spoken to Ben late last night about Stephen's fight. Ben explained that the shifter guy broke up the fight. It had to be a one-off intervention surely?

Honda was punished accordingly and locked in solitary for 4 days. Why did he do it? Roy didn't know. There was no explanation. It was only after Roy had asked Lilian who the victim was, that she had said the new guy was someone called Stephen. Roy thought about going to the hospital wing. He could finish Stephen off now. But no, that was far too easy. He wanted him to experience prison life for a while first.

The shifter breaking up the fight played on Roy's mind. Why did he get involved? They usually had their own little schemes to work on. Things none of the guards could ever prove. They'd never affected Roy's plans. But what if they did now? Silly idea, he thought. They wouldn't want to help Stephen. But, even if they did, he would crush them too.

Roy stood up, massaging his knee and turned to look out the window. It looked breezy outside and the sun was slowly disappearing from view, hidden by the clouds as it dropped in the distance. He looked ahead at the silhouetted towers, outside the prison fence. He knew the powers they held; guns. Could he shoot Stephen from there? No, too easy.

Roy walked back to his desk and opened the second draw, pulling out the framed photograph of his wife. He stared at her face and felt the anguish and pain explode from within, replaced by anger and then optimism. He drew the frame up to his face and kissed the photo once, before sliding it back into the second draw. He opened the third draw, which had paperwork and a small hooded jumper.

He pushed the items to the back and lifted the base up gently, creasing the corners as it scraped the sides. Beneath the panel was a small handgun, wrapped within a small purple cloth. The end of the gun was visible. Roy didn't touch it. He just needed to know it was still there. He just needed to know it was still waiting to serve its master, probably for the final time. Roy pushed the panel back down and closed the drawer.

Roy locked his drawer and marched towards the door. He locked it from the outside pulling the handle upwards hearing the locks click into place as he turned the key. He walked past three guards who were on computers. Roy knew one should be handling reports and appointments. One should be watching the CCTV and he was unsure what the third one should be doing, but he didn't seem to be doing much. Roy ignored them and walked past, heading for the atrium.

He reached the door leading to the next area. It was made of thick metal and had slightly discoloured over the past few years. There was a key hole on the door above a small handle. Positioned on the wall, six inches from the door frame was a small keypad. Roy pulled out his security card and swiped downwards as the little machine bleeped. He then typed in his four digit passcode and the door opened with a small release of air audible as the locks were released.

Roy entered a narrow corridor and repeated the exercise at a similar looking door. As Roy stepped through, a wave of cold air hit him in the face. Roy came to the small security section, which was occupied by two guards, who were standing against the wall watching the prison. Roy walked straight through without communicating and entered the main part of the prison.

Roy held onto the support of the stair case and descended the small flight of steps. He passed another guard and saw the inmates dressed in orange before him. As he reached the bottom, he came out by the television room. He peered left and saw three inmates sitting on chairs, watching a black and white programme. He walked forwards slowly, one step normally, the other at a limp and he crossed the atrium below the cells. He felt inmates gazing at him as he passed them.

He ignored them and reached the centre of the atrium, when his face dropped, and his heart pounded inside his chest, as he came face to face with Stephen for the first time.

26

Stephen looked at the man in front of him. His hair was pure white and in most places, combed back across his head. Stephen thought his face looked young, especially his eyes. His body looked lean and his shirt looked tight across his arms. Stephen saw the man's mouth open slightly as if in shock and he looked panicked.

Lance nudged Stephen again and nodded to the stairs opposite them. They were about to move when the older man in front of them, turned on the spot and walked away and was lost to sight. Stephen looked at Lance, who was smiling, but his eyebrows were lowered; he looked confused. 'That was weird,' Lance said still looking at the spot where the man had been standing. 'That was Roy, the warden. He has been for many, many years. Surprised he hasn't retired yet.'

'He looked embarrassed. Probably because of my face,' Stephen said as he raised his bruised right hand against his cheek bone.

'He isn't the most conversational person, you'll ever meet. He isn't liked, same as I told you earlier.' They both walked towards the stair case in single file and up the metal steps. The prison was beginning to become crowded as more inmates filtered in from the outside and other rooms. Stephen looked over his shoulder briefly and saw a sea of orange, as inmates passed left and right beneath him.

They reached the top of the stairs and Lance stood, holding his arm out to Stephen approaching, as if to say, after you, and Stephen walked into their cell. This cell was the same size as Stephen's previous cell. However, this room had a bunk bed, which was just as small as his single bed. Stephen imagined he wouldn't be able to sit on the bottom bunk, without having to duck his head down to miss the bed above.

The pillows were a dark white along with the thin bed sheet and the thin quilt folded over on top of it. The bed posts were black and worn through years of use. The room had a small window, with vertical bars welded into the brickwork surrounding the windowpane. 'Welcome to your new room,' Lance said behind him.

'Thanks,' Stephen said. His mind whirled back to months before and Stacey came into his view. He blocked the image and was back in the room. 'Top or bottom bunk?' Stephen said looking at Lance, pointing at the beds.

'I'm top one. Make yourself at home,' Lance said laughing. Lance ascended the small ladder attached to the bed and threw himself down, lying on his side, with one arm bent to support his head. 'You shouldn't deal with Roy much. He stays out of it all down here. His orders filter through via the guards.'

'He looked angry,' Stephen said.

'No different to normal. He knows we don't like him or believe him.'

'Why don't you like him?'

'Not today.'

Stephen looked Lance in the eyes and rested his back against the white wall behind him. He knew he had asked many questions, but he hadn't been given enough answers. 'Why don't you like him?'

Lance smiled back, 'you're not giving up now? There are many things, you're better off not knowing yet.'

'But stuff like how I owe Keith, you don't think I deserve to know?'

'You will find out,' Lance said. Stephen remained silent and didn't argue. He bent his head down and started gently rubbing his hands together. The room was silent, until Lance spoke quietly, 'we think, Roy killed someone years ago.'

Stephen raised his head at Lance, who was now staring at his pillow. 'Keith had a friend years ago, Bertie. He wasn't a shifter, but Keith cared for him. Bertie was a big guy. He was overweight and had terrible asthma. He came in here for some sort of fraud within the government.

'Bertie worked in the laundry room. He kept himself quiet and working there was the bare minimum he wanted to do work wise, but enough to make him feel like he was getting his heart rate going. Keith asked him to do something. Something we're not that sure on and it's something that Keith won't reveal. Bertie seemed like he was onto something. Keith was going to meet Bertie in the laundry room'

Lance twisted and lay on his back. Stephen remained as he was, watching Lance staring up at the ceiling not wanting to interrupt the flow of the story. Lance continued, 'Keith arrived at the laundry room and Bertie was on his back. Keith said he was breathing shallow and wasn't moving. However, Keith said,' and Lance stopped for a moment as if to stop himself from choking, 'Bertie had told him Roy had been there with him.'

'Roy killed him?' Stephen said.

'Keith thinks so, but the cause of death was a heart attack. He was overweight and unfit. He had high blood pressure, but Keith always asks why would Bertie have said that Roy had been there with him?'

The room was silent as Stephen digested the conversation. 'When was this?' Stephen said.

'A year ago. Keith has been working on something ever since. Keith was going to kill Roy but he knew he would never get out of here.' Lance now sat up and peered around the cell door to check they weren't being overheard. Stephen also looked to his right and saw the doorway was empty. Lance edged forward, with his legs hanging over the edge, swinging alternate back and forth. 'You can help, Stephen.'

'How?'

'Tell me everything Keith told you earlier?'

'But he hasn't told me anything, Lance.'

'Tell me why he told you he was in here. That may answer the questions I have.'

Stephen looked at Lance, thinking hard. Should he say anything? Had Keith told Lance what he told Stephen? 'Nothing he told me matters,' Stephen said.

'Nothing?' Lance said.

'No, Lance. Keith helped me and as far as I know, I think he told me in confidence. It wasn't anything that was related to his friend Bertie.'

Lance pushed himself off the bunk and landed on both feet, his knees bending as he lowered himself. He stood upright and wiped his brow with the sleeve on his right arm. He walked towards Stephen, still making eye contact and stopped a foot away. Stephen thought he may have another fight, but Lance smiled from ear to ear at Stephen and patted him on the shoulder three times with his left hand, 'come on, we're going to the library. I've got something to show you.'

'What is it?'

'Come on, you will like it,' Lance said as he approached the door again. Stephen brushed his hands down his orange top and breathed heavily as he followed Lance. Stephen felt unsure, but even in the past twenty four hours he had trusted Lance and Keith basically introduced the pair of them.

They descended the same set of stairs and Stephen now had a grin on his face. He felt confident he wasn't being led into a trap but then his mind switched to doubt when he thought about what Keith had told him previously; *the laundry room, contraband room and library are the quietest rooms in this lovely place.* Was lance going to take him to one of the quietest rooms in here to give him round two?

The atrium was busy and inmates bustled back and forth. Stephen could smell cooked food hanging in the air and he realised, he hadn't actually been to the cafeteria yet. Stephen remembered seeing food trays and now he had thought about it, he felt hungry and again uneasy as he followed Lance.

They reached the library and Stephen walked in behind Lance. Lance walked down one aisle towards the far end and Stephen again followed, but with caution in his footsteps. The room felt quiet and undisturbed and darker than before. As Stephen reached the back of the room, he came face to face with the shifters. Lance continued to walk forward and he crouched down next to Keith, alongside Tony and the same three men from outside the workshop.

Stephen could see Lance nodding as Keith's lips moved.

Lance pulled his head away smiling and took a step back. 'Stephen,' Keith said aloud remaining seated, 'did you enjoy the workshop?'

'It's something I will continue with.'

'Good to hear. Wondering why you're here?'

'Yes, a little bit,' Stephen lied.

'I told you before, you owe us.' Keith said, still remaining seated. 'Before that though, let me introduce my friends Laurence, Peter and Karl, boys meet Stephen.' The three remaining shifters Stephen hadn't met stood up together and held out their right hand, which Stephen held one by one for a second at a time.

Laurence was small and wiry, with short, spikey, jet black hair. His eyes were dark and he looked intelligent. He had no wrinkles and his mouth was smiling. Peter was a little bigger than Laurence and his hair was slightly longer and lighter. His mouth didn't move during the hand exchange and he kept his blue eyes looking to the back of the room. Karl was a mix between the other two, but for he had mousy brown hair and was covered in freckles. He blinked several times and his eyes looked kind. Karl was the only one to speak, 'good to meet you.'

'You too,' Stephen said releasing his hand, looking at all three of them in turn. The three shifters sat back down and Keith again took the floor. 'Lance check we're clear' and Lance walked towards the front of the library. 'We said you owe us.'

'I am grateful for you saving me,' Stephen said.

Keith said, 'when I said you owe us, you really do, but before I told you how you owed us, I had to make sure I could trust you. Lance tested you earlier with the finest of details. You didn't reveal the story of how I came in here.'

'I'm not a snitch,' Stephen said glancing at Tony briefly.

'So here's how you can help us,' Keith replied. 'Lance tested you earlier to see if you could be trusted and we feel you can. Now you get to hear the big news.'

Stephen turned around as he heard Lance walking back towards them. Stephen saw him nod to Keith with a smile and say 'all clear.'

Keith looked Stephen dead in the eye, 'we're going to break out of here.'

27

Roy slammed his office door behind him as the glass pane shook violently. Roy limped past the three guards outside his office, his face etched with anger. He was not angry for coming face to face with Stephen. He knew he would need to at some point; it was he who had put him here. No, he thought, it was Stephen who had put himself here. But Roy was scared.

He was scared because everything felt real now. All these months of planning had come to fruition and now he was stood with everything he craved. However, why did he panic? Was he not prepared to meet Stephen yet? It was all he talked about every week to his wife. Roy looked at the door even though he knew no-one had followed him. They knew better than to walk in uninvited. They were all disposable, just like Stephen.

He sat down at his wooden desk, staring forward at the paperwork neatly lined up in a pile, next to the lamp, which was facing in his direction. He stood up and with all his might; he threw the contents of the table onto the concrete floor and screamed aloud. He breathed heavily, feeling sweat run down his forehead.

The door burst open and Lilian surged into the room, 'sir, are you ok?'

Roy kept his eyes focused on a spot on the wall, 'I'm fine, Lilian. I slipped a little, my bloody knee.'

'Causing you trouble?'

'When has it not?'

'Let me know if you need anything,' Lilian said smiling briefly and she exited leaving Roy alone.

Roy looked down at the desk again as his hands tightly gripped underneath the wooden desk. His breathing was deep but he could feel his temperature falling slowly. Roy loosened his grip and fell back into his chair. He pulled his knee gently up to his chest, with his foot resting on the edge of the chair and rubbed his knee cap softly and tenderly.

Roy laid his head back and stared up at the ceiling, continuing to subconsciously rub his knee. His mind started functioning and he began to think about Stephen again. The way he had strutted up the corridor, like he didn't have a care in the world. Surviving should be your number one priority, Roy thought.

Roy pictured Stephen's face looking bewildered and intrigued at the old man before him, who wanted nothing more than to kill him slowly and painfully. He started to rewind to an hour before. He didn't go to the church. He knew he would need too, but it wasn't essential today. Bernard would talk as he was honest and he would divulge what Stephen had talked about. Roy wasn't sure if he was overthinking about the church, but he wasn't wasting all this preparation or leaving any stone unturned.

He looked at the clock hanging in his room. It was white and circular and very basic. It was just before six; Ben, he thought. He would be coming for another counselling session. Another meeting, which Roy knew Ben didn't want, but that he would need if he wanted to stay out of trouble and not in solitary. He lifted himself up off the chair and using the back of his knees, pushed the chair backwards.

Roy took two steps to the left and leant down, his knee shaking as he lowered himself and he picked up his belongings. The light was easy, but the paper had been scattered into several places. He rose and fell in different spots until he had collected all the paperwork. He could feel his heart rate slightly rise as he picked the final piece up and he stood still for a moment.

Throwing the paperwork into his draw, he limped over to the window and stared out, looking at the diminishing sun, low in the background. There was a double knock behind Roy, right on cue. Roy turned slightly and pulled up the knot on his tie, feeling it tighten around his neck as Lilian swung open the door. As she held it open, Roy saw the skinny frame of Ben with his hands in front of him and his head lowered.

Roy watched the tall beam pole figure enter the room. Ben looked up once he was fully in the room and Lilian nodded once at Roy and pulled the door shut. Roy stared at Ben and felt calm. He had another trick up his sleeve for his little puppet that would complete the tasks he needed doing.

Roy held his stare on the small pigmentation on Ben's chin and waited for him to speak. It was psychological as to who got the upper hand. They looked at each other for what felt like an eternity, when Ben spoke low in the room, his left hand scratching his right shoulder, with his elbow sticking upwards pointing at Roy, 'You wanted to see me again?'

Roy smiled and held his arm out, ushering Ben to take a seat opposite. Ben walked forward three steps and sat down in the plastic chair, his legs uncrossed. Roy followed suit and peered just over Ben's shoulder unable to make out the black shapes moving back and forth beyond the glass, 'this is our usual session, Ben. We have things to discuss.'

'What would you like me to do?' Ben said, as he fidgeted with his hands. Ben wanted to find out why Roy was so interested in Stephen. Ben had been told to keep a close eye on him. That was fine. He had a vested interest, but he had to only feed Roy the good parts.

'How did you get on with following our new guest?'

'There's nothing to report. I have seen him a lot today though. He's been hanging out with his new cell mate called Lance.'

Roy thought hard, 'what's this Lance like?'

'He's a straight arrow. He's quiet and he goes to different places, like the workshop.'

'He's been helping Stephen?'

'He's been showing him bits around here, if you class that as helping,' Ben said, keeping the fact Stephen had met the shifters secret for now.

'Did Stephen go to church?'

'Not that I saw. I'll keep watching him. The count is on downstairs, I should go.'

'No, Ben. No need to go downstairs. I have made them aware you are with me,' Roy said. The count occurred every night after dinner as people left the cafeteria for their cells. If you weren't at the count, you were reported on every portable radio in the prison and the CCTV systems were watched with a fine toothcomb. The prison then went into lockdown. They have never had anyone go missing during the count, 'anything else?'

'The shifters are planning something else,' Ben said, 'but I'm not sure what.

'I don't care, as long as it doesn't involve Stephen. Have *they* even properly met him?'

'No,' Ben lied again.

'Then forget about it. If you see Stephen with the shifters, then we will discuss it. It may then be a concern for me. Ben, you need to meet Stephen for yourself. Over the next few days, when he is alone, not when he's with Lance. Lance may forget about him tomorrow, so we shall see.'

'Ok,' Ben said.

'You know what happens if you don't get results?' Roy said opening his wooden draw and pulling out the black metal pole.

Ben was stuck now. He had to push his own personal agenda to the top of the priority list, whilst continuing to feed parts to Roy. He didn't want anything to slow him down. 'I will do just fine.'

Roy replaced the metal object into his draw, 'without results in a week, something will be found in your room. Let's say illegal contraband? That's solitary isn't it, Ben?'

Roy stood from his chair, slowly and delicately, holding onto the desk and shouted loudly, 'Lilian.' The door opened thirty seconds later as Lilian entered the room, 'see Ben downstairs, please,' Roy said.

Ben, head lowered, stood without a word and left the room. Lilian nodded again at Roy and closed the door, leaving Roy alone. Roy felt tired. He wanted to go home. He was up early tomorrow to go see his wife. He would give her all the details and the progress report, even though he had little to offer at present.

He locked the draws and placed the key into his trouser pocket. He untightened his tie knot and tucked his white shirt into the sides of his waistline. He exited the room switching the light off as he went. The room looked gloomy and dark and Roy didn't want it any different. He locked his door with another key, which he also placed into his pocket. He reached the same three people at a desk as earlier. The young man dressed smartly with short blonde hair, filing paperwork, lifted his head and smiled at Roy. Roy didn't acknowledge him.

The second person was an older lady, watching a computer screen, which was the CCTV. Roy walked around the desk, 'busy night?'

'No, sir,' the lady replied.

Roy looked at the screen for a moment and walked away. He took two steps, when he stopped dead on his feet and his heart pounded. He faced the screen and in the bottom corner; he saw Stephen walking next to one of the shifters. The quality wasn't fantastic, but Roy knew the faces. He felt an urge to take his anger out on the three people sat before him.

He kept his composure and walked away, scanning his card and typing in his four digit passcode. He took the staff route to exit the building, with Stephen and the shifter solely on his mind. He ventured through the staff corridors, until he had exited the building. It was darker outside and the sun was out of view, gradually being replaced by the white glow of the moon.

Roy reached his car and heaved himself into his seat. He sat still for a moment, before opening the storage box to look at his wife. He tried to smile, but he felt uneasy. Was this coincidence that Stephen was talking to Keith? Did Ben know all along? He wasn't sure what to believe. But he knew one thing now for sure.

Stephen Farley would need to be dealt with sooner rather than later.

28

Seven days later, Stephen was sat on the bench located by the greenhouse. He saw James knelt down, digging a small hole with a mini hand shovel. Stephen sat with his hands in his lap, still adjusting to the new surroundings, even though he had been here over a week. There wasn't a day that passed, where he didn't think about Stacey.

Stephen looked upwards at the sky, which was scattered with clouds gliding left to right. The patches of visible sky were of a perfect blue and there was no breeze in the air. Stephen felt alone for everything around him seemed quiet. Stephen had done a lot of listening recently and a lot of laborious work, now all he wanted was to rest, but he knew he wouldn't get any of that, maybe never again.

He thought back to a week ago and pictured himself standing at the back of the library. Keith told him they were breaking out of here. At first, Stephen laughed inside, impossible he thought. Keith must have known Stephen would be dismissive of the idea so he had gone into detail for him. The other four shifters sat quiet and relaxed, whilst Lance didn't take his eyes off Stephen.

Keith had talked about the planning. They had decided to breakout months before. Almost a year ago it was mentioned, but it was never put into fruition. However, now the dream had become reality. Keith told them of the research his shifters had undertaken and how help from outside sources was invaluable. They had seen routes out of the prison but there were things to do before they attempted it, starting from now.

Stephen's main questions had been about the guards. How were they meant to outnumber the guards? But Lance had already answered the question; *the guards have basically overpowered us. They don't outnumber us. We only have our hands, but they have weapons and back-ups.* Keith had told Stephen all about the maximum security prison a mile away.

Keith explained how the armed guards come as soon as the alarm is triggered, which could be because of a fire, a riot, a death or a breakout. The prison had only seen two riots before and one death; Bertie. Not one prisoner had attempted to breakout, yet. The maximum facility guards would surround the prison meaning no escape, unless you fancied the potential of being shot.

Stephen had met his therapist the previous day. She had commented on his coolness throughout their discussion, as if the death of his wife hadn't affected him. He guessed she was only there so the prison could say it had fulfilled an obligation for people to talk freely. But Stephen had grown to like her throughout the meeting.

She was a beautiful lady who always wore a smart shirt and jacket, with a skirt down to her knees. She had beaming eyes and although it rarely surfaced, a nice smile. Stephen felt it was nice to have dialogue with a female. It would never be Stacey though. Stephen had one more session with her left and after that he imagined he would be signed off and left alone.

Stephen blocked the pretty therapist from his mind as he

saw Keith and Tony approaching him. Keith was smiling ear to ear and Tony was looking down at the ground. 'Afternoon Steve,' Keith said, 'relaxing are we today?'

Stephen stood up as they reached him and nodded his head. His face had almost returned to its normal colour now and he no longer felt pain in his abdomen. 'Thank you for meeting me.'

'Lance said you had questions?'

'Yes, I've been thinking a lot.'

'Then let's sit,' Keith said and he was the first to sit down on the bench. Stephen mirrored Keith and they both sat staring forward. Tony didn't sit down but looked beyond the greenhouse where you could make out several other inmates wandering the grounds. 'Are you having second thoughts?'

Stephen leant forward and placed his elbows onto his knees, resting his chin on his clutched hands. He looked into the distance at the clouds as they moved across the sky, 'no, I'm in. I trust you, but there are things that have been on my mind.' Keith didn't reply so Stephen continued, 'how would we actually escape from here? I have spent the last week looking at the prison and the towers and the guards, I can't think of an easy route.'

'There isn't, an *easy* route, you're right. But there are possibilities, which we are confident would work. First way, we will show you in a while. Second way, as we said before, is down underneath the prison, we think, near the kitchen, which leads to an old side entrance, that no-one uses anymore. If we get through there, then you're almost out of the prison. The towers were the original sticking point with the first way, but we know if we can turn off the power to the prison, then the lights go out and they can't see us.'

'How can you get underneath the prison if it's no longer used?' Stephen enquired.

'It used to be a corridor used for people bringing things in and out of the prison,' Keith said. 'Things such as food and toiletries, but the prison decided it made more sense for everything to come in and out of the same entrance. No need for more scanners than necessary, so this corridor became derelict.'

'How do you get there?'

'We are uncertain. We don't know where the corridor is exactly, but we will find out soon enough. Then we'll know the whereabouts exactly, of where we arrive when we exit the prison.'

'How did you find out about this exit?'

'A friend, shall we say, told me about it, many years ago. The corridor never crossed my mind if I'm honest.'

'Where is the power trip located?'

'Upstairs, amongst the boilers behind many doors, but that's fine. A guard told someone in the plan once where they are located. We can get access, but that's still the hardest part, getting up the top and then down to the bottom. It may take time, valuable time.'

The three of them remained silent and Stephen looked ahead of him. He could just about make out the sounds of shouting in the distance. 'What about the alarm that triggers maximum security?'

'The power trip you just mentioned also links to that alarm. It may sound too good to be true, but basically the prison is isolated if we cut the power. By cutting the power, the security alarm won't go off and max facility won't know what's happening. This is good as when the power goes off, like a normal power cut for example, the emergency lighting still comes on minutes later.'

Stephen looked back trying to remember all the details he had just been told.

'The prison still gives a certain degree of power, even when the main power line is cut and we need this, as I'm sure you understand or else it would be catastrophic here, see? All the power in the doors here would stop. So we need a certain amount of power. Cut that and we're screwed, no mistakes.'

'Cut the power,' Stephen said.

'Yes, but the only thing I'd say is that people will get hurt.'

'How?'

'Well,' Keith said, 'breaking out isn't going to be a friendly interaction is it? We have to use force and aggression. They will use brute force, but they will no doubt be stretched. They'll be trying to keep us in line and try to get power back on. They'll think dozens and dozens of armed guards are on their way down here, little will they know, the alarm won't ever be triggered. We have to do that bit first, before anything else. I also don't want the woman getting hurt. That assistant of the warden's, Lilian for example, she doesn't mean any harm.'

'How many people are in on this?' Stephen said, still resting his chin on his knuckles, looking ahead as James was back to his original hole.

'We've been recruiting people for around six months, one by one. I think we have fifteen of us minimum.'

'Only fifteen?'

'Not *only* fifteen. It will be everyone when the night arrives. When other prisoners see people causing havoc or trying to

131

escape, they will follow. It would be foolish for us to tell every-one, as it would get out. We only tell a select few. We also need to keep the numbers down as our escape routes could become blocked with too many people.'

Stephen now leant back on the wooden back rest and looked sideways at Keith into his deep brown eyes, 'why did you recruit me?' It was the question he had feared asking the most.

Keith smiled at Stephen and tilted his head slightly, 'your job won you the battle. You were a mechanical engineer, yes?'

'I was.'

'Yes and correct me if I'm wrong, but that must have involved a lot of mental work and problem solving skills as well as being able to make and fix things?'

'Yes, it did.'

'There you go then. You may be key to this whole thing, but don't get me wrong, you're a bonus,' Keith said as he winked at Stephen.

'Will you use weapons?'

Tony sat down next to Stephen and Keith replied, 'we will use weapons to harm, not kill. There is no guarantee this plan will work. If it doesn't, we don't want to come back inside with more blood on our hands.'

'How will you get access to weapons?'

'We,' Tony corrected him.

'How will we get access to weapons?'

'We have access to some already. You will see some soon. The weapons of course can be deadly, in the wrong hands.'

Stephen bounced backwards and threw himself forward at speed, landing with his feet adjacent to the ground. He watched the greenhouse for a moment, thinking of the next question.

'Sorry to ask another question,' he said 'but where do the weapons come from?'

Keith was stood next to him grinning, hands in his pockets. 'Think about it.'

Stephen looked up at the sky and tried to find the same clouds he had followed earlier. He closed his eyes and walked around the prison, the tv room, the laundry room, the contraband room, the church, the gym, the workshop. Stephen opened his eyes and looked at Keith, 'the workshop,' he said.

'The workshop,' Keith said as he slowly nodded at Stephen. 'Recently, we have started making things. That's why Laurence, Karl and Peter, were outside the workshop when you first visited it, they were looking at things. Oli is in on the plan as he plays a crucial part. He is miscounting materials and tools. Clive doesn't have a clue. Oli keeps him sweet.'

Stephen looked at Keith, now nodding himself, digesting, 'it all makes sense.'

'Good. Now let's show you the first escape route. You're ticket number fifteen.' Keith started to walk and Stephen followed. Stephen looked over his left shoulder and saw Tony push his hands off his knees and stand up, moving forwards with them. Stephen was thinking about everything Keith had told them. It all seemed to be real. But was it real enough?

'Here we are,' Keith said. They were all stood next to the greenhouse and James was now wrapping rope around his forearm, dragging it towards him. Stephen waited for Keith to speak. 'This is the baby.'

'The greenhouse? Escape from here? You'd burn before you got out,' Stephen said.

Keith laughed and moved himself to stand directly in front

of Stephen. 'We're about to show you something Steve. We've trusted you and we know you won't repeat it, but open your mouth and all that waits for you is death, I hope that clarifies it,' Keith said, still grinning. 'Come in and see for yourself.'

Stephen stayed static for a moment. He watched Keith duck through the door and Tony mirrored him. James was left standing by the door and he held his arm out, ushering Stephen to follow them. Stephen entered the room and was overcome by the same feeling as before; heat. The room felt humid and musty and free of fresh air. James entered after and said, 'clear outside,' and he leant on a privet opposite Keith.

'Show him please, James,' Keith said still staring at Stephen. Stephen diverted his gaze and watched James move to his left and slide a table, covered in flowers and plastic tools to the middle of the floor. James checked over his shoulder towards the entrance and then knelt down to the floorboards, which looked slightly damp and were covered in dried mud. There were several other plant pots littered across the floor.

James lifted one floorboard and slid it across the floor. He shuffled forwards a foot to repeat the motion with another floorboard. He had done this before, Stephen thought. Stephen felt himself walk forwards slowly as Keith and Tony both remained where they were. James dragged back a plastic sheet and pummelled it into a small ball. As Stephen reached James, his eyes widened, and his mouth dropped.

Beneath the floorboards was a large hole, half a metre in circumference. It was impossible to see down the hole unless you really leant close. All Stephen could make out, were the marks around the edge of the hole, where he presumed people had already climbed in and out. Stephen gaped at the hole and

James after a few seconds unravelled the creased plastic sheet and lay it flat across the hole, followed by the floorboards and the plant pots.

Stephen, still shocked, looked at Keith, 'like it?' Keith said.

Stephen felt unable to speak. It was a magnificent sight. It spelt freedom. It spelt possibilities. It spelt truth. 'I, it's, I can't believe it.'

'That hole is one hundred metres long. It leads directly into the woods. It's perfect. It's been here for a while now. People from the outside can reach it too. It's not easy, but we know people who have been here a few times recently.'

'Not far into the burrow are the weapons,' Tony said. 'There's two by fours, some metal equivalents to a truncheon and some liquids for the right moment.'

'The guards don't have any idea?' Stephen said, pulling the neck of his top away from his skin.

'Not a clue,' Keith said. 'Let's go outside before we all melt.'

Stephen heard the grind of the worktable being moved back into position as he ducked his head out of the door. The air was cooler outside and the sky was clear now, 'do the weapons we have match the guards?'

'Yes and no,' Keith said, 'yes as in by the time they realise what's happening, it may be too late. No, as in if they do realise, then they have much heavier and stronger objects. We're talking proper truncheons, pepper spray, rubber gun pellets and so forth.'

You need to meet Roger and Phil. They've been in solitary recently. Come on, let's go.'

The three of them left the perimeter of the greenhouse, without a word to James, as they began strolling back towards the prison door. Stephen felt a sense of excitement. He thought about leaving tonight but he knew he would be recaptured and only have time added on to his sentence.

'Keith, won't the towers see people entering the woods from this escape?' Stephen said.

'No. We intend to shut the power off when it gets dark, and they'll be sitting ducks. A few will escape from the tunnel and then go for the towers aiming to take full control. Once in, they secure the guards and then show us the signal, which we're not sure on actually,' Keith said as they continued to walk.

'So, we disable the max security alarms and the lights to the prison, which will only leave the emergency lighting on and power to the doors inside, right?' Keith, nodded, his arms folded. 'What about CCTV?'

'Can't be touched as it's linked to the internal power, so remember you're on camera the whole time.'

'Then weapons, will they be kept inside the tunnel?'

'Until nearer the time.'

'All fifteen people will be working on this, all with a personal agenda?' Keith continued to nod. 'So, what's my part?'

Stephen stared ahead at Keith and breathed slowly. He pulled the bottom of his top away from the base of his spine. He felt sweaty and thirsty, thinking about the tunnel to the outside world, which must be unbearable. Stephen watched Keith tilt his head slightly to the side and uncross his arms. 'You have a key part. You need to figure out how to get through that old entrance to the prison.'

'Why do we need it?'

'The greenhouse tunnel may become too crowded. When we find out where it is, you need to go there and check it out.

It may need some, engineering, shall we say.'

Stephen began to walk to the back entrance of the prison, feeling a bounce in every step. He now had a job, which he would start as soon as he could. He looked at the towers on his left and shook his head, knowing he had to trust Keith. He was so lost in if's and but's, that he didn't notice the pair eyes following him across the yard.

29

Ben had been watching Stephen all day. He stayed under the radar and on the outskirts of the prison, as Stephen observed the prison again, stopping every so often to look at parts. Stephen had stopped for fifteen minutes to look at the towers. Maybe he was just interested in the towers themselves, nothing to read into it. Ben watched Stephen pace around the prison walls further, until he was lost to sight behind the greenhouse.

Ben knew not to follow him. The greenhouse was run by Roger and Phil. They were best friends in here and they were not people you wanted to get on the wrong side of. Ben had never mixed with them and he didn't intend to. No matter the task in hand, he wasn't venturing into the greenhouse vicinity.

Ben's plans were straight forward; wait for Stephen to re-emerge and continue to follow him. Ben leant against the fence thinking hard, questions running through his head. He was chewing the skin off his right thumb as his left hand hung down beside him. Did Stephen know not to go into the greenhouse? Or had he been asked to go there? Ben kept his eyes on the pathway.

Ben knew Roy was going to expect updates soon enough. He knew he would only relay things that he wanted to reveal and that Roy, partly, hung off - his arm. Ben knew Roy needed him. Roy couldn't go sauntering around the prison following Stephen, but Ben knew that he could and so he continued to gaze ahead, but more questions surfaced.

Why was Roy so interested in this man? Why did they share the same aim overall; to bring Stephen down? Ben stopped looking ahead, when he saw two of the shifters, Keith and Tony slowly walking across the yard. They looked calm and relaxed. He looked in another direction, still keeping the two shifters in his sights. Ben could hear the whirring in the distance coming from the two towers.

Keith and Tony walked through the small pathway to the greenhouse and were lost to sight. Ben pushed himself off the fence and walked a small curve until he could see straight down the pathway; nothing or no-one visible.

Then he saw someone digging, so he stood still for a moment and started to move carefully, towards the greenhouse.

There was still no breeze and the air seemed to be growing more humid by the minute. Ben wasn't sure if it was the temperature rising, or whether he had become hot and anxious. He stood twenty metres from the pathway and stopped. Ben knew he couldn't just stand here. It was stupid and may draw attention and Stephen may be in there for hours. Ben wasn't even sure if Stephen was meeting up with the shifters anyway.

Ben turned right until he reached the fence and leant against a spot, twenty metres closer than his previous position. He leant his head against the fence, the back of his head, dipping into the small hole supported by the four wires linked together. He started to think about his life again. He had done a lot of thinking lately. He had spent a lot of time alone, trying to plan, but all he arrived back at was his mother, which then somehow linked back to Roy and Stephen. Ben couldn't help but think the three were connected in some way.

The first memory Ben always revisited was from exactly a week ago with Roy. Ben pictured Roy opening his desk draw, pulling that black object from within. Ben thought it was a lead pipe. He had felt some of the pain it could unleash. Ben knew that Roy had his own agenda and that there was more to this than he had let on. But did Roy know Ben was playing games too?

Ben's mind clouded and came back into focus again as he was kneeling- down in front of Bernard praying three days ago. He had visited the church more frequently, praying for luck and health for the future. He would need all the luck he could get. Bernard was harmless, but Ben knew Roy didn't trust him. Bernard probably knew a lot of things. Ben thought his mother would like Bernard. She would have liked anyone connected with the church.

Ben blinked and he was sat looking at several other inmates, all positioned in a circle; his counselling session and his first mistake. Why had the councillor opened her big mouth? Because of her, Roy now had an interest in Ben. Why, he wasn't sure, but in return for information, Ben could picture the promise of freedom Roy had given him.

His mother, Charity, came into view, smiling lovingly at him. Ben looked back at her beaming and happy. He was free and safe. Then, his mother's face changed, and she had aged terribly. She was old and frail and weak. Her smile was replaced by fear, as he pushed a pillow onto her face, and she moved no more.

Ben had been updating his diary daily, filling in every page with detail. He had diaries dating back to when his mother was alive, before she lied. He used to write in the diary monthly, now it had turned into a regular theme. He did it alone and away from prying eyes, like a lone wolf. Ben opened his eyes and saw Stephen and the shifters.

Stephen was talking to Keith, fiddling with the back of his top. Ben could make out Keith's tattoo on his neck, knowing this was what separated him from the other so-called shifters. The other shifter was looking around. Ben twisted slightly and started to stare in a different direction, trying to keep the three of them in his peripheral vision.

After a few minutes, they began to walk away slowly from the greenhouse, Stephen holding a smile across his, usually, sunken face. They continued walking around thirty metres, when they stopped suddenly on the spot. Ben could make out their lips moving and after a few seconds, they split, Stephen travelling in another direction away from the prison entrance.

Ben watched and waited. He wasn't interested in the shifters really. He didn't care in one sense about Stephen talking to the shifters, but he knew he'd prefer Stephen isolated and alone. He started to sidestep left keeping Stephen in his sights. Stephen was casually crossing the prison yard, his hands deep into his pockets and his orange trousers tucked into his white socks.

Ben knew where Stephen was heading; the church. He looked at the looming prison building and squinted, trying to see the large clock face, pinned to the highest point of the structure. He had just over an hour until his next meeting with Roy. He sneered and pushed himself off the fence, following Stephen.

Ben kept enough distance between himself and Stephen and placed his dry hands into his pockets, mirroring Stephen. Ben remained on the outskirts as Stephen entered and was lost to sight. Ben stopped still for a moment and rolled up his sleeves. He lowered his head and walked metres until he was standing at the church door. Ben took, a final deep breath, and clenched his right fist. He was, finally, ready to meet Stephen Farley.

30

Stephen pushed the door open with both hands and entered, being swallowed in darkness. He stood still for a moment and allowed his eyes to adjust to its new visibility when he heard a voice in front of him, 'Stephen, welcome back.'

Stephen knew the voice to be Bernard's and he took six steps forward, so he was fully in the room, 'how are you Bernard?' The room was humid and bereft of fresh hair. He began to adjust his collar and roll up the cuff of his sleeves.

'Fine, thank you, have you come to pray?' Bernard said smiling, cupping his left hand into his right.

'I have actually Bernard. Never done it before, so give me time,' Stephen said smiling back, no longer fidgeting. Stephen hadn't really taken in Bernard's appearance before. Bernard was around sixty years old, with a head of grey hair. His face was wrinkled and weathered, but his eyes looked full of life. He had glasses on, which were black and square.

Stephen looked left to right at the two benches either side and veered right, sitting at the far end. Bernard was reading something, with his head lowered. His left hand was sliding the glasses up and down his forehead as he leant further forward. Stephen was about to start talking inside his head. Was he going mad or was this how everyone prayed?

Stephen leant his elbows forward to the shelf in front of

him and crossed his hands, when the door behind him opened abruptly and assertively. Stephen twisted his body quickly and saw a tall, skinny man standing at the doorway, the light from outside visible between his legs and above his head. Stephen thought it may be Tony.

The new visitor walked quickly and purposefully towards Stephen with his fists clenched. Stephen leant back backwards as 'Ben,' echoed across the room. The man stopped dead in his tracks and looked for the source of the noise. The door closed, blocking any natural sunlight. 'Sit down, Ben it's nice to see you again. Come to pray?'

Stephen watched the man called Ben look at Bernard and then down to Stephen. Stephen could make out a small mark on his chin and he continued to stare back puzzled at the aggressive manner, with which Ben entered. 'Pray?' Ben said.

'Yes, like you do a lot recently. Before you do Ben, this is Stephen Farley, Stephen, this is Benjamin Durant,' Bernard said.

Bernard began descending the small wooden steps approaching the pair of them. Stephen could sense Ben staring down at him and he could hear Ben's shallow breathing. Stephen turned his head slightly and his eyes met Ben's, 'nice to meet you,' Stephen said.

Ben didn't reply. He looped around the edge of the bench and sat down slowly, gripping the back rest, keeping his eyes on Stephen the whole time. Bernard was now standing between them, with his hands gripping the bench as he leant forward, 'Ben has become a bit of regular.' Stephen looked from Bernard to Ben as he watched Ben's eyes roll and his face remained straight and unfriendly.

'No privacy or secrecy though is there?' Ben said. Stephen

thought Ben's voice sounded deep and his body was skinny with no muscle. Stephen thought it was as if he had just stopped growing suddenly as a teenager, 'let me pray.'

Bernard nodded once in a slow movement, his chin almost touching his chest. Bernard took his hands off the bench and walked back towards the front of the church to sit on his own singular seat. Stephen watched him the whole way as Bernard sat down, breathed out deeply and pulled the paper he was reading previously, close to his face. 'Why do you pray?'

Stephen waited for Ben to respond, but Ben was now facing the front of the room, his eyes closed, and his hands placed in his lap. Lance had warned him about inmates and had described some of them as "unstable". Stephen turned slightly in his seat and faced forward.

'I'm not praying,' Ben said out of the silence. Stephen's body faced forward, but he turned his head ninety degrees to look at Ben. 'I don't think praying will do anything,' Ben continued lowering his voice slightly 'I prayed for years and what have I got to show for it?'

'What did you pray for?' Stephen asked, continuing to look at Ben.

'This and that, that and this,' Ben said still talking with his eyes closed.

Stephen closed his eyes and went back years ago; Stacey. He thought about their wedding. The smile on all the family's faces, the sun beaming down upon them, Stacey crying as they swapped their vows. Stephen thought about his mother. He missed her more than he ever knew possible. She was the soul of any party, bubbly, jovial and kind. Stephen wished that life back.

'You're new here aren't you?' Ben said once again interrupting the silence.

Stephen re-opened his eyes and scratched his brow, turning to look at Ben. Ben was now sitting facing Stephen at the end of the bench. He had his right leg tucked under his left on the bench, with his right arm resting straight along with the back rest. Stephen thought he looked nervous and uneasy and awkward, 'yes, I'm new here.'

'Long time in here for me now,' Ben said as he laughed, his body shaking from head to toe with his mouth wide open. Stephen didn't respond, instead turning to focus on the small window again. 'What did you do before here? Ben said.

'Why?'

'Why not? From what I've read, you're due in here a long time.'

'I was a mechanical engineer.'

'So, you're clever?'

Stephen could sense contempt in Ben's voice, 'I wouldn't say clever. I enjoy fixing and maintaining things.'

Ben paused for a moment and replied as if he had been asked a question, 'I never worked. I looked after my mum, till she died.'

'Sorry.'

Ben began to laugh and shake, his shoulders bouncing up and down, 'What, was lifelike, on the outside?' Before Stephen got a chance to reply Ben continued, 'It's been a long time, you see.'

'It was good. I loved my wife.'

'How did she die?' Ben said with no remorse or sorrow in his voice.

'She was bludgeoned to death. I don't know why, to this date.' Stephen kept his eyes on Ben and watched him. Ben looked more awkward by the minute as if he was uncomfortable talking to Stephen. Maybe he was just socially awkward or maybe he was just strange.

'You took the fall?'

'I didn't do anything,' Stephen said. He started to think about the escape again and freedom. He pictured himself running through the woods, throwing his orange jumper in the air as he run freely and purposefully. He only wanted to escape to try and find out what happened to Stacey, impossible as it seemed, he had to try.

'I saw you earlier, behind the greenhouse. You're not allowed round there.'

'Says?' Stephen said looking at Ben.

'Two guys own it. They will end you.'

'Ok thank you. I didn't know that.'

'Why did you go there?'

Stephen tried to think of a response, without it sounding like an outright lie. Ben had obviously seen him and therefore assumed he had seen him talking with the shifters. Why did it matter? How did it help him or affect him? 'It looked peaceful. I wanted to be alone and that place is quiet.'

'Here is quieter,' Ben said.

'I wanted to be outside,' Stephen replied

'How are the shifters?' Ben said. Stephen's suspicions were confirmed by those five syllables. 'They seem to hang around that bit too. Of course, they can, they know Roger and Phil well.'

'I don't know,' Stephen lied looking back at the window near

Bernard. 'I've not really met them.' Had Ben followed Stephen all day? He would need to tell Keith about this, but what if this caused harm for Ben?

'Did you really kill your wife?'

'No. No, I didn't.' The change of subject and random questioning bewildered Stephen and he didn't know where to look in order to hide his confusion.

'My mum died. What's yours doing?' Ben said.

The question itself made Stephen forget all other thoughts and just picture his mother. His mother with her smile and her eyes and the humour, which was all wrapped into one kind, caring lady. 'My mum died, years ago.' Stephen replied, now staring into his lap, feeling sadness and hatred for the world. He could sense Ben moving slightly to his left and he lifted his chin and saw Ben had moved a foot closer.

'How long ago? How?' Ben said.

'Heart attack.'

'Did she ever keep secrets from you?'

'What do you mean?'

'My mother kept a secret from me for years and years and it caught up with her. That's why she died. She couldn't hold the secret in any longer,' Stephen watched Ben fiddle with his hands, pulling his trouser legs away from his skin. He looked panicked and anxious.

'She didn't, no. What was the secret you found out?'

Stephen would never have predicted it, but as soon as Stephen had finished his sentence, Ben leapt up onto his feet and looked down at Stephen. Bernard gently placed his paperwork down and raised his glasses, looking in their direction. Ben didn't wait to be spoken to, instead he turned on the spot and walked for the door leading to outside. Ten long strides and his skinny frame were lost to sight.

Stephen looked at the door for a few seconds, wondering if Ben would reappear at any moment, but it was quiet, all but for the footsteps of Bernard, who was crossing the church floor. 'He's a funny case, that Ben,' Bernard said.

'I don't get him,' Stephen said as Bernard perched himself down to where Ben had sat.

'He blames his mother for a lot of things. We all know he killed her, but he's never admitted it outright. He's made little hints like he did then, but never confirmed it.'

'Because of a secret?'

'It must have been some secret, but, I would confidently say, our parents have always kept secrets from us, to protect us and to serve what they feel best. Maybe Ben never understood that part.' They remained quiet for a moment, staring into nothing when a minute later, Bernard spoke again, 'he seemed quite interested in you.'

'Did he?'

'I think you know he did. You look queasy, Stephen. Be careful, is all I'd say, with any inmate who pays a big interest in you.'

Stephen sat quietly for a moment, thinking about the days ahead. He had more questions for the shifters now. The only comfort he had taken from the day was the fact he knew his mother would had never kept any secrets from him.

31

Roy had seen Ben follow Stephen into the church. Good news, he thought. The boy was making progress. He had been given a week. A week was a long time. During this time, Roy had stayed away from the prisoners below him. He had got regular updates about the prison in general from his newly appointed assistant, Lilian whilst he stayed in his office playing the role of the puppet master. He liked that title.

Roy had been stood behind a fence near the entrance door, watching Stephen go near the greenhouse. In clockwork fashion, Ben then appeared and walked to the opposite side of the entrance and leant against a fence. Roy kept his eyes between the greenhouse entrance and Ben. He could hear shouting in the distance along with laughing and the operating within the overlooking towers.

Then things got interesting.

Roy was sure he'd spotted them first. Ben was looking in a different direction. Two of the shifters were moving forward at little pace, towards the greenhouse. Roy couldn't see their faces, but he could tell they looked comfortable. Once the two shifters had disappeared, Roy observed Ben push himself firmly off the steel fence and walk gently across the dry, sandy ground. Ben stopped dead centre of the entrance and was now staring. Roy knew he was trying to stay under the radar, but he looked like a fish out of water.

Ben was moving again, and Roy was now smiling. He knew Ben was following his orders, which meant Roy had him where he wanted him. Could it be possible that Ben would return to their next meeting with actual progress? Either way, Roy knew Ben couldn't win. The pressure was due to be increased two- fold, in little over an hour.

Ben moved closer to the greenhouse, but he was once again leaning against the fence. Roy thought Ben looked hot and sweaty, maybe even desperate. He watched him rest his head back against the fence and he was sure he saw Ben's eyes close from afar. The next few minutes were completely quiet, but for the sounds of the other inmates. Roy had patience; he'd been patient for years now.

Roy's didn't have to test his patience for too long. He saw Stephen and the shifters exiting the greenhouse vicinity. Roy gritted his teeth and felt the anger pulsing through his worn and aged body, with his mind thinking hard and his wrinkled hands tightening around the cold, dark fence. Why was Stephen with the shifters again? Once, you could argue was coincidence, but to be seen with them twice, was puzzling and dangerous. Was this even the second time?

The three of them were now in conversation. They started walking towards him, so Roy covered his face and was hidden from the unobservant eye. They split up as the two shifters re-entered the prison next to Roy. Roy didn't pay them as much attention as he did to Stephen, who he could still see from his concealed position.

Ben was following, remaining at a distance. Stephen was lost to sight. Roy left his spot behind the fence and then knew where Stephen was headed; the church. Stephen entered the church slowly and carefully followed by Ben. Roy kept his eyes on the church and waited. He waited and absorbed the heat surging through the air.

Roy moved from his spot and tried to go back inside when he saw Ben thunder out of the church door. If Ben re-entered the prison now, he would see Roy straight away and Roy didn't want that. Roy wanted to see how honest Ben would be to him in their imminent meeting. Roy limped up the stairs to the offices. The sound from downstairs was drowned out, as he climbed, and it was replaced by the whirring of air conditioners and his own deep breaths.

Roy reached the top of the stairs and attempted to storm down the corridor back to his office. His leg was aching. He had ventured outside and he thought the humidity had swollen his knee. He was gritting his teeth as his white hair bounced with every other step. He knew the meeting with Ben was about to happen and he had to be ready, calm and ready.

Roy walked past the desk with the three computers positioned at the back of the table, half a dozen electrical cables visibly hanging from behind into a small black box and a plug socket attached to the wall. There was only one person sitting at the desk today; the woman who always seemed to be watching the CCTV. Roy looked around quickly, trying to find the other guy who did the filing.

Roy reached his office and turned the little handle. The door hinges creaked as they held the weight. He gripped the door and swung it shut. He started to feel his breath coming back to him, as well as his temperature cooling by the second. He pushed his chair back slightly and slid in, letting his legs go as he slumped backwards. The chair made no sound and Roy just stared at the door.

The desk lamp, which he had thrown previously, was slightly bent in the middle of the stand. Roy shuffled his paperwork into a small, neat pile and slid them into his top draw. He then opened his second draw, checking that the small black pole was still in reach. He pulled it out, feeling its weight in his palm and he pocketed it. He didn't need to check the third drawer, the gun was safe there.

Roy leant back and thought of questions to fire at Ben. How Ben answered depended on Roy's next move. Like a game of chess, he thought. Your turn, my turn, your turn, my turn until the pieces had been moved into position and one was ready to strike. Roy knew he would be the one finishing the game.

In the end, should he kill Ben, after he killed Stephen? Would Ben surviving be a problem? Would he know enough to repeat it? Roy rested his head back against the rest and asked himself one further question. Why did it matter to him what happened after? Roy didn't expect to survive afterwards. His job was complete. He only then wanted to be with Linda.

The questions stopped instantly, when there was a loud knock on the door. It echoed around the quiet room and Roy could see shadows beyond the glass. *Ben*, he thought. Roy didn't speak; instead he re-tightened the knot on his tie and fiddled with his collar. Roy then leant forward and placed both hands onto the desk surface, took a deep breath and glared forwards.

The door opened and Roy saw Lilian's smooth hand reach round. Seconds later in walked the skinny frame of Ben, which looked shiny and sticky and sweaty. Roy looked at his face as he entered and saw he looked anxious and angry. Roy felt a slight fear nagging at him. What did Ben do?

Roy nodded once at Lilian, who smiled back and shut the door, the creak, audible from the back of the room. Ben walked forwards with his head slumped, as he scratched his dirty hands furiously. Roy noticed Ben didn't raise his head once, but instead sat backwards into the chair and continued to stare down at his feet.

Roy tilted his head slightly and looked at the boy before him, who he thought was weak and almost useless. He would be useless soon enough. 'News, Ben?' Roy said.

Ben didn't respond straight away. Roy was tempted to lean over the table and hit him hard and fast across the head. Roy believed he could kill him, but he didn't need to yet. Roy started to consider the next steps in his plan. He knew what would happen to Ben today, regardless of what he had found out. It was all part of the bigger plan.

Ben raised his head slowly and carefully as if scared to bump his head on an imaginary object above. Roy looked into his eyes and could sense panic as well as anger, 'there's a plan. I know there is,' Ben said.

'News about Stephen?'

'Nothing,' Ben said, and Roy sensed the lie as it left Ben's lips.

'So why do I need to know about this, so called, plan? I told you to watch Stephen.'

'I spoke to Stephen today. In the church, he was sitting in there with Bernard.'

'Yes,' Roy replied, rubbing his left knee.

'He told me about his life briefly. He had a wife, he wanted to start a family, he was happy. He said he didn't kill his wife, but we know he did,' Ben said, trying to sound convincing.

'What else?'

'He prays,' Ben said.

Roy was now looking at his desk, following the dents across the surface, his eyes gliding from corner to corner. 'What else has he been doing to note?'

'Nothing much else, he visits the library and reads things. He is with Lance a lot, but Lance is quiet.'

'What did he say about his wife?'

'He said, she was killed, and he doesn't know why.'

'Did he reveal any wrongdoings in the prison?'

'No.'

'You look angry Ben. What happened? Has he upset you?'

'No,' Ben lied again, 'we were talking, and I couldn't get all the information, but I will.'

'What else has he been doing to note?'

'Nothing else?'

'You are sure, Ben?' Roy said, feeling his temperature rising and his fists clenched as the knuckles started turning white.

'Yes.'

The lie did it for Roy. He un-tensed his fists and just smiled at Ben, who stared back blankly. Roy stood up, his left knee shaking from side to side as he placed his weight on his right leg and grabbed the underneath of the desk. Roy started to trace around the desk towards Ben. 'Stephen has been meeting with the shifter leader.'

Ben didn't respond but continued to swivel his head as Roy moved beside him, 'he may have bumped into them.'

'Them? I only said the leader.'

'I meant him, not they.'

Roy could sense the panic and urgency as Ben spoke

pleading, fear recognisable in his voice. 'You're lying to me Ben.' Roy sensed Ben pause, no doubt trying to think of his next lie, so Roy continued 'I saw Stephen walking with the two shifters earlier. I saw them talking and I saw your pathetic body watching, trying to be inconspicuous against the fence.'

'I was only watching Stephen.'

Roy was now directly behind Ben and he used his left hand to feel the pole, buried in his pocket. His trouser was being pulled down on one side, under the weight of the pole. 'They were together, so, now I have two problems,' Roy said as his left hand reached into his pocket, 'the first problem I have is why does the man I ask you to watch, find himself meeting and associating with the shifters? The second problem I have is why does the man, who I asked to follow him in return for freedom, lie to me.' Before Ben had a chance to reply, Roy swung the pole through the air as the hard steel connected against Ben's right shoulder.

Ben screamed and his face grimaced, as he firmly gripped his shoulder. Ben moaned and rolled on the floor, as Roy looked at the door to see if anyone was coming in. It was silent and no shadows appeared through the glass. 'If you make any noises, then the next blow will be on your head. You'll wake up in a hospital bed, with broken arms and broken legs and I'll still be here.'

'You hit me.'

'You lied Ben. You don't like liars, do you? That's why you killed your mother, no?' Ben didn't respond, but he moved so he was kneeling before Roy. Roy looked down at him and momentarily, he felt sorry for him. 'Now tell me about the greenhouse, Ben.'

'All I know,' Ben started as he tried to pick himself up with one hand. His left hand was still gripping his shoulder and Roy could see his face was a brighter red than he had ever seen before, 'is that they met today, and I couldn't see them. He's been with people and I want him alone. Even in the church, he was guarded. You need to support me.'

Roy listened to the pleading and Ben's sorry tone, 'would you like some alone time, to think about it all?'

'I need Stephen,' Ben shouted aggressively and suddenly.

Roy acted fast as if his body had rewound thirty years. He swung the metal pole down onto the medium part of Ben's spine and felt Ben's body bend under the power of the collision. Roy took two steps back and placed the pole into his pocket, staring hard at Ben who once again screamed in pain. The door behind Roy burst open and Lilian and a well-built male guard entered the room, looking stricken with fear and shock, as they diverted their eyes between Roy, who was breathing heavily and Ben who sliding across the cold, concrete floor.

'He tried to attack me,' Roy said quickly, so I elbowed him in the back. It wasn't the most convincing lie he had ever told, but he was under pressure, 'take him too solitary.'

Lilian didn't need telling twice and she roughly picked up Ben from underneath both shoulders, grasping the side of his chest. Roy could see Ben had tears in his eyes. The male guard raised his knee into Ben's lower back and Ben's legs folded under the pressure, as Lilian tried to hold him upright. They exited the door, leaving it open, some new air circulating inside.

Roy looked down at the floor and back at the desk. He didn't shut the door, but he walked back around his desk limping and using his right arm, he used his sleeve to wipe his sweaty brow as his temperature lowered to normal. Before he could relax, he pulled out the metal pole and placed it into the second draw.

Roy gently pulled the blind to the side and leant against the window. He could see the glass condensate around his fingers as he overlooked the prison and the almost empty yard. Roy kept his eyes on a single spot in the yard, thinking about Stephen and the shifters. Ben had said they were planning something. Was this also a lie?

Roy recounted the stories he had heard about the shifters; the power, the domination of the in-mates, the intelligence behind it all. Roy knew his plan for Stephen may have taken a turn for the worse.

As the male guard lead Ben forward, Lilian held back a second. She knelt- down and fiddled with her boot lace, before withdrawing her notebook to write down what she felt had really happened in Roy's office and how she had witnessed the guard assault Ben. She finished abruptly and shoved the notepad into her back pocket and continued following. She felt there was maybe truth in what she had been told before she had come here.

32

Stephen was sat on a long workbench in the workshop surrounded by Lance, the five shifters and Oliver. Keith was sat at the head of one end of the table, his elbows leaning on each corner with his arms folded and his back hunched. The workbench was furthest from the door, near where Clive was usually sat. The shelves screwed into the wall were empty and they hung obsolete.

Oliver was sat next to Keith and he was resting his chin on his right palm, whilst his left hand held a small screwdriver, making little marks into the table. Oliver face looked burnt and his freckles were prominent across his face. He looked partly nervous and almost scared. They had been talking for over ten minutes. Clive had gone for a walk after chatting to Oliver and he'd left them the privacy of the whole workshop.

Karl and Tony were next to Oliver on the left and Laurence and Peter were the opposite side of the table. Stephen was directly opposite Keith. Laurence's hair was still standing erect, his face intelligent looking. Peter was ever so slightly bigger than Laurence next to him, his light long hair, pinned behind his ears. Karl was stroking his mousy brow hair in circles and he was looking sideways at Keith. Nearest Stephen was Tony, who looked tall even sitting down and he was once again clean shaven.

'So, we don't have too long guys,' Keith said, 'I've called this meeting to finalise the plans. Roger and Phil are on route. Clive has gone to collect a "delivery", we have about forty minutes.'

'Where shall we start?' Oliver said as he pulled a small cigarette from his breast pocket, 'can I?' he said looking at Keith.

Keith nodded back, 'chimney, smoking will kill you one day. Firstly, shall we go through exactly who we have in on this plan?' Stephen nodded as did the rest of the attendees. Their voices carried across the room. 'We have about eighteen people now, I didn't invite every single one of them here, but they will find out in due course, as soon as we've agreed it all today.'

'Will there be a signal for everyone? So everyone knows it's happening,' Stephen said.

'Everyone will know a date and we think taking over the towers will be the signal.' Everyone remained quiet, all now looking at Keith, 'Roger and Phil will tell you about the towers. We originally intended to get some of us out into the woods to take over the towers, but it's not possible. An outside source told us that to get to the towers, you go past about four guards, they wouldn't make it. We're aiming for a bigger distraction now.'

Stephen sat back in his chair and raised his tanned brown hands, rubbing his cheekbones. His eyes were heavy, and he felt tired, but he knew the plan needed his full attention. He lowered his hands and rested them on his abdomen and said 'ok' to Keith.

Keith spoke again, 'now, let's talk escape routes. We have a few options, at the moment. One we are unsure on. Two routes we are confident will work. The first thing we need to ensure happens is point one; the towers. We cannot escape any angle or direction if they are working and covering the yard, so let's say that the tow.' Keith's speech was broken off by the sound of the door, as it opened abruptly, and two large silhouettes were visible as they entered the room.

Stephen watched their knees bent as they crossed over the threshold. One walked towards the group and the other shut the door. It became clear, once they were closer, that they were, Roger and Phil, who he had been told about before; *two people in here, who make Honda look like a teenager, will fight regardless of the cause.*

Stephen couldn't help but stare. They were both huge. They were easily over six foot eight and easily weighed over two hundred and fifty pounds. They were both broad around the shoulders and lean across the body. They were almost identical for most features other than their hair. Keith stood up when they came closer and shook one of their hands. The first person, seemed to grow, with every large footstep.

He towered over Keith, who was not small, and he had a large smile, which stretched from ear to ear. His eyes were dark, and his ears were slightly misshaped. His nose had been broken previously, that was obvious, as it was slightly crooked at the bridge. His hair was also dark, and it was neatly combed back across his head. As he withdrew his hand from Keith's Stephen could see the size of his hands. They were the size of a tennis racket and they looked spotless.

The man's arms were at least the size of Stephen's upper legs and his wrist was twice the size of Stephens. Stephen imagined he didn't have an ounce of fat on him. 'Stephen, this is Roger,' Keith said.

'I'm Stephen.'

'I know,' Roger said. His voice was deep and husky, 'Keith's told me you're in.'

'Yes,' Stephen replied. Roger held his grip on Stephen's hand, covering every inch of skin with his muscly fingers, as Stephen stared upwards into Roger's dark eyes.

'If you're not, then don't let me ever meet you again,' Roger said smiling as he released his grip.

'He's kidding Steve,' Keith said. 'Roger, he's in alright.' As Keith finished his sentence, the other man approached Stephen and held out his hand. He was almost a double of Roger. He had a short, blonde buzz cut, and his ears were also slightly misshaped, and his eyes were dark. Stephen wondered if they were brothers.

'I'm Phil,' the man said. Stephen's right hand ached from Roger and Phil applied a similar amount of pressure. Stephen tried to squeeze back but he could feel his fingers crush under the grip. Phil let go and took a step back, which took him around two feet away from Stephen.

'Stephen,' Stephen replied.

'Good to see you, Roger, Phil,' Keith said as he sat back down. Phil found a seat, but Roger remained as he was. Keith said 'Ok, the routes. Gentleman' and he nodded at Roger and Phil in turn, 'we were discussing the towers.'

'It's sorted. We've obviously been delayed by a week, but our guy, whom we trust, said he will take care of the towers from the outside, but we need a distraction here first and before that the power needs going.'

'We have one distraction,' Tony said to the group. Roger continued looking towards the entrance door. 'The library,' he finished.

'Still going down that route?' Phil said.

Stephen saw Tony look at Keith momentarily, as if checking if he could still reply and when Keith made no sign back to him, Tony continued, 'this prison isn't the most guarded place, I think we can all agree on that. However, I would say that it's guarded enough. There's camera's and there's enough guards to technically overpower us. So, we can't just start a riot. They will have it under control no time.'

Tony looked once again at Keith, who then spoke, 'the first thing, the main thing in fact is the power to this damn place. We switch that off; we're on our way. Your boy on the outside will not be able to gain access to the towers if the lights are on. The lights surround the towers and the yards. They will have every inch of the yard under surveillance. Roger, Phil, you two still going for the power?'

Phil remained seated and he was joined a moment later by Roger, who slid in next to him, his large muscly arms rubbing against Peter's as he positioned himself in the hard chair. 'We're taking control of the power,' Phil said.

'How?' Stephen said. If he hadn't said it himself, he wouldn't have believed it. All nine people at the table turned and looked at him. Stephen looked at Keith who had a grin on his face and Roger leant forward, blocking out the two shifters behind him with his sheer size, 'we've been in solitary for a little bit of time.'

'We knew we would,' Phil said.

'You know exactly where the power cut off point is, Steve?' Roger said.

Stephen looked at Roger, dead in the eye, and knew not to take his eyes off his. He remembered the words he had been told, 'upstairs, behind many doors and codes.'

'Yes,' Roger said. 'Many, *many* codes. But we have *that* code,' as he leant back in his chair, barely a smile on his face. 'We have spent non-retrievable time of our lives, getting this code, but my god it was worth it.' Roger looked at the ceiling beginning to smile more every second.

Phil then told the rest of the story, 'we saw Danny outside one day. He was watching the yard and we had been working out. We knew Danny was the answer. He saw us approach and he smiled at us, asking if we were ok. He must have been twenty- five and after a second he looked scared.'

'We pulled him over to one side and we had, shall we say, a chat with him about the prison. After a minute and after he had taken one of Phil's blow to his stomach, he told us where all power is kept. Then we threatened his family. We said we knew where his mother lived, his girlfriend, all that.'

'We didn't though,' Phil interjected again.

'So, after some gentle convincing, he told us about the codes too. His fear seemed to allow him to go the 'whole hog' and reveal it all. We know where we need to get to, and we know how. No point everyone knowing. It will take a little bit of time, but that should be the signal; when the lights around everyone go out.'

Everyone was quiet but Stephen was sure Keith looked out of the corner of his eyes towards Tony waiting for a response and a second later Keith closed his own eyes and cradled his hands in front of him. Stephen watched everyone in turn. Roger and Phil were just looking ahead towards the front door. The four shifters were all staring at Keith, waiting for their leader to speak and Oliver just sat still staring down at the desk.

'I agree,' Keith said after a minute. No-one looked surprised or shocked; everyone's reactions remained the same. 'When the power is out, your boy and no doubt his followers will go for the towers on the outside.'

'When the prison goes from being a light in the distance to blackness in a second, they will know. The prison will be isolated and then the emergency lighting comes on. The max security guards won't know anything, as the power we leave only supports the lights and the doors. So, when the lights go out, they go for the towers outside, and you lot run for it.'

'We,' Keith said.

'We will catch up with you, but we will have to get back down from the top of here through the doors,' Roger said.

'So then, we have to consider the distraction. The guards will obviously go for the power and they will try to notify max. But we need the distraction to cause havoc, not just for them, but for us.'

'The library is your final choice?' Phil said.

'It works best,' Keith said, 'we want the fire alarms to go off, which they will, and this will go external, we know that, and we can't prevent it, health and safety gone mad. Power goes off, guards panic and when they visit the power room, the cables will have been cut. Then they hear the fire alarms and all hell breaks loose. The doors automatically open because of a fire and by this point; we will be in darkness for a few moments, until the lights come on again. The towers are also dead, and the tower guards will be busy too with your boys,' Keith said nodding at Roger, 'we bring the weapons in with us, the same night and people take them for the escape.'

'Starting the fire?' Phil said.

'Oli here will do this. He's got the lighting stuff,' Keith replied as Oliver next to him nodded confidently. 'Next point to discuss is the escape routes, how we doing for time, Oli?' Keith said.

'Got some left,' Oliver replied still inhaling on his cigarette, the orange amber getting closer to the butt.

'Good. We have two courses at this moment in time, we know will work. The first way is the tunnel. This is by the far the best and easiest route, especially with the towers out of service, they won't see us enter the hole and then it comes out in the forest.'

'We will be staying to help our boys with the towers; it's our repayment back to them,' Roger said.

'And you two will still be using the second route?' Tony spoke for the first time in a while, nodding at Roger and Phil.

'We have to use it; the tunnel is too small for us.'

'The second route is?' Stephen asked.

'We literally cut through the fences. Someone will cut a hole, away from the greenhouse vicinity, so when these two get back down here, they have a route out. We can just use the mini shears in the greenhouse, they're blunt, but sharp enough.'

'Why don't we all break out through this route?' Stephen asked.

'We don't need to, Steve. We can go out of our tunnel and then we're set apart from everyone else. If we all went out together, then we're easier to spot. There are eighteen of us in on this plan. I'd honestly say a third of them want to escape for the same reason as we do; freedom. The others want to be in on this for the trouble it will cause and to get their own back.'

'So, you're only telling a third about the hole?' Lance said, Stephen jumping slightly, forgetting Lance was still here.

'No, we intend to tell everyone about our escape. However,

we will make them aware that the hole in the fence is the way to escape. The guards will go straight for the hole in the fence, whilst we're crawling silently on our way to freedom.'

'That's why it isn't a subtle breakout?' Stephen asked, 'because the prison will have it under control and be able to round everyone up easier.'

'Exactly, the guards will do the count when everything is under control, but remember, that will take hours and hours as they will need to control the fire, which should have burnt the majority of the place down and the power will be off. Plus, they will have no outside support for a while. The maximum security, will see the fire soon enough, so we need to be gone by then.'

'What's the back-up route?' Lance said.

'A corridor underneath the prison,' Keith replied, and Stephen could see the whole room focus solely on Keith now, nine pairs of eyes eager to hear the next part. 'An old acquaintance told me about it, years ago. It was used for bringing things in and out of the prison. But he said, the prison changed the layout and this corridor was left as it was, unused and forgotten. They said the prison covered the old entrance, but we think it's underneath the kitchen. I'll know tomorrow.'

'How did he know about it?' Phil said.

'He visited it enough times. He said the old door was shut, built over and never re-opened. He always said that if you wanted to escape, get through that locked door and you're out of here.'

'So, that's your job, Steve?' Roger said.

Stephen felt more eyes on him now. He knew the job asked of him by Keith and he knew he had to find out the answers soon. 'I'm going to work it out. Keith is pretty confident about where it's located, so I need to get to the kitchen and see if I can find it. Then I can have a look and see what needs doing. Lance is coming with me.'

Stephen saw Lance's head turn suddenly, shocked and surprised and Stephen smiled at him.

'There we go,' Keith said, 'all happy?' The room didn't really answer other than the odd grunt whilst they all nodded in unison. 'Last couple of items and then we're set. Anything else we need to be aware of?'

The room was quiet for a moment, when something sprung to Stephen's mind and his eyes widened. 'There is something odd I've witnessed in the last few days.' Everyone looked at him and Stephen could see worry etched across Keith's face. 'A guy probably about my age, was asking me all about meeting you guys behind the greenhouse and how I wasn't allowed there. He seemed suspicious.'

'Benjamin Durant,' Keith said sitting back, relaxing and breathing once again, 'a nutcase if ever I've seen one. Killed his mother. Completely gaga.' Keith stopped talking and the door opened, slowly and smoothly as two more people walked in, who were much smaller than Roger and Phil. Stephen recognised them as James and Lee. Their hands were dry and muddy, and their tops looked drenched in sweat. 'Welcome boys.'

They nodded around the room and stood behind Oliver with their backs to the door. 'He was asking about my wife too.' Stephen said.

'He was probably fishing for ideas. He saw us together. But I think there's more to it. I've seen him in and out of the warden's office more than ever in the past few months. Something's not right.'

'Talking about Ben Durant?' Lee said.

'Yes.'

'He was watching the greenhouse the other day. He tried to stay out of sight, but he stood out like a sore thumb,' Lee said.

'Must have been when he was watching me,' Stephen said.

'No doubt,' Keith said. 'I think he's working for something and the warden has something over him. Ben always looked disgruntled after they meet.'

'He knew something was being planning but he didn't know what. He seemed more interested in me and my family. He talked about my wife.' At this point Stephen felt himself well up inside and he felt a rush of anger explode through his body, as his fists clenched, and his jaw tightened.

'We'll take care of him,' Phil said.

'No,' Keith replied. 'If you do, you're straight back in solitary, and this time it may be weeks. We're doing this in three weeks from now. Three weeks today.'

'We've changed the plan slightly,' James said to the group, speaking for the first time. 'When I heard about Ben watching, Lee and I made another large hole and threw loads of mud in it. Nothing big, but it's to cover the real hole, which we will put plant pots and other gardening stuff to block the tunnel. It's to hide it away.'

'We'll also make sure that at least one of us guarding the hole during the day and doesn't leave it unattended.'

'Good work,' Keith said.

'The weapons will need to be moved though.'

'The weapons,' Keith repeated, 'of course. They need to go to the library. Everyone agree?'

Everyone in the room nodded. Stephen felt eager to go

now, three weeks felt like a long time away, but he was sure it would come quick enough. He looked at Lance, who was sitting straight faced, staring at the far wall.

'So now, to recap; the power goes off, Phil and Roger. Then the fire starts, Oli. Then the escape begins. The towers are taken care of outside. The hole is cut to the fence and we get down the tunnel and out of here. Sounds simple and it will be,' Keith said laughing.

'We will move weapons tomorrow and gradual. We will split them across the greenhouse grounds for now.'

'Go,' Keith was saying, as the door burst open for the third time and, in walked Clive, who was visibly hot and out of breath, as he held his large belly.

'I forgot you lot were in here, out of here, *now*,' Clive shouted, 'a word, Oliver.'

The whole room disbursed but for Oliver. Neither Roger nor Phil replied to Clive. Stephen assumed there was a level of respect there or was it because Clive was doing them all a favour?

Stephen walked outside and stood for a moment in the rays of the sun. He watched as the shifters paced back to the prison and Roger and Phil, walked another direction. Even though the sun was shining, Stephen still felt a cold chill swoop through the air, making him hold his arms to keep warm. Stephen's feeling that something wasn't quite right at the prison became greater than ever.

33

Six days later, the weather had changed dramatically. The sun had been replaced by grey skies and dark clouds. Rain had engulfed the prison and the grounds were damp and uninviting. The weather had hindered the plans set up in the workshop almost a week ago for the planned escapees. Inmates, for the majority of the day, remained inside, amid the conditions surrounding them.

Everyone in the plan had been working tirelessly to ensure the plan succeeded from checking the routes to the power room, as well as watching the towers from afar to work out the exact direction, they would need to take on escape. Roger and Phil didn't care; they would only escape once they helped their friends on the outside. Stephen knew they all had just over two weeks and he knew he needed to find out answers about the kitchen.

In a different location within the prison was Ben who was cold, tired and angry and was stood leaning against a wall in solitary confinement. He had been confined to the same four walls for more time than he ever imagined he would be, and he had lost the will to live. He had considered killing himself, more than once. It felt like once every hour, but two things kept him going; Stephen and revenge on Roy.

He knew he was due to be released. A guard had told him

the day before and Ben guessed it was because Roy had no more reasons to keep him here. Ben felt wearier by the day and he had caught a wheezing cough, which kept him awake throughout the night underneath the thin blanket and cold, stale air. He was leaning against a wall, waiting to hear footsteps and the sound of keys, which would signal temporary freedom.

Permanent freedom wasn't possible now. He knew Roy wouldn't let him go; not now he felt he had him under his control. Ben's first plan was to find out what Stephen was doing with the shifters. Ben knew he would be a week behind now, so hard work was what it would come down too. He knew he needed to find this out in order to stay out of solitary, also, to stay in Roy's good books. That part would only help him succeed with his real ulterior motive.

He needed someone who would speak about Stephen. Was there even a plan? He had only spun that lie to Roy about the shifters to try and change Roy's target, but it didn't work, instead it backfired, and Ben had spent the past six days paying for it. His first task when he was let out of solitary was to go to the church, then the workshop. They were the two places Stephen visited the most. Ben wanted to learn everything he could about Stephen.

He heard the scuffle of shoes echo down the corridor, followed by the jangling of keys, which grew louder with every second. Ben pushed himself gently off the wall, holding his shoulder and looked at the steel door. He waited for a moment, breathing in the stale air. A second later, he heard a metal ping, as a key was forced into the keyhole of his cell door and it swung inwards.

Two people stood before him. One was large and pale, with

a red beard, around an inch thick. He had a name tag that read Matthew. The other person was Lilian. Matthew overlooked her by over a foot. 'Out,' he said, 'turn around.'

Ben turned and felt two sets of hands grab his right and left wrist in turn and pull them behind his lower back. Metal touched each wrist and with a little click the handcuffs were tightened. Ben didn't speak. He didn't need to. They thought he was someone who had just attacked their boss. They hadn't seen anything yet.

Ben was led down a dark corridor and past other cells, identical to his own. Some doors were ajar, but the majority were closed. As Ben reached the end of the corridor, they came to a large single door. Matthew stepped forwards and punched in a few digits and the small light above the door turned a pale green. Matthew grabbed the handle and opened it for Ben and Lilian to walk through.

They ascended a dozen metal steps, leading up to the main prison body. Lilian held Ben's arms and pushed him, so his elbows were high in the air. As they reached the top, Ben felt the other guard squeeze past them and walk to the next metal door, where he repeated the exercise with the keypad. The light above the door went green and they all walked through again.

They reached two guards sitting on wooden chairs. 'Here's the one who thinks he can knock us about,' one guard said. Ben looked back at him and didn't change his gaze; he kept it straight and level. 'If we didn't have cameras here, I'd beat your face, so you were unrecognisable. Get him out my sight.'

Ben was grabbed heavily by Matthew and Ben felt the pain and swelling rise under the force. He tried to grit his teeth as his eyes adjusted to the lighting in the new room. Ben was now stood in a single room, which was painted white and was filled with halogen bulbs. To the side was a desk with some little bits of machinery scattered across them along with some folded orange clothing.

The new guard patted Ben down from head to toe, feeling every inch of his body. Ben grimaced in pain and tried to keep his knees and back straight. When the guard finished, Matthew re-grabbed his arm and led him forward alone, typing in a small digit code into a number pad, attached to the wall as this door opened sideways.

'You need to visit the warden again, an hour from now. I'll be there this time to keep an eye,' Lilian said smiling serenely.

Ben walked through the door and stood still as he heard the door close behind him.

Lilian watched as the door closed and she nodded at Matthew. As he walked back towards the other guards, she withdrew her pen and the small notepad and made a few neat notes. She underlined the word violence and nodded satisfied. She placed the pen and pad into her back pocket and quickly followed Matthew.

Ben looked ahead and realised he was somewhere near the main atrium of the prison. He gently moved forward trying to get feeling into his body again and he came into the actual atrium. He recognised it straight away and shuddered at the look of the inmates surrounding him.

Ben kept his head down and headed for the outside. Ben could sense in-mates staring at him from every angle; maybe he was the talk of the prison? That wasn't a good thing. Ben wanted to complete this mission alone and unknown. Ben walked straight to the outside door, which had two guards both sitting down next to it, watching Ben's every step. The corridors were quiet and seconds later Ben found out why.

The torrential rain soaked him within seconds from his head to his feet. His hair came down to his eyes and his top was skin- tight to his chest and arms. Ben, actually felt, a sense of calm with the rain; as if the last week was being washed away with every pounding drop. With every short step, Ben felt his rubber soles, sink further and further into the muddy ground beneath him.

He stopped for a moment, trying to work out the best place to visit first. The church was closer, but the workshop was more important. He veered left and aimed for the workshop and shelter from the storm. The yard was empty. Ben could see no orange suits or any guards.

He reached the workshop and stood next to the wooden sign. Beyond that Ben could see the greenhouse and he was sure he saw a flash of orange moving inside. The towers were overlooking the whole yard to his right, but Ben kept his focus in front of him and walked in the workshop, which was encircled by puddles and ferocious drops of rain.

Ben didn't knock, but instead walked straight in, keeping his head down to hide his eyes from the last exposure of rain. The workshop was, more or less, as he remembered it; relatively large and uncomfortably bright. Ben felt an instant headache along with his heavy cough and he felt tired from a weeks' worth of poor sleeping conditions.

Oliver was inside and he was moving things from the desk he was sat at, into a small blue, rubber box on the floor. Ben also saw a small stick on the floor, which was orange at the end; a cigarette. Ben looked at the room and tried to act plausible and realistic as if he really wanted a job here. He looked at the desks, which were clean and tidy, revealing the dents and marks scratched into them by many in-mates.

The three wooden shelves pinned to the walls were unoccupied and below them stood two small gas pumps, along with a sink and two taps, which were small and dark. 'Hello,' Ben said taking two more steps. Ben pulled his orange top away from his chest, which was heavy and saturated. Below him was a small puddle expanding along with small drops falling from his wet hair.

'Hello, Ben. What are you doing here?' Oliver replied from the front of room. Ben looked at Oliver and tried to keep calm and tried to rehearse his story again.

'You have a towel?' Ben said. Ben saw Oliver blink several times as if surprised.

'No, I don't. What you, doing here?'

'I'm looking to work here'

'There are no spaces, sorry. We have a lot of people here now. The church may need help,' Oliver replied, and Ben watched him fiddle with something on the desk. Ben took another two steps forward until he was stood right underneath a bulb, which created a shadow on the floor around Ben's whole body.

Ben was meeting Roy in an hour and that hour would pass quickly. He wanted to go with something, just something to give himself more time. Sadly, what he wanted was entwined with Roy, except for Ben didn't know why Roy was so attracted to Stephen. To give Roy anything, was to share things he wanted secret. He needed to know about a plan, he was sure was happening.

'I can work hard here. I've been thinking, this is something I'd be really good at.'

'Only now? You've been in here years,' Oliver replied.

'I've had time to think.'

'We know you've been in solitary.'

'How?'

'You don't think the prison talks? Come on Ben, why are you really here?'

Ben was lost for a moment. The last six days of planning, out of the window with a simple question. He looked at Oliver who was staring back at him expressionlessly and Ben wanted to turn around and run, but he couldn't; he'd run away all his life, but not now. 'Tell me the plan.' Ben said.

Oliver didn't confirm nor deny, but instead leant back in his chair and crossed his legs, 'what plan?'

'Something is going on, I know it,' Ben said. 'Does Stephen come here? Has he met the shifters here?'

'Ben, calm down. Nothing, is going on, I don't know if they've even met.'

Ben felt his body shake and his anger erupt, 'I CAN'T ACCEPT THAT,' he roared across the tables at Oliver, who looked taken aback. 'YOU'RE PLANNING SOMETHING AND I WANT TO KNOW WHAT.' Ben finished his sentence and sunk to his knees. He felt tears form in the corner of his eyes and he felt his physical pain disappear. Ben was just crying into his hands.

It seemed like an eternity, but Oliver was stood next to him resting his right hand on Ben's left shoulder, 'what's wrong, Ben?'

Ben stopped crying for a moment and became immobile. He had let his guard down completely. The only time he ever done this was to his diary. He rose himself upwards, brushing Oliver's hand high into the air and out of nowhere he hooked a right fist, hard into Oliver's temple, which knocked him over and against a desk leg.

Ben looked down at Oliver, whose face was shaken and surprised. Ben turned around, running into a new batch of rain, which he knew wouldn't be able to wash away the problems he had just caused himself.

34

Stephen had been sitting in the library with Lance avoiding the rain and wind. They both had their heads bowed over a newspaper from two days ago. There was nothing positive on any of the pages, it all seemed downbeat. The weather forecast suggested the poor conditions were unchanging. It wasn't ideal but the escape wasn't for two weeks, so there was still hope.

Inmates around them, were all talking, and this didn't help them. The library was usually quiet most of the day, but the poor weather conditions had meant everyone had hidden there for shelter. The escapees had no real chance of meeting to discuss the plan, but Stephen was confident Keith would still be working away in the background.

It seemed a lifetime that Keith had told them they were breaking out. At first, Stephen hadn't believed him, but Keith had, seemingly, told him everything. Three of the inmates in the room, pushed their chairs back, the wooden legs scraping on the flooring beneath them as they exited the room.

Stephen and Lance took their chance and picked up the newspaper, which then revealed two pieces of large paper folded in half. Stephen kept flicking between the paperwork and inmates, which hadn't allowed them to concentrate. Lance kept looking towards the door, peering in between the aisles.

Once Stephen and Lance were confident, they stopped being

so cautious and began re-looking at the paperwork. Stephen unfolded the first piece of paper, which was a drawing, dated six years ago. It was a bird's eye view drawing of the prison, showing the whole layout from every quarter. Keith called it the blueprint.

Whenever Keith got these drawings and information, he'd been storing them in between books under certain genres. The genre changed every three days, and this was communicated to Stephen and Lance immediately. Stephen didn't know where Keith got this information from and he didn't want to ask. He knew Keith had external sources and that Keith wouldn't likely reveal it anyway.

Keith said the disposal of this information was such an important part of the plan. If any of this paperwork was lost or found by a guard or even an inmate who wasn't in on the plan, then the breakout couldn't happen. Stephen glanced at the paperwork, looking at every room as he went from the library to the contraband room, which was listed as the illegal and unauthorised belongings room.

Stephen's eyes hovered over the cell section for the first time. He stopped for a moment to appreciate the sheer size. There were several rooms and several floors, which Stephen didn't even know existed. It showed the solitary confinement rooms where Roger and Phil had been kept weeks ago, just off the atrium.

The diagram showed their position in the library compared to the kitchen. Stephen looked an inch to the right and saw the staff quarters, which were based on the second floor. It also showed on the same level, where the power was located. Stephen knew the power was the biggest part of the plan, but some argued it was the towers. Stephen didn't envy Roger and Phil's task.

Stephen's eyes were concentrating on the kitchen, 'reckon it will be easy?' Stephen said.

'Of course, it will,' Lance replied grinning, 'we will have a look and see if we can get through. If we can, then we will have a look today yes?'

'Yes, that makes sense, before we meet Keith tomorrow.' Stephen felt getting into the back of the kitchen may be the problem. It was twined onto the actual food hall, which was vast in size. Stephen knew from his countless visits to the food hall, that it was now open plan. These prison drawings were dated six years ago, so Stephen knew things had changed.

Lance pulled out the other piece of paper, as Stephen took a quick look around the room. The remaining four inmates were still sat in a huddle talking. Stephen leant to his right and looked at the paperwork. It was another birds-eye view picture, but from a higher position than the previous one. It showed the prison, as- a- whole, along with the surrounding areas.

Next to the prison were the two towers, which were drawn in two large circles. Then there were short road markings leading to the towers; the place where Roger and Phil would have their battle. For a wide radius beyond that, there seemed to be nothing else. In the top right- hand corner of the drawing Stephen read there was a train station ten miles away and a motorway around seven miles away. Stephen tried to recount his trip to the prison, but he didn't remember a thing.

'What you think?'

Stephen tucked the pieces of paper underneath the newspaper and rolled them up tightly, 'I'm not sure. I think the main one for us is the first drawing. We need to see the kitchen properly. Dinner isn't long from now, so we need to get in early and have a look.'

'Just think, six days of thinking about this kitchen and we're almost there,' Stephen replied.

'Keith is always one step ahead,' Lance said.

'You mean the greenhouse search?'

'Yes, it's like he knew it would be searched so he moved it all. Obviously knowing that Ben guy was watching helped. Two birds with one stone.'

'Come again?'

'Well the only good thing of the search was the fact we know the guards think something is going on and that Ben is helping them. He, has to be. The towers apparently reported nothing strange either Keith's outside source informed him.'

'Who is his source?' Stephen asked, 'is it the same person who has been helping him all this time, or does he have several?'

'He doesn't really say, but I think it's one person, who I think knows the prison well. He knows people who have come and gone from here and I think they stay in contact. I never asked you Steve, Keith said you read about the max security part of the prison, why?'

'I told Keith that I thought it may be a good idea to have a quick look at the layout and how it works, as a back-up to the back-up plan.'

'Did you find anything?'

'Nothing really and he expected that. He said the greenhouse was a perfect escape and the kitchen was a good back-up, subject to today.'

'He like the thinking though?'

'I think so; he said every angle needs to be covered. I get the feeling he's done all the thinking himself, but he was just being polite to me.' Stephen had a question for Lance. He wasn't sure how to ask it, 'you told me you'd only ever go to the max facility if you needed to. That's when you knew about this plan wasn't it?'

'Yes, I know if we get caught, we will go down there for a long, long time. Maybe even get moved to somewhere more secure.'

'Are you doing all this because Keith saved your life?'

Stephen saw Lance turn his head slightly to react to the question and then look up at the ceiling, as if staring into another world. 'Yes, if I'm honest. I don't have a reason to escape and I wouldn't do this if it wasn't for Keith.'

'What did you try to do?' Stephen said, 'sorry, that's a bit personal.'

'I was lost in my mind. I had bad anxiety issues and was down the whole time. Coming in here was the final straw. I had to take my life, to really be free from pain.'

'Sorry.'

'Don't be sorry. Keith had watched me a few times, taking wires out and he came to my cell as I was about to do it. He stopped me and took me under his wing. So, when this plan came out, he told me, and I volunteered to help.'

'Lance, can I ask why you are in here?'

Stephen could sense pain in Lance's dark brown eyes. Stephen kept looking at Lance, the glow of the lights above him reflecting off his wrinkled scalp. 'I was stupid. I set a club on fire, as a warning really to someone. They were, messing with my sister, and I didn't want it continue.

'So, I set a boxing club on fire, middle of the night thinking it would be empty, but it wasn't. There were five of them in there. They didn't get out in time. It wasn't meant to end this way. My sister never spoke to me again.'

'Sorry.'

'Don't be, it's my fault. If we get out of here, I'll find a way to her and a way to survive. Shall we go check out the kitchen bit?' Lance said wiping his brow, quickly changing the subject.

To their side, they heard the library door open and heavy footsteps approach them from one of the aisles. Stephen saw Lance pull the paper towards him and hide it underneath his orange top. Stephen saw a shadow from the middle aisle and, as it grew closer he saw Honda walking towards them with long strides. Stephen swallowed hard and felt a sense of panic; now wasn't the time for round two. Honda nodded at the two of them sitting down and he veered right and sat down at a small table on his own and pulled out a small book from his pocket.

'In a minute, one more question I want to ask you, in privacy,' Stephen said. Lance kept his eyes on Stephen and didn't answer or invite a response. 'The shifters have the power in here; they even have the respect from the toughest people in here, like Roger, Phil, Honda. There must be more to it?'

'There is.'

'Tell me, please.'

'In privacy? Never to be repeated?'

'Promise.'

Lance pushed his chair slightly out from underneath the worn and used table and crossed one of his legs. He looked at the desk and remained quiet for a minute, as if working out the order of the words, 'they help people in here. They always have.'

'Like?'

'People come in here for a reason. People still need their outside lives to a degree. They supply people who need things.'

'Drugs?'

'Amongst other things. They bring in contraband like fresh meat, fruit and vegetables. They get drugs in. They get steroids in for the yard. They help people. Only five people know how they do it; them. I don't know, Roger and Phil don't, only them.'

Stephen remained quiet, thinking about Keith and his past. He was glad he was on their side, because he was pretty sure if he wasn't, he'd be dead.

'Come on, let's see the kitchen. Keep what I told you under wraps or I'll commit another murder and it won't be accidental this time,' Lance said grinning as they both stood upright. Stephen felt grief for Lance. Lance had killed people in his past, not on purpose and he'd paid for it ever since. There were more questions Stephen wanted to ask but he felt he'd asked Lance enough.

They began to exit the library, passing through the heavy door and the contraband room and the laundry room. Stephen could make out Malcolm sitting on a washing machine folding clothes into a neat pile. Stephen thought of Bertie and then the warden.

The noise of talking and muttering grew louder as they reached the atrium and it was busier than Stephen had ever seen previously. There were more than a dozen guards also patrolling the floor, and as Stephen looked above, guards were standing against the railings, some looking down, some watching their own level.

'Lance,' Stephen said, 'do a lot of visitors come here?'

'Rarely,' Lance said as they both turned right at the atrium and began walking around the inmates scattered across the large hall. 'I've never had one. I guess we are just too far out. We're basically miles from anything, as you saw on those maps. Would you want a visitor?'

Stephen didn't really have to think about his answer, 'my wife, she never can. She's dead.' Lance didn't reply and Stephen's mind opened into another world. Stacey walked up to Stephen and stood on her tip toes kissing him full on the mouth, as her small wrists wrapped around the back of his freshly cut hair.

Then out of the distance came Stephen's mother in a lovely blue dress with a beaming smile etched across her youthful face. She tiptoed, just like Stacey had, and she whispered, 'I know you didn't do it, Stephen, I know.' Stephen hugged her hard and long. After a minute, Stephen let go of her as she patted him on the shoulder smiling at him sullenly. 'Stephen,' she said, 'dad would be so proud of you. Stephen,' she said again, 'Stephen.'

'Stephen,' Lance said, and Stephen opened his eyes to brightness and noise, 'hello, where have you been?'

'Nowhere, what's happened?' Stephen replied.

'We're outside the kitchen; I've been calling your name for about a minute.'

'Sorry, I don't know where I was, but Stacey was there and my mum and my mum knew I didn't kill, Stacey.'

Lance was looking at him puzzled with a wide grin across his face, 'I think you're going mad mate, come on.' Lance waved his arm towards the kitchen door. Stephen followed, regaining his bearings. He was stood at the edge of the atrium now, near the television centre and he was surrounded by other inmates and guards.

The food hall was now open and as he walked through the open doorway, the tables were only a quarter filled. The smell of processed food wafted through the damp air as Stephen and Lance approached the back of the kitchen. Stephen saw a guard leaning against a wall centre of the room, underneath a circular clock, which hung around twelve feet in the air.

Stephen noticed that the same four men, which he had always seen working here, were stood behind the shoulder high glass counter. They looked disinterested and bored. They passed twenty tables and reached the counter. They joined a small queue and waited until they were first in line. Stephen took a glance around and imagined what the room would be like in twenty minutes.

Three people slid their trays across the metal rails in front of them, which were slightly spread apart. They picked up their trays and left the line, aiming for a seat from which they had plenty of choice. Lance was first in line and he said something to one of the canteen staff, who was wearing a white apron and a small white hat. Stephen had spoken to the man named Johnny several times. Johnny nodded and walked away to the far end of the counter.

Stephen followed Lance and kept his head down as the other three remaining canteen inmates moved left and reshuffled themselves to serve the small queue forming. Stephen reached the end of the counter and bumped into Lance who stopped abruptly in front of him, 'calm it Steve,' he said, 'we need a slight distraction to get behind here without being suspected. Johnny's going to do it now.'

Johnny sauntered round the counter and across the cafeteria floor and to the complete surprise of everyone in the room but for Lance; Johnny slapped an inmate's tray clean in the air. The inmate jumped to his feet as those within a metre radius were showered in beans and other slop and shouting erupted within the cafeteria.

The inmate grabbed Johnny, shouting in his face. The guard ran across the room as a semi-circle was formed partly around the pair. The three people who were working behind the counter stayed stationary. Lance pulled Stephen's arm beyond the counter and out of sight from the commotion. 'Why did he do that?' Stephen asked as they veered around one corner and past a pair of large, silver fridges.

'It was staged, Steve. Johnny did it to someone expecting it. They are both in on the escape,' Lance replied.

'Where are we going now?'

'No idea, but I'm hoping we can find out,' Johnny said, 'go, round the first corner, and be quick.'

'Why didn't Johnny do any homework for us?' Stephen asked.

'It's our job firstly and secondly, he's the only one in on the plan from the canteen lot. The other three or so don't know about it, so for him to come here would arouse suspicion.'

'Let's go down here,' Stephen said pointing at the far end of the room. As soon as they reached it, Stephen knew this was the room Keith had described so long ago. The wall before them looked almost new and the paint looked fresher than the rest of the room. 'Can we get through?'

'Not through the wall, no,' Stephen said as he looked at the wall and pictured a door behind it, with a long corridor, leading to a door and to freedom. 'They couldn't have just shut it off. There would be health and safety risks. Move some things in here.' They both began moving wheeled tables and food containers, full of long life mash and porridge.

Stephen found what he was looking for a minute later, 'Lance here.' As soon as Lance arrived, Stephen pointed at a small freezer, where visible just beside one of the wheels was a dark grey drain. 'This is what we need. Where's the slop?'

Lance turned around and directly behind them, on a shelf was a small bucket, which had slop poorly written across its face. 'In here?' Lance said.

'Keith said so,' Stephen replied, and Lance plunged his hand into the bucket and pulled out a medium sized, industrial screw- driver and a little piece of metal, which Stephen presumed was an attachment. Lance shook his hands into the bucket and using a towel, he wiped his hands one by one. Stephen turned his attention to the freezer, and he heaved it away from the drain to full reveal it.

'Does anyone go in here?' Lance said.

'Keith said no. Johnny doesn't think it goes anywhere.'

'Open it up.'

'I'll try,' Stephen said as took the screwdriver and attached the mechanism. He knelt- down and placed the tool over a bolt on the corner of the drain. He twisted and felt a slight shudder as the bolt moved. Stephen moved the tool back and forth and then with his fourth twist, the bolt loosened and was out the ground.

'Three to go,' Lance said. Stephen nodded without looking up at Lance and he loosened the other three bolts. 'We will just rest the bolts back into place when we leave. We can't afford to have to undo these again if we need to go out this way.' Stephen gave the tool back to Lance and with ease, he hoisted open the drain, which was light.

'You've done it,' Lance said.

'We need to check things out,' Stephen said as he sat down on the edge of the hole. 'It's too dark in here to see. We can't leave the drain open, can we?'

'No way, Steve, if someone comes back here and sees the drain open, then it could be game over. We're back to one or two escapes.'

'When I go down, rest it over the hole. Hold on,' Stephen said sharply. Stephen looked below him and dropped. The fall was around eight foot and Stephen could see an air vent, a metre away. The space Stephen occupied was small and empty, 'Ok cover me.' Stephen heard the drain fall on top of him and he was enclosed in darkness. He wandered slowly forward to the air vent, unable to make out a single thing or where Lance was either. 'Lance?'

'Still here, you, going on?'

'I only want to get a look so we can at least provide Keith with some good news.' Lance didn't reply so Stephen stepped slowly forward, sliding his feet on the floor as he reached the air vent. The vent felt cold. Stephen fingered the edges of the vent trying to grip his fingers between it and the actual wall.

He found no points to grip or heave at round the outer edge of the vent. Stephen imagined down here was sound- proof so he took a big step back, rocking on his heel and he drove his right heel into the centre of the vent, where it shuddered. He repeated the motion again and the vent flew forward, into the next room.

Stephen listened for noises from above, but it was quiet. The corridor smelt musty and like a room, which hadn't been used for many years. Stephen imagined the walls were mounted with mildew. Stephen's eyes adjusted to the darkness and he tried to imagine how large the room was, although he didn't know how far it was to reach each opposite wall.

Stephen felt his foot kick something below him, which clattered along the floor as he walked. It was something small and metal and the sound of the metal bouncing against the concrete reverberated around the hollow room. Stephen held his palms out in front of him and moved forward. Even though Stephen's eyes had adjusted to the darkness, he was still barely able to make out anything in front of him.

Stephen became hotter and hotter the more he ventured into the room. Stephen reached another door and felt for a handle. There was nothing attached to the door, which Stephen guessed from feeling it was wooden. Stephen felt near the edge of the door and as he felt once again for a handle, the door swung open away from him.

Stephen could make out a small light at the end of the tunnel, which he guessed was about thirty metres away. Then he was joined by noises surrounding him, which made him stop dead. He could hear little scurrying noises across the floor; rats, he thought. He didn't want to hurt them, so Stephen dragged his feet across the floor, trying not to tread on them.

He gently let the door go back against the frame and it made no sound. Stephen could sense dark patches against the walls, and he could sense rooms too. Were they old prison rooms? Doubtful, but the plans he had read didn't show this detail. Would it be the key to getting out? Stephen, really hoped not, he hoped the greenhouse tunnel was good enough.

As he slid onward, the light grew closer. He reached the end of this corridor and turned into the next and ahead of him was another door, with light creeping in around the edges. Stephen was covered in sweat, and his hair had, fallen into his eye, on one side, as it was wet and un-kept. As Stephen trudged forward, feeling his throat dry more every second, he could see into one of the rooms, which had a small window.

The room was very small, only about ten- foot square, in size. He couldn't make out the contents of the room, but he was sure there was a long table, with wheels attached to four legs on the bottom and a white sheet lying across the surface. There was nothing else of note within the room, so Stephen headed for the door and the light.

He reached it, quickly, as he was able to see more clearly now. He could hear footsteps outside and two men talking. Stephen didn't move and waited for the sounds to pass. As the conversation grew fainter, Stephen started to check the door, feeling for the handle. He found a small round knob halfway down the edge of the door. Stephen slid his hand across the wall and found a metal bar bolted across the door.

The door had also been locked in five places. It was impossible to get in from the outside, unless you drove through it. The prison was confident that it had it protected enough from the outside. Stephen turned around and started to walk back to Lance. He curved around the corner and came to the door, which had opened quite easily. He put a gentle amount of pressure on the door and it opened away from him again; a revolving door, easy to go both ways.

Stephen, softly moved through the hole, where the air vent was based and he could see a small amount of light above him.

He slid his feet across the dry, dusty floor trying not to inhale the distinctive smell of dust floating in the air. He walked beneath the drain, 'Lance,' he whispered.

The drain flew open instantaneously, and Stephen blinked several times, seeing Lance leaning over the edge. 'Up here. Johnny said we need to move,' Lance said, lowering his right hand into the hole. Stephen gripped his forearm and using his left hand he jumped, grabbing the edge of the hole as he pulled himself upwards.

Before he had chance to talk, Lance manoeuvred the drain back on top of the gaping hole. Once it was positioned correctly, Lance then knelt- down and re-did the bolts, giving it one tight turn on each corner. Stephen now started to walk back where they had come from to check they were alone. Stephen ran back to push the freezer back over the drain. Lance dropped the screwdriver and mechanism, into the slop, and they stared at each other.

They both bounced out of the room and over the doorway and Stephen watched as Lance brushed himself down and they stood amongst the whirring of the fridges and the kitchen appliances. They both didn't speak until they reached the last corner, both peering around to look at the actual kitchen area.

Johnny was stood facing in their direction. The other three canteen workers had their backs to them and were facing the crowd. Johnny moved his arm in the air and Stephen and Lance took long strides until they were in the open area and on the front of the counter. 'Amazing,' Stephen said.

'Indeed,' Lance replied as they both started to exit the food hall. 'I'm not hungry, let's find Keith.'

'Why didn't Johnny get taken away by the guards?'

'He doesn't. He's been here for years and the guards don't want the paperwork. Plus, as soon as we'd got through the back way, Johnny would have hugged Daniel and then it would have all been forgotten about,' Lance replied, 'let's go to the library.'

They both headed in that direction, both smiling, satisfied with what they had found, just as Roy began walking to the workshop.

35

Roy left his office quietly, telling his staff he had something to check before clocking off. Roy had met Ben less than an hour ago and Ben had finally made some progress. Ben had been down to see Oliver and had returned as a soaking wet, poor excuse of a person, sad and obviously in pain. The first twenty minutes of their meeting, Lilian had joined them as they talked about Ben.

Then Lilian left and Roy moved straight for Ben, telling him what he expected from him in the next few days. Roy said he wanted concrete evidence about any activities around the prison, not just about Stephen but from everyone. Roy didn't tell Ben that he had had the greenhouse searched and that he had the guards keeping a close eye on the shifters.

Ben discussed how Oliver denied any wrongdoing within the prison. Ben told Roy there were cigarettes in the workshop. Roy wanted to check this out for himself. He had no doubt contraband was being brought into the prison, but now he had proof. Oliver would need to talk. Roy thought about Oliver and if he was mixing with the shifters, whether Roy would then have more trouble on his plate than he had catered for.

The past six days for Roy had been quiet and uneventful. The greenhouse had turned out to be a dead end. The prison guards had undertaken random searches, including two of the shifters bunks, but nothing surfaced. Roy had seen Stephen walking and talking with Lance a considerable amount. Roy let Ben go and said don't be late for the count, but Roy didn't share where he was headed.

The rain had helped Roy as most of the inmates had remained inside. He had started to think about if killing Stephen in here was a bad idea, but it would be easy when he got him alone. He wanted to tell him face to face, why he had to die. He needed an opportunity when the shifters attentions had turned.

One of the nurses within the prison didn't turn up on some previous work days . He had no back up and he had no news of her quitting. Then the following day after she didn't turn up again nor the day after that; first the guard quitting a few weeks ago, now her. Something just didn't feel right.

Roy crossed the yard and was instantly wet. The ground was muddy, and the puddles were wide. Roy tried to stride across the yard, his leg holding him back with every other step. As he reached the workshop door, the small roof above the door protected Roy from the enormous rain fall. Roy didn't knock, but instead just pushed the door open and stepped over the threshold.

He saw Oliver sitting at the back of room. He threw something on the floor and his right foot covered it quickly; a cigarette? 'Oliver, I need a word.' Roy pushed the door behind him and ambled into the room. Roy hadn't been in the workshop for a long time and he realised why. It smelt musty and sweaty and of burnt metal. The lights were bright, and Roy felt if he stayed too long, he would have more than a headache.

'What's wrong?' Oliver replied.

'Why are you not at the count?' Roy said as he looked around the room. The metal wired tool cabinet was locked and the rest of the room was empty. The desks were clear of any materials and behind Oliver on the floor were two large rubber boxes.

'The count? It's not due for another thirty minutes?'

'New rules, Oliver, I want everyone there early, that includes you.'

'I'll clear up here and I'll leave.'

Roy stepped closer towards Oliver and noticed a large red mark across the side of his cheek. Roy tensed a little and thought about Ben. 'You've been hurt, your face, it's bruised.'

'O nothing, accident with my tools.'

Roy moved to one side of room and kept his eyes firmly on Oliver's. Oliver was thinking, but Roy knew Oliver could never outsmart him. Roy leant against the side next to the sink and taps. Roy looked left slightly and made out the two gas pumps used for mechanical work. 'There's more damage to you, than what a tool could have done, especially by accident.'

Roy watched Oliver look back at him carefully and pause before he replied. Roy simply rested against the work surface and waited. Roy now had a good idea. He thought Ben had looked angry and scared when he came to his office earlier on. Roy assumed he was just nervous to meet him again after their last episode, but maybe there was more to it.

'I know what happened,' Roy said. Oliver didn't reply again. Roy could smell tobacco hanging in the air and he could sense the fear in Oliver's posture. 'Ben Durant did this, didn't he?'

'No,' Oliver said.

'Why lie? He spoke to you earlier, he told me. He told me he hit you,' Roy lied 'but he didn't say why.'

'He got angry with me. I wouldn't let him work here.'

'Strange that someone sees fit to hit you because of a simple no, don't you think?'

'That's him though isn't it? Everyone knows he's a fruit cake,' Oliver said.

'No, I think there's more to it Oliver, I really do,' Roy said. 'Something is happening in these four walls. Something, I'm sure, that involves a lot of you and Ben knows it. Now I can either ask you politely to tell me what's happening. Or I can ask the guards to close this place down and you'll get no tokens or pleasure. Or I can put you in solitary for a week, your choice.'

'Why do you or he think something is going on?' Oliver said.

'You're a poor liar, Oliver. Very poor indeed.'

'You can't put me in solitary for knowing nothing about some, socalled, plan.'

'I can for smoking though,' Roy replied. Roy looked at Oliver who looked surprised. 'If I asked you to lift your foot up, I'd find a small butt and don't even deny it. Ben is being dealt with now for hitting you. I don't want Roger and Phil getting hold of him.'

'He's working for you, isn't he?'

'No,' Roy grinned back at him.

'What do you want?'

'I know something is going on and now you've given the game up, I'll have this place closed down tonight. You'll go into solitary for two weeks until you've got some answers. Smoking contraband is a bad crime to commit in here.'

'You'll find out nothing,' Oliver said.

Roy knew Oliver had answered it exactly how he had predicted; denial and confirmation in one sentence. 'Oliver,' Roy began.

'Trying this with me won't work. I won't keel over like Bertie did,' Oliver interjected.

Roy's eyes narrowed and he remembered Bertie and that laundry room. 'Bertie was ill and had poor health, nothing more.'

'We know you did it,' Oliver said.

'Did what?' Roy said smiling.

'You'll find out nothing,' Oliver said again.

Roy felt in his right pocket and pulled out a fifty pence piece. His final piece of the plan was in motion. He threw the coin at Oliver underarm and watched as it soared through the air and landed on the concrete and bounced along.

As soon as Oliver leant down to pick up the coin, Roy twisted the small cap off the tiny gas pump. He watched as Oliver rose from the floor holding the coin. The gas pumps were silent and deadly as it invaded the air, 'a coin?' Oliver said.

'For solitary,' Roy said and he paced for the exit. He knew he had to rely on Oliver to execute the final part to the plan. Roy knew a few minutes after he'd left; Oliver would light his final cigarette. Roy opened the workshop door and saw the rain pouring down in front of him towards the prison, 'ten minutes, Oliver,' Roy said and he walked out into the open.

Roy bowed his head down and walked for the prison, wrapping his jacket around his body. His feet, were sodden and they sunk into the muddy water, which was getting deeper every second. Roy reached the entrance to the prison and ignored the two guards who were sitting down, and not looking, anyway, and he walked into the atrium. He reached the centre of the atrium, just as he heard a deafening explosion and his face lit up with a sinister smile.

36

Stephen was standing in the centre of the atrium next to Lance. The prisoners were subdued and wary of one another. They had heard the explosion last night as the majority of them were, either in their cells, or in the food hall. As soon as the bang echoed through the prison walls, everyone run to see what the noise was.

Keith was one of the first on the scene, Lance had told Stephen. Keith was in the food hall talking to a few friends, when a bang erupted, sounding like twenty trucks beeping their horn at once. Keith reached the exit and saw the workshop in flames. He ran to the workshop followed by others, but the fire was too strong.

Lance said the only way it could have happened was from a gas leak. Lance said Oliver wasn't stupid with the gas pumps; you always had to be on full alert. The whole prison had been stood in the atrium, listening to the warden discussing last night's ordeal. The warden said external police were coming back, to look into the matter in more detail.

'I can't believe it,' Stephen said.

'Oli was a mate. If it blew because of the gas, I can't believe he was that stupid. He knew not to smoke in there, unless he checked the gas first,' Lance replied.

Stephen didn't reply as he had no answer. Stephen didn't

know if it was the gas that had caused it, although it seemed like the only probable cause. Smoking inside could have ultimately been the final straw for Oliver. There was two weeks left till the breakout and Stephen wondered if the business with Oliver was going to hold them back. Stephen felt the warden looked almost happy about breaking this sudden news to the prison population.

Roy made a promise to find out exactly what happened and that he would serve justice where it was due. Roy said he was waiting in his office today for some police officers to check the workshop vicinity and that the area would be out of bounds for over a week and no-one was to visit the area. Lance tapped Stephen on the shoulder and, as Stephen turned around, he saw Keith marching towards him, darkness around his eyes and anger across his face.

'Library in five minutes,' Keith said, and he walked straight past the two of them.

'He's not ok, is he?' Stephen said.

'No, he's not,' Lance said as he pulled Stephen's elbow sleeve in the direction towards the library, 'Oli was a little prodigy for Keith. Keith needed someone who had access to tools and equipment and Oli was that man. Oli got cigarettes and Keith got the man. Keith will be angry about lost weapons and tools, but more so that one member of the plan has gone.'

They both walked towards the library. The laundry room had a few people folding up clothes with Malcolm, looking for a place of peace and quiet. Stephen walked through the large door into the library and headed for the back of the room. It was empty in there, but for one person, who sat cross legged at furthest table, placed right in the corner; Tony. Stephen saw

Lance nod once at Tony, so Stephen copied. Lance pulled a chair next to Tony and Stephen sat next to Lance.

'Keith's not happy,' Tony said.

'We gathered,' Lance replied, 'is he calling an emergency meeting?'

'No, he wants to know about the kitchen as it could be more important now. Oli was going to get the fence open subtly. Now he's gone, the only other thing we can do is wait to see who's working in the workshop, but they may not get anyone working there for weeks.'

Neither Stephen nor Lance replied, and they all remained seated, looking downwards and not daring to talk. The silence had gone on for around five minutes when abruptly the library door banged open and in walked Keith, a face full of fury and rage. Stephen thought he looked five years older and ready to fight.

Keith pulled out a wooden chair and threw himself into it, 'I'm pretty jacked off. Oli was a good lad. He meant no harm to anyone. He's gone and so have a few weapons.'

'Anything else missing?' Tony said.

'Well, luckily, we have one pair over but the bolt cutters Oli had for us have obviously gone up in smoke. Now we have shoddy ones. Going to take longer for Roger and Phil, but not much we can do. The tools, I'm not as worried about as we have enough now.'

'What do Roger and Phil think? We still on for two weeks?' Lance said.

'We cannot push the date back and they wouldn't want to, I don't want to,' Keith replied. 'Stephen, tell us about the kitchen.'

'I think it's a good back up. It is accessible now, especially during a mini riot, but getting through it is another story.'

'Why?'

'You go to the back of the kitchen amongst some of the freezers and food storages. There's a drain, which is loosened now. Once you jump down, it's very dark, but you can just about see enough to move. Then you come to an open hole. Keep walking and you reach a door, which opens both ways. Then keep walking down the corridor and around the corner, you're at the door to the outside. Having looked at the blueprints, we then come out in a small parking lot.'

'Interesting,' Keith said. 'Tell me about the door.'

Stephen said, 'It feels like a big, thick metal door. It has five locks bolted across the frame and the door and one big lock in the middle. I was thinking that the middle one needs a key to unlock it, but there's no key- hole. You'd need to saw through it and then you're out.'

'Can we get through, Stephen?'

Stephen looked into the dark eyes of Keith and sensed the pain of losing another friend and thought carefully of his answer, 'It's possible, yes.'

'Possibly is better than no. How do we get through?'

'So, if we need the corridor and that's if, I doubt we will, based on the greenhouse, but let's say if, one of us needs to take a hacksaw. That would do it. We need to cut through soon.'

'How soon?' Keith said.

'Like now soon,' Lance replied.

'Do we have more than one hacksaw?'

'We only have one, ideally for the hole to the towers.'

'The prison will replace the workshop tools?' Lance said.

'Eventually, but maybe not for weeks,' Keith said.

'Well, let's hope Keith. Let's hope that we have some for two weeks' time,' Stephen said.

'And if we don't?'

'Let me and Lance worry about it,' Stephen said. 'Give me the hacksaw now and I'll go down one night before dinner. I need help to get in and out of the hole, but Lance is with me.'

'When?'

'Tonight,' Stephen replied. 'I'll take the saw and I'll work through the five. It shouldn't take longer than an hour. When I was, down there, I saw an old table. I'll block the door from opening and I'll be back up in no time.'

Stephen smiled at Keith, trying to put a lot of words and feelings into the smile and Keith smiled back at him, ducking his head. 'You're a good lad, both of you are. I'm so angry with Oli, so angry. He smoked all the bloody time. I used to call him the chimney. But I always told him to make sure everything was switched off before he did and dispose of the butts properly. It was nothing scientific, it was common sense, but he didn't do the gas this time.'

'Mistakes happen,' Lance said.

'No. I agree mistakes happen, but it shouldn't have with Oli.'

'Why?'

'Oli was a clever guy. I'd like to think you have to be of a certain mental level to have been considered for this breakout. Oli was and we needed him and that's what got him over the line. I'd been getting him fags for a while and his repayment was to make me things and for me to be able to use the workshop as a contraband place. He did it for a long time and he did it well. The workshop was a key location for us; not far from the greenhouse and was always being maned by Clive, who doesn't give two hoots.

'But something doesn't rest easy with me. Oli was the only one who used those pumps. They were so small and so obscure, but they were powerful. He was only allowed to use them when Clive was in the room and he didn't need them for our plan, so why were they on?'

Stephen remained quiet and on the edge of his seat waiting for the answers. 'I don't know,' Lance said.

'Someone turned them on when Oli wasn't looking. Someone Oli knew, that he didn't expect to do it. Someone who knew Oli smoked and wanted something from him.'

'Someone like Ben,' Stephen said without even thinking. It was the first person who came to his mind; all the stalking, the questions, the strange activities. But was Ben capable of another cold murder again?

'Exactly. The lad has been hovering around for weeks, asking questions, being suspicious. He may have tried something with Oli, who didn't bite, and he blew him up. I'll find out though, but my problem is, I can't do anything, nor can anyone else, as solitary waits for the person who hurts him,' Keith said rubbing his eyes with both hands. When he took his hands down, Stephen noticed how tired he looked and strained; like he hadn't slept a second last night.

'One other thing,' Keith said, 'I think the warden knew about it.'

'Roy?' Lance said, his eyebrows moved an inch upward.

'Yes, him. His speech today, I didn't buy it, and one thing he said sent my mind crazy, Laurence said the same. He said he would *serve justice where it was due.* How does he know it wasn't an accident? He didn't know Oli from anyone else in here; Oli, could have been a clumsy fool, he didn't know him.'

The last sentence made Stephen think, maybe Keith was right. The warden has seemed sympathetic and angry that someone on his watch had died, but his statement, now Keith had highlighted it to him, stood out like a sore thumb. Stephen had never met the warden in a face to face capacity, nor did he wish to, but if he was also capable of murder, Stephen didn't feel anyone was safe.

Tony uncrossed his legs. He looked tired too, as if he had been up with Keith for the whole evening. 'What else do we need to discuss?'

'The kitchen door, Keith,' Stephen said, 'it didn't need any mechanics to get out the door, it's old school. Anyone could have done it.'

'Maybe so, but I wanted you to do it,' Keith said smiling at Stephen.

'That's really, nice, but anything else of importance?' Tony said.

'We've stopped recruiting,' Keith said. Stephen wasn't surprised really and judging by the reactions of everyone else in the room, neither were they. 'After last night, Roger, Phil and I decided we should keep a close-knit group now. No-one else is to find out.'

Tony leant forward leaning on the table as he peered up one of the aisles, 'James and Lee will reopen the tunnel on the night just before dinner, when everyone is together. Then it should be quieter for Roger and Phil to get upstairs and storm it, just as it's going dark.'

'My source on the outside has told me some of the things the guards may have, range from rubber pellets to batons to pepper spray. We need to combat against it. We're thinking about it all, but above us, we have more than enough weapons and we have the element of surprise,' Keith said. 'I'm going to lay down, be vigilant' and he turned on his heel leaving them behind.

'The last time someone died close to him was Bertie. He knows he may never find out how they died, but he won't rest, even on the outside, he will keep going.' Tony stood and nodded at Lance first and Stephen second and he departed the room. Stephen thought he saw him look over his shoulder as he walked up the aisle and Stephen had the fear that he and the other escapees may all be doing that for the next two weeks.

Lilian had watched the crowd disperse across the atrium, whilst Roy limped back towards the office quarters. She had watched his body language as he delivered the news to the inmates. She turned over a fresh page in her notepad and scribbled her thoughts from the day, before she tucked it away and made her way outside.

37

Stephen had completed the mission of cutting the locks away from the door located deep beneath the kitchen. Stephen had used a hacksaw, which was silver and black, but it looked almost brand new. Stephen worked on the largest lock, weaving his saw into different positions, weakening it from every angle. He pushed his arm back and forth, rocking the saw firmly on the metal lock, which slowly showed an indent as the sawing gained momentum.

Stephen could feel his wrist aching, but he knew he couldn't stop. It took Stephen around twenty-five minutes to cut through the main lock. As he rocked forward, he fell with his momentum as the lock broke and a tiny piece of metal hit the floor beneath him. He knelt- down and went to work on the other four locks.

The rest were considerably easier. He sawed quickly and the smaller locks fell, leaving Stephen with time to spare. Stephen knew the door could be opened with a key or either by force. Stephen didn't want to open it now as he would burst open into the car park. Stephen saw the table covered in a white cloth. He grabbed the table corners and pulled it backwards, easing it through the wide door frame.

Stephen dragged the table until it was pushed tight against the door. After recovering the saw with the same, dirty cloth from the greenhouse, Stephen walked back to Lance with pace and he no longer slid his feet. He knew he had to get back to Lance as quick as possible, even if they had been given an hour.

Stephen whispered when he came back to the drain and Lance first took the saw and then hoisted Stephen back up into the kitchen. They got the key back to Johnny and arrived back at their cell. It had taken fifty- eight minutes, start to finish. They both looked at their cell door for the next thirty minutes, anxious and sweaty. Lance kept gently punching the wall, as they waited to see if anyone came up to their cell. After an hour, they gave up and left for dinner.

Two days later, Stephen and Lance were both sat on Lance's top bunk talking and playing with a pack of cards. Stephen was always good at cards, but Lance was something else. Stephen thought he had more tricks up his sleeve than a magician. Stephen had been sat in their cell for around an hour, thinking of his wife and his old life, when Lance came into the room looking happy and positive.

They had been playing cards around fifteen minutes, making sure the coast was clear before they began talking about the plan. Lance had been with Keith outside for about an hour looking over the workshop, which was cordoned off. There was hardly any part of the structure still erect and Lance had said he doubted they would get it up again in the next year, let alone before the breakout.

Lance smiled as he beat Stephen once again, before relaying his chat with Keith, 'there were the five shifters, James, Phil and I. Lee stayed at the greenhouse and Roger was digging deep about last minute things. Keith told me his suspicions about the warden and Ben. He hasn't yet shared this with anyone else.

He wants to know he's right first.'

'Has he seen either of them?'

'The warden, no, but Ben, yes, but he's in the church a lot. Keith would talk to Bernard, but he said he'd hold him back probably.'

'I can speak to Bernard,' Stephen said.

Lance continued as if ignoring the final statement from Stephen, 'the police have almost finished their investigation; accident they say, gas wasn't turned off and they found cigarette traces. They put two and two together.'

'How does he know this?' Stephen said in awe.

'Sources are what he told us. The main thing is the breakout date. It's been moved forward to this Saturday.'

'This Saturday?' Stephen exclaimed, 'that's four days away?'

'Sorry, did you want to go and shout it out from the roof-tops?' Lance replied hitting Stephen in the chest, the deck of cards flying all over the bed. 'Yes, this Saturday, Its a week earlier, but Keith reckons if anyone has an incline on our escape, this will throw them all out.'

'Are we prepared?'

'Keith thinks so. He wants us to go for it, nothing to lose.'

'Why Saturday?'

'The element of surprise Keith said. He said that on Saturday, a lot of people won't want to be there, so their guards will be down. He's hoping I think, but he's usually right.'

'What else is new?'

'The prison has had some additional guards allocated here because of the workshop. Keith said his source told him once before, if they ever employed more guards, it's because they were nervous of something.'

'How many?' Stephen said.

'About thirty, nothing major, but enough to cause disruptions,' Lance said.

'We can really do this can't we?'

'Yes, we really can. We'd be history makers,' Lance said, and he squeezed Stephen's left hand, 'heroes.'

Stephen smiled back at Lance and felt a sense of purpose now. 'What is the deal with weapons? Did he say?'

'To be left at the library and we will get them before dinner.'

'What if we can't access them?'

'Then were either screwed or we fight bare hands, possible I guess with the likes of Honda fighting.'

'Honda's fighting?' Stephen said loudly again.

'Keep it down. He isn't in on the plan, but as soon as he sees a commotion, he will be all over it, no question. Don't forget also,' Lance said lowering his voice, 'when Roger and Phil go upstairs, they are going to try and take some of the big weapons with them; the rubber pellets, smokers, pepper spray and that. If they get a few of them, I think were halfway there.'

Stephen remained still for a moment thinking of the entire plan and where he would be throughout. He intended to remain close to Keith throughout. Stephen hoped they would all be quick in their escape. 'You worried about the tunnel? Stephen said.

'Not at all. Lee went down it the other day, peered out into the woods. If we go quietly, the police won't even spot us.'

'The codes are all shared now?' Stephen said.

'All perfect. The people who need it have been told and Roger and Phil have the spare key card too, I feel sorry for those working upstairs.'

'Everyone still in?'

Lance didn't immediately reply to this. Instead he remained seated and looked ahead at the opposite white wall. Stephen stared sideways at him, waiting for an answer as people outside their cell walked down the corridor, their footsteps coming and going hastily. 'They are,' Lance said. 'But you can tell who's in on the plan. I think Keith got everyone so riled before, that we've all distanced ourselves from the non-planners. Keith doesn't want this. He wants one big prison family.'

'Why distanced? I haven't noticed.'

'I think everyone has a sense of remembrance for Oli. To get close to other people, disrespects Oli, I don't know. But one thing for sure, we need to stick together. May as well hold a big white sign up saying, we're about to escape, over here.'

Stephen laughed and looked out the door as two more people walked past their cell, 'what is Keith doing about Ben or the warden?'

'He isn't sure. He can't, touch either of them, or he'll go to solitary or even worse, the max security facility, definately. But he can't, really, even talk to them, because if he does, it may arouse suspicion. I get the impression the escape is more important to him,' Lance said.

Stephen nodded and understood the sacrifice Keith was making. He wouldn't find out if either was involved, but he would escape, just like Oli wanted. 'So, we've got about four days left then, Lance?'

'Yes, four days. Hopefully no more surprises until then.'

Just at that moment, an officer was stood at their cell. He looked large and experienced and he had an expressionless face. He looked directly at Stephen and said, 'you've got a visitor.'

38

'Me?' Stephen said.

'That's what I said, murderer,' the guard replied, and he was gone.

'I've never had anyone visit, Lance.'

'Who could it be?' Lance said.

'I honestly don't know, but I'm a little worried now,' Stephen said.

''Well, let's go see,' Lance said as he shuffled forwards and jumped off the top bunk, both feet landing harshly on the floor.

Stephen stayed still momentarily, thinking about the visitor, unable to think of a single person who would come to visit him. Was it a trap? Was he going to go the same way as Oliver? Stephen moved to his left across the thin mattress and took three steps down the worn, metal ladder. He landed on the floor next to Lance who was smiling.

They both walked out the room, Lance with a small spring in his step, Stephen almost trudging trying to avoid the meeting. The corridors were busy, and Stephen saw people walking left to right below him. They both descended the stairs and walked past two guards who were both leaning against the railing. Neither guard acknowledged them.

Then Stephen stopped dead just as they reached the bottom of the stairs, 'I don't even know where the visitor room is Lance.'

Stephen saw Lance turn on the spot and look at Stephen smiling. 'I don't think anyone showed you during your tour. It's past the TV room. The visitors come in the side way. Steve, stop worrying,' Lance patted Stephen gently on the shoulder twice and then crossed his arms, leaning his head in the direction of the visitation room.

Stephen followed and walked past a few people he recognised. He saw Honda talking to someone Stephen didn't know against the atrium wall. Stephen also saw Karl and Peter talking as he approached the television room. Both Karl and Peter saw Stephen and Lance, but remained in their private conversation.

The television room was busy, with some sitting back against their chair, some having turned their chairs around, and resting the chests against the back rest. Stephen now regretted having never been in the television room. It was a large room, much bigger than the workshop and the church. Like most rooms, it was pure white. Stephen promised himself if he ever got out of here, he'd never want to see a white wall ever again.

Lance walked through a doorway, which were just the frame and no door. When they got through, the prison walls brightened slightly, and Stephen knew they were in a different part of the prison. 'It's simply a cross over the threshold but its nicer here for the visitors. I reckon the prison wants the visitors to think we're all in a lovely, bright, warm place, so they doll it up a bit. Load of rubbish,' Lance said.

'Where now?' Stephen said.

'Down that corridor and you're there.'

'Do you want to come?' Stephen asked.

Lance didn't reply for a moment. He looked at Stephen with barely a smile, 'I'd love to, but they won't let me through.

They're not my visitor. If my mum was sitting there, I'd give all I could to see her again.'

Stephen smiled back, as they headed for the visitation room. The lights were built into the walls and they were protected by thin metal bars. Stephen reached the end of the corridor and came face to face with four guards. He looked at the area around them and saw multiple metal scanners being maned by one of the guards. The other three were stood facing Stephen and one of them was the same man who had come to Stephen's cell.

'You've not signed anyone up to your list?' Lance said bewildered.

Stephen didn't move for a moment, 'no. I didn't have anyone to add. Everyone I cared for had been taken away from me.'

'Arms up and come here,' one of the large guards said. He was tall and square with a black bushy beard. Stephen looked at Lance who didn't say anything. 'You here to see someone power puff?' the guard said to Lance.

Lance didn't reply, 'can he come with me?' Stephen said.

'Let me think, how about no. You're here to see some-one alone.'

'Steve don't worry. Go and see who it is. I'll wait here for ten and see if you're back then,' Lance said.

'Won't be long,' Stephen said, and he walked forward two paces. The guard dragged him forward by his shoulder and began to pat him down. Stephen saw another guard walk forward a few metres standing to side of Stephen, with a baton held by his side. Stephen tried to think of a way to get Lance's attention, but he didn't want to make it obvious.

The guard stopped at Stephen's left leg and said 'clear.' Stephen walked forward, craning to see Lance who was smiling, leaning against the wall. Stephen went through one of the scanners, which remained silent and he was now on the other side of the boundary. 'Go down there and someone will sign you in.'

Stephen strode in the direction the guard had pointed at. Stephen could hear noises down the passage, the sounds of conversations and chattering. Stephen started to feel nervous and worried. He could honestly admit he didn't know who was waiting for him ahead. He had no relatives left, no family. Had Keith organised this? He would have said, surely?

Another guard asked Stephen for his name. Stephen signed a small piece of paper pinned to a pad and entered the large room, which was filled with around twenty people. He saw windows to one side, revealing a car park. This seemed like the closest Stephen had been to the real world for a long time.

Stephen froze with shock. He knew who his visitor was immediately. They were just looking at him with no expression, their hands cupped in front of them and their shoulders hunched. The man sitting down was Clifford Lovell; Stacey's father. The last time Stephen had seen him was at his trial.

Stephen knew that his mouth was wide open, and he must have looked as if he had seen a ghost. He took three steps forward arriving at the wooden table. The table legs were drilled into the floor. There was another guard around the outer edge of the visitation room, all watching the prisoners closely.

'Cliff,' Stephen said still standing upright.

'Sit down, Steve, before they tell you off,' Cliff replied. Stephen was so pleased to hear his voice. It hadn't changed in the last few months and it reminded him of his previous life.

'Wh-what are you, you, doing here?' Stephen said.

'You look terrible son. How times change.'

Stephen leant forward. He couldn't help but feel that at any moment Clifford may lean over the table and hit him. Stephen knew he didn't deserve it, but he also knew that Clifford was hurting, and Stephen understood. 'I hope it sounds ok, but I'm pleased to see you.'

'I never thought I'd be pleased to see you either son,' Clifford replied.

'Why are you here?'

'To chat with you, son. You've not had any visitors and you've not cared for yourself, that beard. Stacey wouldn't have stood for that,' Clifford said, and he smiled solemnly, looking downwards at his hands. Stephen felt himself looking at the man ahead of him, who had felt just as much as grief as he had.

'I didn't do it Cliff. I honestly didn't.'

'We know.'

'You've got to beli-,' Stephen said, finishing mid-sentence. 'You know?'

'Marina and I were and still are, heartbroken. Our little girl, our intelligent, funny, bubbly, little girl is gone and we will never lock our gazes on her beautiful, unique, piercing eyes. But the first few months were hard, horrific in fact.' Stephen stared at Cliff feeling his pain and anger rise. 'But two weeks ago, we started to talk about it. Talking about not how it happened, but why.'

'I'm sorry,' Stephen said.

'Why would you do such a thing? What gain was there to you? Was every angle covered by the police? Trust me, when something like this happens, your mind doesn't stop.'

'What I've had to go through doesn't compare to what you both have. She was your daughter.'

'She will always be our little girl. But we know you must have thought about nothing else too,' Clifford said.

Stephen felt guilty now. He had thought about Stacey every day since being imprisoned, but lately the breakout had been at the forefront of his mind. 'She has never left my mind.'

'Tell me what happened that night son,' Clifford said, still looking at this palms.

Stephen looked at the old man before him. He looked, exactly, the same as when he had first met him, except for his eyes. Stephen thought his eyes looked strained and wrinkled around the edges. Stephen closed his eyes and wound the clock back to the last time he entered his front door. 'We had an argument over nothing. I left to go to the gym, but I felt bad, so I came home.'

Clifford raised his head and looked into Stephen's eyes. Stephen thought the way Clifford was looking at him was as if he was x-raying him. 'Then I went through the door and saw her.' Stephen started to cry for the first time in what felt like a long time. Stephen felt the tears run down his cheek and Clifford's expression remain unchanged.

Stephen felt as if he was in his own world and that no-one, let alone twenty other people surrounded him. Stephen continued to cry and felt a weight leaving his body, a weight he had borne, for longer than he would wish on anyone, 'what next,' Clifford said.

'I tried to see if she was alive, but she was gone from me. I pulled her close and I squeezed her and squeezed her and wished her back in place for everything I owed.'

Clifford at first didn't move. He instead remained neutral looking at Stephen and Stephen felt as if he was still working him out. Stephen felt ready to leave and go back to his cell. He raised his arm and wiped the tears from each cheek, blinking several times as he started to regain his composure. Stephen wouldn't have believed what he heard next, if he hadn't seen Clifford's lips move.

'I believe you.'

'You do?'

'I do. Marina is coming around to the idea, but I do. You two never argued and nothing, knowing you and her, would have ever meant you caused harm to her.'

Stephen's heart thumped in chest and the relief was evident as his muscles relaxed. Stephen kept looking into Clifford's eyes trying to convey everything he felt inside, 'thank you.'

'Don't thank me. I will find out what happened to her. If it's the last thing I do. With my dying breath, I'll find out.'

'I aim to find out too.'

'Bit hard, being behind these bars son.'

Stephen decided not to tell him the plan, 'it's all I can aim for. How did you get in here?'

'A lot of work is how. I asked a week ago about visiting people and then I mentioned you. They didn't know who I was first. Then I had to go further up the line. I said I was related to you as an uncle and they signed me up eventually. Marina doesn't know I'm here. I don't think she's ready to know yet.'

'I'm sorry to ask, but how is she? Sorry, that's a silly question.'

'She's not the same. We haven't spoken properly in a long time. She lost her only daughter and she wants payback, same as we all do. Even if you had done it, imprisoning you wouldn't have been enough for her. She believes in an eye for an eye.'

'I'm sorry,' Stephen said again.

'Now, I came here to see you. You need to go do something, maybe two things.'

'Anything.'

'First, go shave and tidy yourself up. My girl married a handsome man.'

Stephen laughed and nodded, 'done.'

'Second, I want you to remember, I believe you. I always did and always will. I trust my judgement and I'm trusting your word. I will pay all the money we own to rerun the whole trial again. For closure, for Marina, for Stacey.'

Stephen couldn't hold it in anymore. He didn't want to reveal the break-out plan, but he wanted to help Clifford, 'wait a week.'

'A week?' Clifford replied.

'Please, just wait a week and I'll help you with it. I want to know just as much as you. I honestly don't know how we can really find out, but there has to be an answer somewhere.'

'You're in here though?'

'Yes, but, trust me. You said you trust my word. Trust me when I say I'll help you.'

Clifford nodded as a bell ran loudly in the corner of the room. 'Time to go I imagine,' Clifford said nodding at the bell.

'Thank you. Thank you for everything.'

'A week and I'll hear from you.'

'A week,' Stephen said.

Clifford smiled at Stephen and stood upwards slowly as he held onto the table and Stephen saw his knee wobble beneath him, 'I'm not as strong as I was. I took Stacey going, hard, to begin with, but now I've got the mental will. That counts more than physical strength.'

Clifford held his right hand out towards Stephen and shook it. Clifford's left hand shook violently in the air as he brought it upwards and cupped Stephen's hand. Clifford released his grip and followed the other civilians into freedom. Clifford exited the room without looking back. He was patted down and let through a small turnstile.

Stephen was ordered back where he came from, patted down and ushered through the detector. Lance wasn't in the corridor anymore. Stephen looked ahead at the hallway, leading back into prison but for the very first time he felt happy to return to his cell for he felt hope and another reason to live.

39

The following day, Roy was sat at his desk feeling anxious and angry and tired. He hadn't visited the prison quarters for days, avoiding any potential trouble. Instead, he remained closed away in his office thinking of his next chess move. He chose not to talk to anyone, other than when Lilian gave him updates. She was very competent and hardworking.

Roy felt anxious because he hadn't been able to get close to Stephen. Roy was at breaking point with him. The police coming into the prison didn't help as it kept Roy pre-occupied. He dealt with the police in a quick and timely manner, trying to remove them from the premises as quick as he could so he would be left to his own devices. Roy wasn't sure on how to get Stephen alone. He had no reason to.

Roy's anxiety grew larger when he thought about his boss. His boss never even visited the prison, rarely did he even contact Roy, but now he was in regular daily contact. He was comfortable and relaxed about the way Oliver had died. He knew the gas and fire explosion was the cause, but he wanted Roy to check the rest of the prison for similar and potential risks. He then wanted updates on how he intended to prevent it from happening again.

Roy felt angry. He felt angry with himself more than anything. Oliver's death was something he didn't care about at the time, but it had caused him problems ever since. Roy knew Clive would need to take the blame. He should have been in the room. Oliver was unattended and that wasn't allowed. Roy's boss said he would contact him in the next two days to, 'close down', this event and Roy didn't know what that meant.

Roy started to feel a mixture of anger and anxiety; Stephen had had a visitor. Someone said they was his uncle. Roy knew Stephen had no family. To visit someone, you simply had to complete a few forms and Roy had checked these forms internally; they were fake. The old guy who came would never be found again unless he reappeared, which Roy highly doubted.

Roy felt tired too. He hadn't slept in over a week and the round the clock working on Oliver's death had taken its toll. The scotch he had drunk over the past few days hadn't helped him keep calm or relaxed. Instead it fuelled his wild thoughts. His boss had asked so much from him and he didn't want to provide it, but he couldn't see a gap to get close to Stephen; he was truly snookered.

Lilian had told Roy that people were venturing outside again, due to the brighter weather. Lilian had said some inmates were angry and some were suspicious about Oliver's death. Roy knew he wouldn't be suspected, but it gave him an idea, an idea that would remove one problem in his life. A problem that, at first, he thought he would be able to use to his advantage. But the problem had turned bad and his original plan backfired. A problem he couldn't afford to kill, like he did Oliver. A problem called Ben.

Roy hadn't seen Ben or heard from him in the past few days. He knew he would likely be in the church making useless prayers of some sort. Roy now knew the way he could remove

Ben from his life. He had a perfect reason to put him in solitary, and a way to keep him from messing with his future plans; he would frame Ben for Oliver's murder.

Roy shuffled with the panel of his bottom draw, revealing his handgun still wrapped in the oiled and dirty cloth. The gun was filled with six bullets and Roy intended to only use two; one for Stephen and one for himself, only when he was free. He knew the time to kill Stephen was imminent. He would let the dust settle with his boss, and attack.

He leant down to reach for the gun when the door in front of him burst open and Matthew stood there, slightly panting and out of breath, 'boss, we've got a problem.'

40

'What?' Roy replied quickly, slamming his desk draw, feeling the blood rush to his head. Roy was looking directly at Matthew waiting for him to continue, 'what,' Roy said again.

'It's your boss. He's here. He's coming to see you.'

'What, he's here now?' Roy said with eyes bulging and his heart racing.

'He's arrived downstairs. They're checking him in. They phoned through to tell us,' Matthew said.

'Warn us more like.'

'Apparently, yes. He wants to chat to you and Lilian.'

Roy looked down at his desk, his breathing becoming shallow. If his boss was here to see him, then it wasn't good news and Roy felt a tint of fear; his boss could cause the biggest unexpected problem. Roy was determined that if his boss caused a problem, that he would fight his corner and he was sure Lilian would too. Why did he want to see Lilian?

Roy's boss was called Frederick McCanus. He was a heartless, power ridden city boy. He had worked under him for fifteen years and during this time Roy thought he could have counted on both hands the amount of times they had met. They spoke occasionally on the phone regarding updates, but Roy liked to keep things quiet here and Frederick was happy with his work.

The only time Frederick had, unexpectedly, turned up at the prison was after the death of Bertie. Frederick was no doubt coming because of the explosion. Roy knew the way the game was played. If the prison was quiet and uneventful, Roy was, seen as, a fantastic warden. But when bad things happened, there was only one person to blame. Roy knew Frederick was only worried about one thing; his reputation, and that would no doubt be at the forefront of their discussion.

'Boss, he's down the hall now,' Matthew said as Lilian entered the room looking troubled.

'Let him come,' Roy replied still concentrating on his desk. He envisaged pulling out his gun and shooting Frederick, then Ben, then Stephen. He wiped the thought from his weary mind as he heard a man's voice outside the door.

'He's in here?' Roy heard and he knew it was Frederick. Roy moved inches to his right and fell back wards into his chair. The room had daylight shining across the floor, silhouetting Roy behind his desk. 'Roy,' Frederick said as he entered the room carrying a black, leather briefcase in his right hand whilst holding an umbrella in his left hand, 'pleased to see me?'

'It's a surprise to see you,' Roy said coldly as Frederick approached him.

'Lilian, it is nice to meet you finally, do you need a chair? Or are you happy to stand?' Frederick said.

Roy looked at Frederick and watched him closely. He hadn't changed over the years. He had light hair, which was perfectly folded across his head and he wore black, square glasses, above a small, trimmed, moustache. His chin was pointed, and his ears were small. He had a smile stretching from ear to ear, which radiated arrogance. 'So, how can we help?' Roy said leaning back.

Lilian closed the door behind Frederick and walked to the side of the room, leaning against the wall with her hands behind her back. Frederick placed his umbrella on the wooden table and his briefcase against the chair, 'I've come about the explosion. Bad business, Roy to be honest, we're the talk of the prison faculty. An unattended workshop, which has tools and gas and other hazards, goes up in smoke. You surely didn't think questions wouldn't be asked?'

'We have carried out a further risk assessment and the officer who was meant to be manning the workshop will be punished.'

'Punished how?'

'He will be given a week's leave.'

'Do you think that will be enough punishment?'

'It's my decision and my prison.'

'We will come to that, Roy. Updates for me first, what have you got? Frederick said.

'Nothing else, the rooms are all safe. I have been thorough,' Roy replied trying to evade Lilian's confused gaze in order to conceal the lie.

'Ok, I'd like the report on this please, today. I also want the report on the explosion, today.'

Roy looked at him angrily. A sharp pain shot through his leg and Roy clutched his left knee, gritting his teeth. 'I haven't done the reports yet. That's my job tonight.'

'Tonight? Roy has something else been occupying you lately?'

'He has been making sure everyone is ok, sir,' Lilian said.

Frederick didn't reply, but instead swivelled in his chair and crossed over his legs. He then turned to look at Lilian with a self-important smile. Roy saw the egotistic man before him and shook his head at Lilian who dropped her head.

'Nothing else has been on my mind. It has just been a lot of work, but we will get there.'

'Getting there isn't *there* though is it, Roy? Roy answer me this, have you been drinking?' Frederick said rotating in his chair again.

Roy breathed deeply and knew he couldn't hide the fact. He probably smelt of scotch and his eyes may have been bloodshot, 'I had a couple to help me concentrate.'

'At work? Oh, it just gets better and better doesn't it, Lilian?'

'It won't happen again,' Roy said calmly.

'Damn right it won't,' Frederick said as he pushed himself off the arm rests and began to pace the room. 'My manager wanted answers and I gave them to him. The cause of the explosion was obvious, but that doesn't hide the fact it was unattended, and no officer was on duty there, all under your watch.'

'I will sort this,' Roy said coolly, trying to remain calm and placid.

'No, you won't,' Frederick replied icily as he looked out the window at the dark skies. 'I need to make sure this doesn't happen again, and I want someone to check this prison from head to toe.'

'What are you saying?' Roy said as he noticed Lilian's eyes flick between the pair of them.

'There's good and bad news, Roy. Bad news first, shall we? Frederick said smugly. 'Bad news, you are being taken out of this prison for two weeks.'

'What?' Roy, shouted, his emotions obvious in his tone. 'You can't do that to me.'

'It's come down the line. Even if I wanted to keep you here, I can't, but there's good news. We're unable to get anyone else here before Sunday morning. So, you will remain here until Saturday night. You may wish to try and fix some things now, just in case I allow you to return here.'

Roy was stunned. He felt hurt and he felt angrier than ever. He knew he had three days to go. Three days to live. Three days to get Stephen. 'Fine,' Roy replied casually.

'You understand, Roy?' Frederick said grinning.

'I understand completely. It makes sense.'

Frederick's eyebrows jumped an inch as he digested what Roy had said. He nodded his head confused, 'Roy, I will contact you in two weeks from Sunday and we can see where we are. The drinking, is something I will not share for the moment, but sort it out.'

'Thank you for coming, Fred,' Roy said, 'I will wait to hear from you.'

'Before Sunday I want you to sack Clive for gross misconduct. He isn't to be given a week's leave,' Frederick said. Frederick walked back to the desk and picked up his umbrella and bent down to pick up his briefcase. He placed both items on the desk and stroked his suit, 'three days Roy and your life changes.'

Frederick nodded in the direction of Roy and smiled conceitedly at Lilian, then he left the room. 'Roy,' Lilian said.

Roy lifted his head, and he contemplated Lilian, who was beautiful and appealing. She was soft and kind, something Roy used to be, 'thank you, leave me for a while please.' Lilian nodded slowly and departed the room. He pulled open his bottom draw and looked at the gun. He had listened to one thing Frederick had said and he had believed every word; three days Roy and your life changes.

Lilian shut the door behind her and stood in the silence, breathing heavily, whilst digesting what she had heard. Roy had been suspended. Not immediately, but soon. She was running out of time. There had to be more to it than what Frederick was letting on. Lilian wrote the final points of the day in her notepad and cupped her hand over her mouth. She knew she almost had enough to nail Roy, but she couldn't prove it yet. She imagined Frederick couldn't either.

41

Stephen was leaning against the metal link fence near the church. The weather was overcast and cold, but it wasn't raining and that was his biggest relief. Everyone else thought the weather was changing and that rain was imminent. Stephen was looking at the sky picturing himself in next few hours. He felt nervous yet optimistic.

It was just over two hours until the breakout. All the plans were made, and the next step was the actual escape. He hadn't really seen Roger or Phil around, nor had he seen Keith today. Lance was the person he saw the most and he could tell Lance was uneasy and edgy and Stephen knew the feeling.

Stephen raised his right hand and aimed to scratch his beard, but all he felt was a small hint of stubble growing through. Stephen had grown so attached to his dark, un-kept beard that he subconsciously attempted to continue playing with it. But after his meeting with Clifford, he had used his tokens from the labour at the workshop to buy razors and shaving cream and had removed it straight away.

Stephen started to think about his meeting with Clifford. He had made a promise, which he didn't intend to break. He had asked Clifford to hold on for one week. A week would allow him enough time to hide away and let the dust settle; Stephen knew he would be a highly wanted man, once they knew he had escaped.

It was only after Stephen had relayed the whole conversation to Lance that Stephen started to ask himself how he would help Clifford. What was Clifford going to do? The police felt they had enough evidence to slam dunk the case, but Clifford must have felt there was more? Stephen thought he could enlist the help of Keith. That was if he were still on the run. But how would he be able to contact Keith after the breakout, how could he contact anyone?

Stephen had been outside for around an hour. He just wanted to watch the world go by and relax before the hard work started. Stephen guessed the shifters were inside working. The only dampening thing for the prison was the funeral of Oliver, which had been held in his home- town yesterday. No-one from the prison had been allowed to go and Stephen had been told the reason for that was because of a management restructure. Stephen didn't know the exact details, but Keith had been told that the warden was going to be absent for a short time period.

Stephen hadn't had any dealings with the warden and Stephen knew the warden wasn't interested in him, but this change was positive for the breakout. Whilst the guards were all reshuffling, the inmates would strike but Stephen still had the feeling something wasn't right. However, he would never dare relay this back to Keith, purely out of respect.

Stephen, missed Oliver, actually. It seemed a long time ago since he first met Oliver, all before he knew the true importance of the workshop and Oliver himself. Oliver's death hadn't been taken lightly by most in the prison and Keith had said the escape was now in the memory of Bertie and Oliver; two of his friends.

Stephen had started the day in the canteen talking to the shifters and Lance. The prisoners seemed a little subdued. Stephen wasn't sure if it was nerves because of the escape, Oliver's funeral or because it was early in the day. Stephen and Lance hadn't slept much the previous evening and they weren't sure if this was due to the same reasons.

Lance had been whispering to Stephen and going over the plan time and time again. Stephen could have recited every single detail now; he wasn't complaining, but he could have done with some sleep as he didn't know when he would get the chance to sleep again. Lance had made a good point regarding the aftermath of the escape, with sleep deprivation being high on the agenda.

Keith said he wanted to do it without hurting people. Lance completely agreed with this, but he told Stephen he was unsure how they wouldn't be able to not hurt guards or how they would stop the guards from hurting them. "They ain't going to handcuff us all, there isn't enough cuffs in the prison", Lance had said. The only thing they could do was break away quick and if this wasn't possible, Lance said it was either them or us.

They had rerun through the plan from start to finish and Keith relayed this to everyone else of importance. Roger and Phil would start with the power first and take it out of action. They said they knew how to cut through the wires and the doors and as soon as the darkness surrounded the prison, then the fire in the library would start.

Keith had given the responsibility of starting the fire to Laurence who would light the books up as soon as he was in darkness. As soon as the darkness came, Roger and Phil's boys on the outside would go for the towers. It seemed to Stephen as if everything rested on Roger and Phil as without them, the other parts of the plan couldn't and wouldn't work.

Then it was a case of getting outside as soon as possible. The greenhouse was the first aim, but they also had to cut through the fence. This would be easier once the towers were preoccupied and this hole was imperative for Roger and Phil. Stephen remembered Keith saying half of the inmates escaping wanted to for freedom and half wanted to cause havoc. Keith said in the end it was down to the individual and once outside, it was every many for himself.

Stephen had to talk for a brief period during the meeting. He discussed the kitchen escape and how it could work. Stephen had said if there were any problems with the greenhouse then the kitchen was the only option. Johnny had hidden a hammer in the freezer, which was to be used for the final door if needed. Stephen hoped it wouldn't be.

Johnny was due to unlock the bolts to the drain an hour before dinner and then reposition the freezer over the top again. Johnny said it was stupid to undo the bolts if everyone was going out of one exit, but Keith shot him down and said it was imperative that there was another exit inside the prison. Johnny didn't argue at this point and he nodded, understanding his task.

Stephen was pleased they had covered what felt like every angle and he was confident the kitchen escape wouldn't be needed. Stephen also knew the fire alarms would cause a big problem to the guards as they'd have an escape on their hands and a fire somewhere in the building. Keith said escaping quickly was imperative as the fire may spread, endangering them all.

Stephen pushed himself up, climbing the metal fence with his hands behind him and stood in the chilly breeze. He started to pace towards the church, which stood tall. Stephen saw no-one around him or anyone coming in or out of the church. He wanted to say his final prayers and speak to Bernard, who he hoped never to see again for all the right reasons. Stephen reached the church door and turned the handle to walk in, just as the clouds above him darkened and the rain began to fall.

42

Lilian was sat in her car on the phone to her boss, 'we're taking care of Roy tonight?'

'We have to,' her boss replied. Her boss was a middle-aged woman who had gained the respect of her entire crew through a fledgling career. Lilian didn't want to let her down and she knew she had to get this right.

'I will stall him as long as I can. His suspension starts tonight. We need him before that.'

'Just hold off until we reach you.'

'Ok,' Lilian replied.

'This is great work,' her boss said.

'Thanks, ma'am,' Lilian replied, and the line went dead. Lilian opened her glovebox and threw the phone inside. She took a deep breath and wrapped a scarf around her head. She exited the car, ready to fulfil her final duties.

Roy drummed his fingers on his desk. The room was becoming darker as the rain fell and the black clouds glided across the sky. Roy had his tie slightly loosened around the collar and he wore a dark blue jumper over a white shirt. He was tired, but he knew he would need one more blast of energy and he knew he could conjure it from somewhere.

Frederick had contacted Roy regularly over the past few

days, asking for progress, ensuring he had passed on certain responsibilities and mainly Roy thought, to gloat. Roy laughed inside at him; he no longer cared to be here. If he had been asked to leave immediately, then he would have had a problem, as that would have meant two weeks of Stephen running free and alive. Roy had already let him live far too long.

Roy's double checked his gun was fully loaded, although he knew he'd only need two bullets; one for Stephen and one for Ben. He wasn't sure what order he should do it in. Stephen should probably be the last one, it felt right. After all, Stephen had changed the course of his life completely.

Roy imagined himself leaving the prison after committing the murders and whether he would get out in time, before the bodies were found. Roy knew the staff here trusted him. All he had to do was get Stephen and Ben alone and then the rest would all fall into place. How to get them alone was the question he kept asking himself over and over, again? Someone knocked on his office door.

Roy looked at the door, still drumming his fingers on the wooden table as Lilian entered looking windswept, 'Ben is due in five minutes, anything you need me to do before we let him in?'

Roy contemplated the idea of killing Ben as soon as he walked through the door, but the gunshot would be audible across the offices. He needed them both close and he needed to be in the prison quarters where loud bangs were the norm. 'Nothing, Lilian, you check out if you need to.'

'No, it's ok. I'll stay as long as you do.'

'You've been good to me, Lilian. I wish you all the best.'

'Thank you, sir,' Lilian said, and she left.

Roy had already cleared his desk contents away. He had the photo of his wife now stood up on the desk. He shredded the paperwork, which had been neatly filed in the draws and now all that remained was the black pole, he had used on Ben and the gun, still wrapped in cloth. Roy still had his mobile telephone in his left pocket.

Roy waited for Ben. Ben hadn't done what Roy had hoped for. Roy felt he had his own agenda. What was Ben trying to accomplish? Roy pictured exactly where Ben would die, and he smiled happily. Roy looked at the picture of his wife knowing in a few hours, that he would be with her again and that the vow that he had promised to her beside her gravestone was fulfilled.

There was another knock at the door and Lilian opened it once more. Ben entered the room, looking as frail and skinny and helpless as ever. He had his head down and he looked bereft of confidence. He walked straight into the room and without invitation, fell back into the visitor's chair.

'Our last meeting,' Roy said resting his wrists onto the table, 'we will not be long today.'

'Why do you treat me like this?'

'Like what, Ben? Have I not treated you well?' Roy said pausing for a response. 'I asked you to keep an eye on Stephen and tell me what he was doing. You had time to watch him. Instead you told me about plans relating to the shifters. But you damn well *knew* these involved Stephen. I sit here today still not knowing the plan or even if there *is* one.'

'There is one. I'm done trying to convince you,' Ben replied.

'No need to convince me Ben, I'm done trying to help you. In a few hours my shift here shall end and I won't be returning, so tonight will be the last time we meet.'

'You're leaving?' Ben said lifting his head for the first time.

'You've not heard the rumours, no doubt, circulating the prison? I am leaving tonight. Once the count has happened, I have two things to do and I shall be gone.'

'Forever?'

'Forever, Ben. This shall be your last night here too; you will never get your freedom.'

'My last night?'

'You can't remain here anymore, not after what happened to Oliver.'

'Oliver?'

'Yes, Ben, Oliver. The prison has you pinned as suspect number one. You told me you had punched him, but I didn't know you'd go and kill him.'

'I didn't and you know it.'

'Do I? Here's what happened, you were so desperate to follow something on your own agenda, but he wouldn't play ball, so you punched him and went back later to finish him off. That's how I've written it down.'

'You can't do that. The prisoners suspect you for the murder. They know we're working together.'

'Delusional, as well as useless, they can think what they like. If they do think we're working together, that only looks bad for you. Working with a warden or spying on your in mates. They won't tolerate it, Ben.'

'You can't do that.'

'Tell me one thing, Ben, why did you always lie about Stephen and his plans?'

'Because you were right about one thing, I did have my own agenda.'

For the first time since Roy had met him, Roy felt Ben was oozing confidence. He stared angrily at Roy. 'What agenda was this?' Roy said.

'You'll never know. I won't go down for Oliver's murder and you know it. Once I'm done being accused then I'll finish my business with Stephen.'

Roy sat still for a moment. He considered opening his draw and shooting Ben in the dead centre of the eyes. Roy had the metal pole deep in his pocket and he could feel it resting against his thigh. Roy pushed his chair back and limped behind the desk and to the window. He looked out across the skies, which were becoming darker and the rain was falling heavily above them. Roy felt a sense of anger in his body.

'You have a problem with Stephen, I understand. But tonight, you will be in solitary. Your problem is only recent. Mine goes back a long time ago,' Roy said turning to face Ben.

'You think you know everything don't you?'

Roy turned around and took one step forward, two, three, four and five until he stood next to Ben. Ben looked left and upwards at Roy, smiling. Roy smashed the pole across Ben's temple, just next to his eyebrow. Ben fell out of the chair and Roy felt adrenaline pumping through his veins. He roughly jammed the pole into his pocket and looked over Ben, who was conscious. Blood was running down his cheek.

Ben had to be removed immediately, 'Lilian,' Roy shouted and within seconds, she was back in the room, accompanied by Matthew.

'What happened?' Lilian said anxiously, looking between Roy and Ben who was stirring on the floor.

'He murdered Oliver. He just admitted it. I reacted out of

instinct. He's dangerous,' Roy shouted. 'Lilian, Matthew, take him too solitary, please.'

'What did you hit him with?' Lilian said.

'My elbow,' Roy replied panting.

Lilian stood still for a moment processing what Roy had said. She then nodded as Matthew walked forward, picking up Ben from the floor, blood seeping into his hair and across his face. 'Come on scum bag, murderer.' Ben didn't reply, as he was dragged from the room.

Roy walked to his desk and threw the metal pole firmly into the bottom draw, the large thud audible, in the room. He started to think, what next? Now Ben was taken care of, Stephen had to be next. He would no doubt be in the atrium area, easy to reach but Roy wanted him alone. Roy's mind ticked and he froze as he hit the jackpot. He would ask Stephen to come up to discuss a letter the warden had received on his behalf. Roy felt that would be enough.

Then when Stephen sat there in this very room, Roy would tell him everything he needed to and then he would shoot him. So, what if people heard the gun shot? It wouldn't matter as Stephen would be dead. Before all of this, Roy had something new on his mind; Ben. Ben had said he had his own agenda with Stephen. Roy walked towards the door about to go and remove things from Ben's quarters, unaware of what had always been before his eyes.

Now Lilian was worried. Ben was bleeding heavily, and she knew an elbow couldn't have done that damage. She had told Matthew to take Ben to the hospital ward, but he laughed and said he would only follow his boss's orders. She couldn't make notes in her book, so she tried to write the sentences in her head. She needed to call her boss and tell her what had happened. She knew she finally had enough evidence on Roy.

43

Stephen entered the church, having just missed the onslaught of rain. Bernard was looking at the door, as he sat below the window at the front of the room. Stephen smiled at Bernard. Bernard had always been kind to him and found time to speak. Stephen knew this could be the last time he stepped in this church or ever saw Bernard.

The church was light enough, but the darkness outside was making the room seem small and derelict. Stephen hoped the rain would stop soon. He imagined people crawling through the tunnel and out the hole, soaked to the bone and covered in mud. Stephen was worried the rain would slow them down.

Stephen shook his hands, small drops of rain falling to the floor. The church was dry but inside it was very cold and Stephen could hear the rain thundering against the roof above them. 'Hello Stephen, bit wet tonight, shouldn't you be inside?' Bernard said.

'Shouldn't I ask you the same? Stephen said walking forward to the side of the closest bench.

'I'm not going inside yet. I have things to do here,' Bernard replied smiling, his hands cupped, and his legs uncrossed. Stephen could see Bernard looking at him over his square glasses.

'I've come to pray, is that ok with you?' Stephen said.

Bernard stood upright and moved his lower back as if

stretching. He placed his hands in his robes and walked down the steps until he was next to Stephen, 'please sit.'

Stephen sat down and shuffled along a couple of spaces and Bernard followed him, still smiling with his eyes as youthful as ever, even though his wrinkles revealed his true age. 'Are you praying too?'

'I shall. You don't ever need to ask me to pray. You've always been welcome here. It has been nice to have got to know you.'

'Thank you.' Stephen held both hands together in a large fist and leant forward leaning against the bench before him and he closed his eyes and prayed. Stephen prayed for his wife to be with him the whole way. He needed a guardian angel to hold his hand, to tell him she knows he didn't hurt her and that she forgave him for the argument. He wanted one more second with her.

He prayed for the breakout to be successful and for no-one to get hurt. He wanted to get his head down and run for the tunnel. He wanted to grab Lance and be gone. He prayed for a safe place to hide after escaping and he prayed never to return here. Stephen envisaged himself in a small cottage somewhere with Lance, hiding from the outside world. But he knew he couldn't adjust to the freedom because he had to find Clifford, whom he had made a promise to, Clifford who believed him after all this time.

Minutes passed and Stephen felt the words swimming through his head. The stubble around his neck was starting to itch, but Stephen remained static, still thinking about everything over, and over again, but he couldn't wipe Clifford from his mind. Stephen made one last prayer; let the truth come out so Clifford and Marina can be at rest.

Stephen leant back on the bench and opened his eyes. He felt out of breath and tired, but he had created a sense of purpose within himself. 'Finished?' Bernard said beside him.

If Stephen hadn't seen him originally, he would have forgotten he was there. 'Thank you, for everything.'

'I want you to know I'm behind you all the whole way,' Bernard said still smiling warmly.

'Sorry?'

'It's ok son, I know about the plans.'

Stephen paused for a second and stared deeply into Bernard's eyes. Did Bernard really know? He had a lot of people visit here, maybe someone had told him? Did Ben know or was Bernard involved himself? Stephen studied Bernard's eyes and he believed him. 'How do you know?'

'By the man who seems to tie us all together; Keith. He told me shortly after Oliver's death, he came here angry and told me of his thoughts. I hadn't seen him so enraged since poor Bertie. I calmed him down and told him a close secret of mine and he told me about the plan,' Bernard said.

'I'm sorry I didn't tell you,' Stephen said feeling ashamed and embarrassed.

'Not at all my boy, not at all. Keith told me under strict confidence too. It seems a good plan.'

'I sense a but' Stephen said.

'Not a but as such, but I think everyone needs to be aware of what will happen if they are caught.'

'I think half the people know.'

'Why do you want to escape? What's your intention in the outside world?' Bernard said twisting slightly in his seat.

'I want to find out what happened to my wife. I had a visit

from my father-in-law. He believes me and I want to find out for both our sakes, and his wife. Are you escaping?'

'No,' Bernard said bluntly. 'I have nothing on the outside and I enjoy it here. I help people like yourself, although I am involved in the plan now.'

'How?' Stephen asked.

'Keith asked me to fill in for Oliver.'

'You're cutting the hole?'

'Indeed, I am,' Bernard said pulling out a pair of large bolt cutters from his white gown. 'I had these years ago and I said I would do this as my gift to you all.'

'You say it as if you will be gone yourself soon,' Stephen said.

'That's the news I told Keith, Stephen, I am dying. I am terminally ill with mere weeks to live. If I wasn't, I still wouldn't break out nor would I participate in this plan, but I have nothing to lose, God has helped me choose my path.'

Stephen remained quiet, looking at Bernard with his mouth open. Stephen couldn't believe it, he felt anger and anguish, but he had a sense of gratitude that Bernard was doing this to help the others. 'Bernard, I'm'...'I know, but do not be sorry for me. It is the path god had chosen for me.' Bernard placed the cutters into his pocket, which looked baggy. 'Keith has been to see me every day since. He wants to make sure I'm ok. I've known him as a boy really. He was fond of Oliver and so was I, smoking really did kill him.'

'So, what's next for you?'

'The lights, go out, I leave here and I walk to the towers. Once I do that, I walk back in here and dispose of the cutters. Keith said it is simple, but I will make sure I'm quick.'

'Thank you,' Stephen said.

Bernard shifted himself along the bench. He placed his right hand on Stephen's knee and looked at him dead in the eye, 'I have a favour for you, a similar one, which I asked of Keith.' Stephen didn't reply and just remained looking back at Bernard, 'Benjamin Durant.'

'What has he done?'

Bernard took his hand off Stephen's knee and shook his head slowly, he was no longer smiling but instead he looked sorrowful. 'That poor boy has had so much misery thrown upon him. He has never told me why. He has been in here every day for the past week. He stays for a long time, he doesn't eat, drink, but just continues to be angry. Then he told me he would be suspected as having murdered Oliver, but he didn't do it, he couldn't have.'

'How do you know?'

'He was here, Stephen, with me. He was here all evening sat right where you are, his eyes closed. I think he was sleeping. The explosion woke him up and startled me. He didn't do it.'

Stephen processed the information trying to make sense of it. 'Did you tell Keith this?'

'Every word. He believes me and he should, Ben didn't do it.'

Stephen felt an element of guilt. He sat forward and rested his elbows just above his knees and breathed out aloud. 'Everyone thought he did it, him or the warden.'

'It was an accident. We saw no-one near the building and Oliver always smoked.'

'So, what do you want me to do?' Stephen asked looking forward at the dust on the benches.

'I want you to help Ben. I want you to take him with you, Keith will understand,' Bernard added as Stephen looked at him puzzled.

'Take him through the tunnel?'

'It's all I ask from you. Benjamin is a harmless man and he seems to have a slight obsession with you. He never told me why, but I'm sure he would tell you. You remember all those weeks ago, you two sat here talking and he left abruptly?' Stephen nodded as he hadn't forgotten, 'I think he wanted to tell you something, but never could as I was here.'

'Bernard, I don't know.'

'The last wish I ask from you. Keith has promised to me to stop harm coming to him, but he said he wasn't going to help him out. I had the feeling and wisdom, which comes with old age son, that you would come here tonight.'

Stephen sat immobile and thought about the options. He jumped from the tunnel to Ben to Lance to Keith and everyone was screaming at him. The room was filled with shouting and blood covered all of them. Stephen looked left at Bernard who was helping them all escape, 'I'll help him out of here.'

'That's all I ask. He doesn't know about the breakout, so you'll need to grab him and go.'

'I will. If I get caught, then I'll be back here.'

'You won't. Keith's too smart and you're too clever, Stephen. Now go, you'll be late for dinner. There isn't long left,' Bernard said pointing at the clock.

Stephen raised himself as did Bernard. 'Before I go, may I ask you a personal question?' Stephen said.

Bernard said, 'you may.'

'What did you do to get in here?'

Bernard chuckled slightly and crossed his arms. 'I knew you've been wondering that ever since we met. It probably doesn't sound, as you kids say nowadays, as cool as you think it will, but a long time ago I robbed a bank. I took a shotgun and I got caught. I was locked away for a long time. Longer than others who have committed worse crimes. But it is what it is.'

Stephen looked ahead at the old man, unable to imagine him being aggressive, pointing a shotgun at a room full of people, demanding money. Bernard took a step forward and held his arms wide and Stephen hugged him firmly. 'Thank you,' Stephen said, 'for always talking.'

'Thank you, for helping out others. Go.'

Stephen walked past Bernard who moved into the aisle and Stephen stood facing the door with his back to Bernard. He didn't know how to say goodbye and he knew it really was goodbye. Bernard would probably remain here for his final weeks, whereas Stephen and the others may never return here, whether in a good or a bad way.

Stephen pushed the door open and watched it swing back and forth, as it closed behind him. All he would need to do was get Ben and Lance and escape. What Ben did on the outside was his business. Stephen paced towards the prison until he reached the doors and felt the rain soaking his overalls. He tried to shake rain off himself, like a dog, and looked at the two guards sitting at the side of the bottle neck. Stephen turned and walked down the corridor and reached the atrium. He looked over the half-filled atrium, trying to catch a glance at Ben.

Stephen didn't know Ben had just been thrown in the furthest room in solitary, covered in blood and barely conscious.

44

Stephen stood in the centre of atrium, unable to see Ben nor Lance or Keith or any shifter. He looked towards the back of the prison at the corridor before the library and then towards the television room. Stephen folded his head down resting his chin against his chest and thought of Ben again. He couldn't help but feel Ben would be so hard to find.

Stephen walked towards the food hall, which was a third full and the majority of these were the inmates aiming to escape. A few smiled at Stephen as he trudged into the room, leaving footprints behind him and others kept their heads down looking at the tables. Stephen saw Keith at the end of one table, as he moved his arm in the air to call Stephen over. Lance stood up suddenly from one table and surprised Stephen who hadn't see him there in the first place, 'you're soaked, idiot,' Lance said.

'Church duties,' Stephen said smiling back. They both walked over to Keith who was surrounded by other inmates. There was one guard at the side of the room and he was overlooking the entire room. He was middle age and looked capable of defending himself. Stephen reached Keith and a few inmates shuffled along allowing two extra spaces to be created.

'You're late,' Keith said angrily. 'What happened?'

'I was with Bernard,' Stephen said affronted.

'I'll come to that. Dinner is being served in ten minutes.

Eat if you like.'

'I won't,' Stephen said.

'Me either,' Lance said.

'The plan will start as soon as Johnny bangs his drum. Then its belt and braces. We run for it,' Keith said.

'Keith, where are the other shifters?' Lance said.

'In the library guarding the weapons, they will start the fire and bring the weapons to us and we go from there. Bad news though.'

'How bad?'

'More guards are here tonight. The rumour about the warden leaving was true. Been relieved of his duties my source tells me, but it's all hush-hush. So, they're changing over. They're about fifteen guards stronger, my source reckoned.' Stephen stayed quiet as did Lance who looked even more nervous. 'You've spoken to Bernard then?' Keith said.

'Yes,' Stephen said.

'He asked of you?'

Stephen paused for a moment and then looked at Keith who looked concerned. 'He wants me to help Ben escape.'

Both Keith and Lance sighed and looked deflated. 'This isn't good news,' Keith said.

'Why? Where is he?' Stephen said.

'He's just been taken to solitary and he didn't look good. He had blood on his top and three guards moved him very quickly,' Lance said.

'Why?'

'We think he's been with the warden. That was the direction he came from,' Keith said.

'Bernard says he was with him all evening,' Stephen said.

'I believe Bernard,' Keith said.

The three of them all sat quietly thinking. Stephen felt agitated and more troubled than he ever had in the past few weeks. To rescue Ben from solitary was almost, a death sentence. 'I can't let Bernard down.'

'Then get him and get out of here. The majority of guards who work in solitary, will leave when they hear about the fire, so there's your chance. You need the keypad code.'

'We've got it,' Lance said, 'I'll be with you Steve.'

Stephen didn't reply but just smiled gratefully at Lance; his closest friend.

'Steve, you will need a key to get into his cell. I'm confident at least one guard will wait by his cell.' Stephen sighed and looked back down at the table. 'No-one will wait for you to get out, it's everyone for themselves,' Keith said, 'I'm sorry.'

Stephen, heard the sounds of cutlery and plastic in the background, as he envisaged the food being served up ready to be plated. He knew this may be the last time he got to speak to Keith, and he had one last question. 'Keith, where will you go on the outside?'

Keith laughed quietly and pursed his lips together before grinning widely, 'I shall be staying with my lady source.'

'Your source is a woman?' Lance exclaimed.

'A fine woman whom I owe so much to,' Keith said.

'Amazing,' Stephen said laughing.

'You've met her, Stephen, remember?'

Stephen looked taken aback and started to file through his mind to when he would have met her. He looked down at the table for twenty seconds when it him in full in the face, 'the *nurse?*'

'The nurse,' Keith said nodding his head, confirming the answer. 'How else did you think I got to your hospital bed? Anyone else could have killed you, but she let me in quietly to get to you. She's told me everything I needed to know. She only got a job here because of us shifters, bless her. She's left; I made sure she got out well in advance. She's far away and she's safe.'

There was a bang behind them as Johnny hit a large spoon onto a serving dish and it reverberated around the room. More inmates were entering the kitchen now and it was almost two thirds full. Stephen watched as people started to form a queue next to the guard, at the start of the serving area. Stephen didn't need to look for Ben now; he knew where solitary was, and he knew he would have to be quick.

He turned away from the people queueing just as he saw Roger and Phil sneak out the room, with their hands in their pockets.

45

Roy reached the inmates' quarters, his pulse racing. Some people were sitting in their bunks and others were leaving, presumably going to dinner. Roy walked down the second floor of cells and reached the last room on the left. He was not far from the atrium and if he walked back thirty feet, he could overlook the main hall. Roy knew Stephen's cell wasn't far either.

Roy walked into Ben's cell, which contained a small bunk bed, a toilet and a sink. Roy knew the bottom bunk was Ben's as Roy knew Ben liked to be able to see his cellmate and the whole room. His bed was covered in stained white sheets and a thin bed quilt, which was also browning at the edges. Ben didn't look after his room that much was clear. Next to his bed were small pieces of paper covered in drawings and some with poems scribbled across the creased pages.

Roy picked up the paper, trying not to bend down and he looked at the drawings. He felt nothing but revulsion for Ben. He placed the paperwork on the pillow and looked around the cold room. The walls were an, off- white, colour and each wall had odd graffiti and stain marks from years of abuse. Roy looked at the bunk, which had a metal frame and each of the four legs were pinned tight into the dusty, concrete floor.

Roy wanted to take Ben's items, so he had an excuse to go

and see him later. Maybe he would even use Ben's pillow to kill him; give him a taste of his own medicine. Roy tried to think of any other items Ben would have left here. Roy tried not to touch more than necessary, but he grabbed two corners of Ben's bed quilt and shook it violently in the air.

A small black pen flew into the air and landed on the floor a metre away. It rolled in a neat circle and went under the bed. Roy threw the bed cover into a pile on the floor. He stepped to his left and grasped the pillow, which was small and lumpy in places and he threw it on top of the quilt. No belongings. Then his instincts kicked in from all the years of patrolling these four walls.

Roy walked to the bottom of the bed and lifted- up the light mattress. Underneath the mattress was just a thin piece of wood, used to support the weight above it. At the opposite end of the bed was a book. Roy let the mattress fall, dust particles soaring through the air and he walked to the head of the bed.

He heaved the mattress up again with one hand and looked down at the book. It wasn't the only book; there were three. One looked old and discoloured. One looked older but the spine hadn't yet faded and one looked new and hardly touched. They were standard books you could obtain with your tokens. Roy leant down slowly and one by one, he picked up the books, gripping them all in his right hand.

Roy looked at the door, for a moment, but the corridor was quiet. He sat down on the edge of the bed and gazed at the eldest looking book, which was crumpled around the edges. Were there poems inside, drawings?

Inside was a diary.

He opened the book around a third of the way in. The

255

page was covered in neat, unfinished sentences. It had been numbered in the bottom corner. Roy skimmed forward until he reached a heading, which was labelled *later life*. Then he skimmed backwards towards the front pages, moderately shaking as he laughed, thinking of the useless impunity writing in this. Roy reached a heading called *daddy* and he started to read.

The words were generously spaced, and the writing was clear to understand. Had Ben started these before he came to prison? He had probably brought this book in with him. Roy continued to read as Ben started to discuss his father, but not in much detail.

Ben described his life without a father, how it was just him and his mother. It mentioned weekly church visits and the fact his mother tried to look after him. Roy turned the page and read the top line, *I think mum takes us to church as we don't have dad with us. She doesn't know what happened to him, but I think he's been taken off us by the angels.*

Ben was not allowed to discuss his father. To do so, meant punishment. His mother would reference his father a lot by his surname, but Roy couldn't see any mention of his surname in the book. Roy skimmed the final part of the page trying to see if anything jumped out at him or caught his attention.

Roy pictured Ben sitting at an old desk writing down his thoughts and feelings into a useless book, which wouldn't reply. Roy thought about Ben coming back to his cell each night and filling in the blank pages. Was he excited when he wrote? Roy thought about Ben becoming who he was now. What would his life have been like if he hadn't killed his mother? Would his mother still be alive now? No, Roy thought, she would have told him this precious secret at some point. Roy made a mental note to ask Ben what the secret was before he killed him.

The next page was based three months later, and Roy raised his eyebrows an inch trying to understand the jump in events. Roy placed his finger on the page and turned for the next heading, which was then dated a year after the first part Roy had read. He shook his head, confused. Did Ben not get time to fill in his diary, or was it a case that he only did it when he had things to say?

Roy went back to the previous page and read a small snippet about Ben at his first job. It seemed as if Ben had been a labourer for a small building firm. It discussed his wages, which in a month, were what Roy earned in a week, but Ben said he was happy. It said how the other men were crude and how they laughed at him for being, what they said, was different. Roy felt no feelings towards this; he was just pleased that he hadn't been the only one to single out Ben.

Roy skipped half an inch thick of pages, and came to the heading *mother had to go*. Roy knew this story and he decided he had to read it, but not now. He didn't know how much time he had left in here and he didn't want to waste it reading old stories.

He reached the final third of the book. Roy knew Ben had written this one since being in prison. It referred to prison several times over the first two pages; *it's adjusting to sharing a room and toilet with random people that's the hard bit.* He then saw that Ben had referred back to his past, and how he missed his mother and wished he asked more questions. Roy looked ahead, what questions?

Roy threw the first book to one side and picked up the next book, which looked the second oldest. The spine was wrinkled, upon close inspection, and Roy started reading from near the begining. This page had no heading. It mainly discussed the prison. It could have been written years ago, for it mentioned random days of walking the prison grounds, lying beneath the towers and reading in the library. Roy had never seen Ben do any of this.

Roy took another number of pages in his hand and turned them over until he was two thirds in. The pages were still white. It looked more than five years old and Ben had scribbled through a lot of the previously written words. Roy saw the heading *little grass* and wondered where Ben's head had been all this time. He flicked across the page until he saw his own name mentioned and he read slower.

The page described their first meeting in the warden's office and how Ben told Roy about the lady dying in his village. Ben described the anger etched across the warden's face and how he told him only what he wanted to tell. Roy gripped the booked tightly reading on. Ben said, *I came up with a great idea. I want to see Stephen and so does he. I told him who he is, but not exactly who he is. It's worth a try.*

Roy quickly turned the page and landed on a heading called *the son is calling.* Roy knew Ben was abnormal and peculiar, but the heading was enough to make him read more. Roy read lines about the one person he had been so interested in himself; Stephen. Ben had written down his opinion on how Stephen was imprisoned. Roy's eyes followed the page; *I don't think Stephen has done anything. I told the warden about him and he was in here months later. It's strange but it's all to my advantage.*

It then described how Stephen was closer than ever and how Roy himself had masterminded his capture. Ben said how he couldn't wait to meet Stephen and reveal everything he had held secret for so long. Now Roy felt strange and uneasy. He finished the page at pace and now he started to worry.

Why did Ben want to meet Stephen? What secrets had he held for so long? Roy knew the only secret Ben had, was the one about the man who had killed his wife. Surely this must be the secret? If Ben told Stephen this secret, then Roy was surely going to be involved. Roy gritted his teeth and scratched his temple as he thought of all the time Ben had wasted. All Ben was doing was trying to tell Stephen the real reason he was inside.

Roy landed on Ben's counselling sessions. Roy kept reading at speed and read stories about him and how the counselling meetings were *completely pointless and done for the warden's own benefit.* Ben obviously knew Roy had a high interest in Stephen and Roy was reading about how Ben knew he was happy to deny him this privilege. Roy read further down the page about Ben wanting to talk to Stephen for his own benefit and how he would only feed Roy the bits he wanted to.

Roy felt a surge of anger run through his body and he slammed the second book shut, throwing it on top of the first. He sat still for a moment and heard a clunk from downstairs, *dinner* he thought. He needed to be quick and he picked up the final book and opened it on the first page, where it read Ben C Durant across the page. Roy never knew Ben had a middle name.

The first heading was labelled *shifting* and Roy's eyes moved to the next line, which was dedicated to the shifters. Ben talked about his admiration for them and *how much power they had inside the prison.* He said they were more powerful than the old warden, who had no idea what was going on. Ben said the shifters met daily and were always together. Ben said the guards didn't do anything about it.

Roy turned the pages, which were crisp, and he saw a small sub-heading called *plans*. Roy read about Ben's suspicions, which were, exactly, the same, as he had relayed to Roy. Ben said his main suspicion was that the shifters were importing things into the prison and that Oliver was storing them.

Roy read how Stephen was heavily involved with the shifters and that they seemed to care for him. Ben talked about how he never had anyone care for him or look out for him like Keith does for Stephen. Ben said he wanted a friend just like Lance, but *to trust anyone again, you had to prepare yourself for disappointment*. Roy knew years ago he would have felt sorry for this adolescent person, but now he felt nothing.

Roy saw nothing of note on the other pages. It said that Stephen visited the greenhouse, the workshop and the library. Then Roy's eyes caught the words at the bottom of the page saying *too much, too late*. Roy looked at the date, it was only a week ago. The first line got straight to the point and begun with Oliver and how he had died in an explosion in the workshop. Ben said, his regret was that he had hit him, and he wished he hadn't.

Roy pictured Ben, out of nowhere throwing a hard punch to Oliver's head and he imagined Ben feeling invincible and a man for the first time. Ben then described his own predicament; *I'll be done for this murder, wait and see. I didn't do it and Bernard knows it. I was with him when the place exploded, but I've not done what he needed me too. Wait and see.* Roy smiled. At least Ben had got something right.

Roy found the final heading in the book. He skimmed the remaining pages, which were blank and empty. Ben would never be able to finish this diary. He went back to the last heading called *a different life, maybe*. Roy scratched his eyebrow, knowing he would need to leave any second. He read on about how Ben had spoken to Stephen only once since being inside.

Ben then described Stephen as being safe. Ben said the warden wouldn't be able to touch him whilst the shifters were involved. Ben said the warden was suspected for the deaths of Oliver and Bertie and that if Keith got him alone, he would kill him. Roy smiled; *good luck* he thought. Then his mouth fell open as if hitting the floor.

Ben said he could sense how Stephen was feeling. Ben wrote *we are related, in one way, or another*. Related? One way or another? Roy now felt fear bubbling. Ben said he was going to have one more chat with Stephen on Saturday night and then he would go himself. Go where? Roy knew Ben would be 'gone', or dead by his hands only.

Roy turned the page, which was only half full. The top of the page read *ha-ha-ha-ha-ha*. Roy wasn't laughing in the slightest. He felt a small pain in his chest, *damn heartburn, not now* he thought. Ben's last paragraph was the one, which sent Roy's panic into overdrive; *I think this will be the last time I write in you, forever, I think. Thank you for always listening to me. Either I'll be moved soon, or I'll be dead, and I'll be with my mother.*

What would my mother say about all of this? She would laugh at Roy. She would laugh at him for his stupidity. Imagine if he heard the true story behind why I killed her. He wouldn't be so big then. He'd be the little man. He will never know. Her story is what made me. Roy dropped the final diary and blinked several times, trying to understand what he had just read.

Roy palmed the third book away and picked up the first again. He picked at the brown edges until he reached the same heading he had paused at; *mother had to go*. He unturned the folded page corner and read the words written by Ben. Roy's head moved slightly side to side as he read and his eyes flickered back and forth, re-reading words and little scribbles.

The bottom of Roy's jaw was gradually falling lower and lower and his eyes were widening with every line. Roy read about the real reason why Ben had killed his mother. He saw the secrets she had kept, and Roy understood why she had died. He closed his eyes for a moment, thinking about Ben and how he had been sitting metres away from him for so long, all that wasted time.

When he opened his eyes he felt his chest still pounding. He read on and he imagined he was in the room with Ben and his mother. His mother was called Charity and she told Ben she had always loved his father and that he left of his own free will. She would never stop loving him and she told Ben that his father had always loved him.

Ben then said his mother revealed why he was called by his full name. Roy knew it only as Benjamin Durant, he had filled in enough paperwork, but what was the "C" for. Roy traced over the page with his right forefinger trying to see a mention of the name and he didn't see it. He turned the book over and read the back of the book, which was blank.

He rotated the book until he was looking at the front and he opened the cover. The inside read Benjamin Chester Durant, and Roy leapt from the bed with murder in his heart.

46

Stephen remained seated on the bench and watched as more inmates entered the food hall. Stephen was hot and uncomfortable, not sure if he could go through with it. Ben was locked away somewhere in solitary, bleeding, but Stephen hoped he was awake and conscious. Stephen looked at the queue behind him, which was becoming longer.

Keith got up and tapped Stephen once on the shoulder. He stepped over the bench seat and walked to the adjacent bench and leant in between two people. Honda was sitting on the same table. Was Honda involved with the breakout now? Stephen had never asked. One of the men who Keith was talking to turned slightly and Stephen recognised him as Malcolm.

Stephen stood up and Lance looked upwards, 'you, feeling ok?' he said.

Stephen stayed quiet for a moment, 'I'm fine. I'm just a bit worried about getting Ben out of here. How on earth are we going to get down there? You really don't need to come,' Stephen said.

'Look, we have the code and Keith's sure a guard will be there, who will also have a key. If not, we'll come back out and get one.' Lance continued to talk after seeing Stephen look unconvinced by Lance's plan, 'we will grab him and drag him out the doors.'

'That's it though,' Stephen replied, 'what if we have to drag him out? Keith said he was barely conscious.'

'We've done all this planning, over all this time and we can't let this get us down. Block it off,' Lance said squeezing Stephens arm just above the elbow. 'Shall we get some dinner in case we can't eat for a while?'

'I don't want to eat, don't think I could. You go on.'

'No. Stop thinking you're doing this on your own. We're in it together. If you don't make it out, I don't either,' Lance said squeezing Stephen's arm harder.

'Thank you. We can do this,' Stephen said.

'We can. We've had the five cleverest people I've ever met behind this. Everyone is riled now. Keith was telling me before you came in, a lot of the people escaping want to do it in order to fight and then escape. He said he can't control what they do, but they know the score,' Lance said.

Stephen looked at the clock. They had been in the food hall for around thirty minutes. Stephen stepped over his seat. He stood, on tip-toes, scanning over the heads of the inmates. There were dozens of inmates sitting, heads bowed, talking quietly. Stephen looked to his left at Lance just as the lights above them went out and they were engulfed in darkness.

47

Roy walked into his office and dropped the three diaries onto the desk with a thud. He could feel his heart racing, the beats vibrating against his palm, feeling as if his heart was beating twice a second. He paced around the room. His legs felt tired, but his mind now felt awake. He felt stupid and above all else, angry.

Roy considered ringing Xavier to ask him to confirm what he already knew. Xavier would be able to talk to the people he needed to, and they could check the history books to just add the final nail to the coffin. Xavier would be able to look at who Ben really was. He could confirm exactly where Ben had come from. He could tell Roy exactly what he needed to know.

Roy traced his fingers across the table- top. He didn't want to involve Xavier any more than he had done already. Xavier knew far too much, but it was necessary to have been able to get to this stage. Roy closed his eyes and knew his secret was safe with Xavier, no-one would ever know the truth behind Stacey's death.

Roy picked up the oldest diary one more time and reread the caption *mother had to go*. He read it slowly, trying to digest the words. He felt more anger and pain this time. Roy reached the final part and bounced the book gently in his hand. He knew he had to kill Ben too now. Roy knew if he didn't, he would regret it for the rest of his life.

Roy placed the diary open onto the desk and tucked his hands into his pockets. He firmly gripped his mobile phone and walked towards the window. The lights shining from the two towers, overlooked the entire yard. He looked at the glow and he smiled for the first time in a long time. Roy knew he would miss this place. It had been his home for a long time.

As the rain pattered against his window, Roy changed his mind, pulling out his mobile phone. He felt calmer, but his chest and arms were starting to ache more than ever. Roy unlocked the small hand device and dialled the number saved in the phonebook. Roy listened to the small intermittent ringing tone and remained staring out the window, his face close to the glass so he could see clearly outside.

A voice answered on the fifth ring and Roy knew instantly, that the receiver didn't sound happy. 'What do I owe this pleasure?' Xavier said in a deep, husky voice with an air of arrogance.

Roy didn't return with any niceties, but instead got straight to the point. 'Any price you name, I need you to look someone up for me, quickly.'

'Need more help, Roy.'

'Just do it for me, Xavier,' Roy said furiously. He clutched his chest and heard shallow breathing down the phone.

'Twenty- five grand then,' Xavier said.

'Fine, now hurry up, please,' Roy said trying not to sound desperate. 'I need you to look up someone called Benjamin Durant.'

'Hold on,' Xavier replied, and Roy could hear the sound of things moving in the background. 'Benjamin Durant?'

'Yes, yes,' Roy replied checking over his shoulder towards

the office door.

'It's loading,' Xavier said. 'You're a tricky guy. I told you to never contact me again, but if you're offering this sort of money, I'll do you weekly jobs old man.' Roy didn't reply instead he closed his eyes, trying to remain calm. 'So, middle age, prison for murder.'

'Tell me about his childhood. I need current and previous names.'

'He's got no middle name, just a forename and surname.'

'Nothing at all? Roy said confused.

Xavier didn't reply and all Roy could hear was his breathing. Then Xavier's voice sounded animated, 'it does say that when he was very young, actually, his surname was changed. It's now Durant.'

'What was it before?'

'Twenty-five grand for this?'

'I'll give it to you tomorrow.'

'It was changed by his mother. She was called Charity Chester.'

Roy closed his eyes and breathed out wearily. He took the phone away from his ear and watched the call time increase. Roy pressed his finger to the little red button and the phone switched off. Roy turned around and stood in front of his desk. He opened the top draw and threw his phone into it as it skidded along the surface.

He grabbed the back of the chair and leant over bit by bit until he reached and found his gun. Roy straightened up and looked at the gun. He pushed a small button on the side, which released the clip underneath the gun. Roy looked at the clip, which was loaded with six bullets. He forcefully inserted it back into the gun and made sure the safety mechanism was on.

Then the room went pitch black. Roy stood motionless for a moment, as his eyes adjusted to the darkness. He looked out onto the yard, which was covered in darkness. Roy couldn't make out the towers or anything beyond them. He imagined a power cut and he tried not to scream. He stood breathing uncomfortably, his chest aching.

Above him a small light came on and he knew it was the emergency lighting. He took two steps forward, about to exit the room to find Stephen, before he visited Ben. A guard burst into the room, panting and breathing heavily, 'they're trying to escape.'

48

Stephen's initial reaction was to duck. A majority of inmates didn't understand what was going on. It stayed dark for what seemed like minutes, until the room lit up and Stephen looked upwards, making out small, shining lights spaced across the ceiling.

Stephen looked towards the entrance to the kitchen and he saw several men in orange thundering over the threshold. He felt Lance tug at his sleeve, and they attempted to follow. Stephen peered around trying to find Keith, but he couldn't see him. Then every thought was wiped from his mind as a deafening bell rang around them from every angle; the fire alarm.

Stephen covered his ears momentarily and tried to block it out. The guard who had been standing near the queue was on the floor holding his stomach and Stephen saw an inmate kneeling beside him talking into his ear. He must have been shouting as there was no other way to communicate.

Stephen believed what Keith had said; *people will get hurt.* He started to pace across the room, as Johnny passed him at full speed. He hoped never to return to the kitchen, and he imagined a lot of people felt the same. Just before they entered the atrium, the inmates in the kitchen began to fight between themselves. Stephen felt Lance pull hard at his sleeves and they walked into the busy atrium.

The shifters were sliding little pieces of wood around the room as well as metal. Stephen could see Keith pinning a guard down on the floor, punching him repeatedly in the face. Tony was next to him, hitting another guard on his lower back. The guard collapsed to his knees and Tony hit him on the shoulder, knocking him almost unconscious.

Stephen saw an orange glow ahead of him; the fire. Stephen could feel the heat from across the room and he could hear people screaming from that direction. Two guards appeared and they ran into the library holding fire extinguishers. Stephen's ears had almost adjusted to the noise above him and he could see people's mouths moving but he was unable to make out the words.

Stephen looked at the end of the atrium, which lead outside, but he knew he couldn't go. He had been given a job, and made a promise that he couldn't forget. Several more guards ran into the atrium, holding batons, with small belts across their shoulders and chests. They circled a group of inmates and began batting them down, but the inmates didn't relinquish ground; they started to use their own weapons.

'Come on,' Stephen shouted at Lance who was stood rigid. The heat was growing hotter by the minute. Stephen was next to a guard who was holding down an inmate. Stephen could just about hear someone shouting, from the guard's little device, pinned to his chest. He heard something about the cafeteria and atrium being overrun with inmates.

Stephen and Lance headed towards solitary and to where they knew Ben was hidden. As they tried to move through the crowds, Stephen saw Keith pinning another guard to the floor, hitting him repeatedly in the ribs with a baton. Keith then lifted himself up and waved across the room, before he began running towards the exit leading to the yard.

They came across the room, jogging, whilst trying to avoid the oncoming guards. Two new guards appeared from their targeted door. The two young guards were looking around the room wildly, confused and almost scared. Stephen thought, no matter your age, this was a different experience. The guards both focused on Stephen and Lance, and Stephen knew it was time to fight.

He took a step forward, knowing he didn't want to fight, but it was him or them and he had worked too hard to let it be the former. Lance was holding his fists in front of him, when suddenly Honda rushed past them and knocked the two guards to the floor. Honda picked up the closest guard and threw him across the floor.

Honda picked up the remaining guard and hoisted him high into the air. Honda said, 'now, we're even,' to Stephen, and he threw the remaining guard in the opposite direction. Stephen didn't return anything to Honda. Instead, they ran forward at pace, reaching the keypad. Lance punched in a four- digit code and they roughly pulled at the door as it slid sideways. When it was half open, they shuffled through.

Once inside the room, the sounds from the atrium were muted significantly. He could still make out shouting behind him and he was sure he could still sense the fire burning wildly behind them. Stephen knew they would need to be quick. Stephen's ears were ringing loudly, and he looked at Lance who had his right forefinger in his ear. 'You ok?' Stephen said as they stood in the bright room.

'We need to get moving.'

'You think they've taken the towers?' Stephen asked.

'I imagine they will. I didn't see Roger or Phil though.'

'Me neither,' Stephen replied.

'They'll be fine, come on, Steve,' Lance said.

They walked past a couple of vacant chairs, presumably belonging to the two men Honda had almost killed. They reached some metal steps, which dropped deeper into the prison. They could feel the air become cooler the further they descended. Stephen wiped his brow and pulled his shirt away from his chest. Stephen kept his eyes on the steps as he tried to keep his breathing calm.

When they came to the bottom, they reached another metal door. Lance didn't need an invitation as he typed in the same four- digit code and a tiny light above the door turned green. Stephen kicked the door as it swung open. They both burst into the room and saw several cells lined up next to each other. As he approached the first cell, a guard walked out of the opposite cell and hit Stephen hard on the shoulder with his baton.

He screamed in pain and fell to one knee under the blow, turning his head to see the guard. As Stephen tilted his head, he watched the guard fall and skid along the floor on his back. Lance came into view, shaking his clenched fist as he knelt over the guard and hit him on the nose. Stephen placed his right hand flat on the floor and pushed himself upwards, feeling his shoulder immediately swell.

Lance was picking at the guard's belt, pulling off the small radio device, and what looked like pepper spray. The corridor was dark, and Stephen had his eyes partially closed, still feeling the pain in his shoulder. Lance felt in the guard's right pocket and pulled out some keys, which jangled in the air, 'search the rooms,' Lance shouted, his voice echoing throughout the cells.

Stephen checked the left side of the cells and saw that the majority of them were open. He was moving slowly through the room, leaning on one side more than the other. Lance was doing the same on his side. Lance came to a closed door and jammed in a key, which didn't work. Lance repeated the exercise with another three keys before the fifth one worked, but the room was empty.

'Ben,' Stephen roared, his voice carrying throughout the semi darkness. At first neither of them heard any response. Stephen saw Lance turn his ear towards the far end of the corridor, trying to listen for sounds. Stephen took three steps forward when he heard the noise he had hoped for.

'Hello,' a voice said from the far end of the corridor.

Stephen tried to move his shoulder in a circular motion as they travelled further into the room. They came to a cell located right at the back of the room and Stephen could sense someone beyond the door. 'Unlock it Lance, quick,' Stephen said waving Lance forward. Lance roughly inserted the key and turned it, as the door lock clicked.

Stephen placed both hands over the inside width of the door and pushed it open. The door offered no resistance and it rolled open, picking up pace as it revealed more of the room. Stephen walked in first and looked at the skinny man before him, who was sat leaning against a small metal basin, covered in blood and barely breathing.

49

Roy tried to remain calm and collected. Lilian had attempted to sound the alarms. Lilian said two large prisoners had managed to gain access to the power rooms where all that followed was darkness. The two men had then descended the stairs leading to the prisoner quarters. Roy told Lilian to lock down the prison indefinitely. Then the fire alarm rang throughout the room, making Roy duck slightly through complete surprise. Lilian yelled, 'the doors to the outside are open still.'

Roy screamed at Lilian to get straight onto the officer in charge of the towers and to make sure they had all eyes focused on the yard doors. Lilian turned around and began screeching into her radio. Roy could hear loud bangs over the alarm. Roy picked up his gun and door card. Making sure that the safety mechanism was on, he placed the gun into his pocket along with his mobile phone. Roy gently pulled his trousers up by his belt, which felt heavy due to carrying the gun and metal pole.

Lilian, faced him, fear written across her face. She looked petrified. She looked like a little girl, who had been given the worst problem in the world, knowing she would never be able to solve it. 'The towers aren't answering. We cannot reach them. I can't even reach max facility.'

Roy looked back at her angrily, 'what's working?'

'All we have working is the keypads to rooms, the emergency

lights and the alarms above us.'

'The fire service will be here in thirty minutes and then the police about forty-five minutes,' Roy said.

'What shall I do?'

Roy could feel his pulse racing and his chest pounding. 'Go downstairs and try to calm them,they can't get out of here, the yard is solid. Even if they did, there's nowhere to run. Just stay safe and do what you can,' Roy said knowing it would be last time he ever saw Lilian. Lilian nodded once and left the room beginning to stride.

The fire alarm above Roy was deafening, but he shut it out as he kept his thoughts solely on his only aims; Stephen and Ben. Stephen or Ben first, Roy kept thinking. He couldn't think who was the best person to target first. Stephen was the answer he gave himself, as he was running free downstairs, whereas Ben was locked away in solitary. Roy needed to find out why the fire alarm was going off.

Roy walked out the already open door and left the diaries on the desk along with the photo of his wife. He wasn't worried about any of it now. If anyone read them, he'd be long gone anyway and nothing else would matter. Roy could feel the gun clunking against his mobile phone. Roy could feel the sweat on his brow and his hair was static in the air.

Roy quickly limped across the empty room, looking around, gazing up and down, left and right. The staff who worked here were gone. Whether they had run downstairs to help or gone home he wasn't sure. He was very confident in the knowledge that they would have gone home. They wouldn't have wanted to get involved in a potential breakout and Roy didn't blame them.

Roy looked at the computer desk. Paperwork was neatly stacked, and the computers were just showing a small pattern, which was gliding across the white screen. Roy looked at the CCTV screen next to him and he stared in shock. He could see guards and inmates colliding inside the atrium and he saw weapons being swung around the room.

Roy started to think about the worst outcome in all of this if he remained where he was. Would Stephen escape? Would he meet him again? Would he get the chance to get this close to him? Roy shook his head answering his own question and he moved in closer trying to make out the faces on the computer screen, but they were blurred, and he felt weary.

The siren was still reverberating around the offices. He sensed it was a false alarm. Maybe the power cut had tripped a wire. Roy picked up a portable radio device lying on the desk and held it to his ear. He closed one eye and tried to listen for any sounds. He heard nothing until the radio crackled and Roy made out the words "fire" and "library" and "wounded".

Roy strode away from the desk and reached the steel door leading downstairs. He swiped his little door card and quickly typed in his four- digit passcode, which was his wife's birthday. The door lock released, and he walked straight through and down the corridor until he arrived at another door and he repeated the exercise. Roy peeped through the side of the door, looking to see if anyone was on the other side.

The other side was empty, but for one guard who was hanging over the bannister watching below. Roy was engulfed in heat and the hot air smothered him as soon as he was further onto the landing. 'Get down there,' Roy shouted at the guard.

'I can't, it's burning the prison down,' the young guard shouted back.

'What?' Roy replied.

'The fire, there's a fire in the library, it's spreading. We can't get out our normal ways.'

Roy looked back at him in utter shock. He had to be quicker than quick. The route Roy was taking downstairs came out by the television room and this was too close to the library for Roy's liking. 'Move out of the way,' Roy shouted trying to break into a run, but his leg wouldn't let him. As he left the guard behind, he stopped abruptly on the spot holding his chest, which was throbbing and stinging. Roy tried to move forward as he gripped his chest by the sternum.

Roy furthered down the steps, hopping every other on his good knee until he reached the first floor of cells. He almost ran down the next set of stairs, holding onto the bannister until he reached the lower floor. Roy looked across the room unable to see Stephen. Roy didn't want to join any battle. He ducked into the television room and hid behind the wall. Guards came running in and out of the library, carrying fire extinguishers and brandishing batons.

Roy looked inside the television room, seeing a few orange suits screwed into a ball on the single arm- chair. Roy had an idea that he wasn't sure would work, but he had no choice. Roy grabbed an orange top and threw it over his head, shaking his arms through the sleeves. Roy felt disgusted by his appearance, but he was desperate.

He felt for his gun and his metal pole and walked out into the atrium. Inmates were running away from him towards the outside exit. The atrium was quieter than it had looked on the television monitors. Roy looked up the corridor leading to the library room and felt his heart skip a beat. The fire was spreading uncontrollably. The cladding wasn't preventing the fire from dispersing.

Roy knew he couldn't diffuse the fire and he saw guards trying to spray extinguishers over the flames, but it didn't work. They were being pushed further into the atrium. Roy knew that the fire brigade would have been alerted and he knew this was the least of his worries. He started to walk beside the walls towards the yard doors, which seemed far into the distance.

Out of the food hall, Matthew came running out holding a baton in one hand and his radio transmitter in the other. Roy thought he looked red and angry and his face was covered in soot. His arms looked cut and grazed but he looked alert and ready to fight. 'Boss,' he shouted above the alarm, 'we have a number of inmates in the kitchen, who are under control. We have also managed to gain power to the outside doors. They are now closed,' he said not smiling. 'You're wearing prisoner gear?'

'Yes, but don't worry about that now, Matt, how did you get the doors closed?' Roy said.

'Back up power, the two thugs didn't cut everything. We've got some power back, but I can't turn the alarm off. Boss, the towers are under siege. They were attacked by a dozen masked people and they gained access. They have our men pinned inside.'

Roy didn't reply but breathed out loud, uncaring about the towers, 'where are the two who got into the power room?' Roy said.

'They got outside,' Matthew said.

Roy nodded and walked towards the kitchen to see if Stephen

was there. He had everything crossed he was just so he knew he was within touching distance. Roy stayed on the outskirts and took out his metal pole. He was ready to use it. He reached the kitchen entrance and he was knocked back by at least twenty inmates in orange suits running into the atrium, surrounded by guards trying to hit them back into the kitchen.

Roy hit the nearest prisoner to him, and he saw the man fall to his knees as a tiny blood splatter landed on Roy's face. Roy brought his right hand up and wiped the blood off his cheek just as he saw Stephen standing outside the door from solitary confinement carrying an exhausted person that he knew was Ben.

Lilian had been on her way to her car. She needed her phone. Her head was telling her to wait for her boss. Her heart was telling her to confront Roy, for what he had done to Ben. Then things got surreal. A guard was screaming about two inmates accessing the power rooms.

Lilian ran for Roy's office. She instinctively told all guards to trigger the alarms, but they confirmed they had already tried. Even the doors to the outside were permanently open. She had tried to contact the towers. She had tried to contact maximum facility. Nothing. She descended the stairs, with escaping the only thing on her mind.

50

Stephen rushed forward as did Lance. Ben was stirring next to the sink. Stephen saw dried blood across Ben's face and his eyes rested at a two- inch gash above Ben's eyebrow. 'We need to move, quickly,' Stephen screamed. Stephen was sure he could hear the roaring fire alarm above.

Stephen had never ventured this deep into the prison. It felt cooler down here compared to any other part of the prison. The cell Ben was in was small and was very similar to his own cell. The sheets were soaked in blood, from where Ben had been thrown onto the bed and just left. Ben was shaking and one of his eyes was closed. 'What are you doing here?' he said weakly.

'Come to get you out of here. The prisoners are escaping,' Lance replied as he gently placed his hand under Ben's armpits.

'Escaping? How?' Ben replied.

'Don't worry now, come on, move,' Stephen said.

Ben tried to get onto his feet, and he stood upright, 'my head hurts.'

'You've been thumped by someone,' Lance said as he held Ben steady and balanced himself.

'The warden done it,' Ben said taking a small step forward. 'I feel fine, honest.'

'We owe you an apology,' Stephen said.

'Why?'

'Oliver, we know you didn't do it,' Stephen said.

'I didn't.'

'We know,' Lance said. 'Bernard told Steve you were with him. We're getting you out of here.'

'I need to tell you something Stephen,' Ben said gripping the back of Stephen's shoulder. 'Can we stop?'

'No,' Stephen said. 'There's a fire up there, that may spread, and guards may be swarming us soon. Police, fire officers and all sorts, come on,' Stephen finished dragging Ben by the elbow out of the room. Ben was grimacing under the pain. It was dark in the corridor, but Stephen could have sworn that Ben had gone whiter from being moved.

Stephen could hear a tap dripping somewhere within one of the rooms and the corridor smelt damp. Stephen felt they had to rush to get upstairs and as mad as it sounded, closer to the fire. Ben was ice cold and his body felt limp. The walls around them were dark and unfriendly. Some inmates had spent a week at a time in here.

'There's a fire?' Ben said speaking with more strength in his voice, 'that's what you had all been planning?'

Stephen tried not to laugh, 'yes, that's what everyone's been planning.' They arrived at the guard who had hit Stephen. He was lying on his side, eyes staring at the ceiling, with his nose broken. Stephen knew he was in pain as his lower body was slightly turned, his knees scrunched up and his arms folded. He then turned to look at the three of them and closed his eyes swiftly.

They stepped over the guard and Stephen felt his shoulder becoming more rigid and harder to move as they came to the exit of the solitary confinement. Stephen was holding Ben under the arm even though Ben was walking on his own two feet. Ben still held onto Stephen's wrist for assurance. Stephen tried to keep him moving so that his legs wouldn't become stiff.

Lance typed in the code to the door and the light above the door turned green. They quickly pulled the door open and walked through. They went either side of Ben and heaved him up, so he was fully supported and the three of them ascended the metal steps. Their footsteps echoed to begin with, but the further they climbed, the louder the siren wailed.

Lance let go of Ben's arm and they walked past the vacant chairs. They continued to move at pace as they arrived at the white painted room, which was empty and still without speaking, they walked past the desk containing prison outfits and they quickly retyped the code in for the third time this return trip and the door slid sideways.

As the door revealed the atrium, Stephen's world stopped. He saw flames from the library coming out into the atrium and spreading above them into the first level of cells. Stephen looked to his left and Ben's face was shocked and dazed. Lance's face looked outraged and scared, as if he couldn't have ever comprehended that this would happen. Lives were now at risk.

The majority of the escapees were, probably outside and the majority of the group were crawling or had crawled through the tunnel. The last person was probably covering the hole now and trying to catch up with the others. Stephen thought about the two towers. He had heard no gunshots. Was that because none had been fired or because the fire alarm in here drowned it out? Stephen saw the flames, licking the prison walls but he couldn't move.

Stephen's mind spun away into a different world. Stephen started to think about everyone he'd gotten close to. Keith could be miles away from the prison now. Stephen wasn't sure whether he'd ever meet him again. He had grown to really like Keith. He was the first person who he'd properly spoke to in here and someone who had looked after him.

Stephen wasn't sure whether the other shifters would remain with Keith on the outside. He imagined they would, for they had been together for a long time and Stephen knew it was more than friendship. Stephen didn't know where they would rest or where they would hide. Would they go back to their original roots? Or would they go far away and hope never to be found, ready to start a new life under a new alias?

Where was Bernard now? Stephen liked Bernard a lot, maybe just as much as Lance. Bernard had always taken the time to speak to him when he visited. Stephen felt a sense of worry for him. Bernard was involved now. He had surely cut the fence apart and was probably casually sitting in his church trying to watch the riot in the distance.

Stephen's mind clouded for a moment and then an older man with white hair, green eyes and a dramatic limp entered his vision. Stephen had never spoken to the warden nor did he want to. But now Stephen felt as if he'd love to. Stephen was angry for Ben. Stephen wanted to relay some of this pain to Roy. But there was bigger pain to inflict; escaping.

Stephen wondered if the warden would keep his job after all of this. Probably not, was his first reaction. He had lost full control and questions would be asked. Stephen hoped that Roy wouldn't have the answers. He thought if he saw Roy, he would go to him, only to ask about three people; Bertie, Oliver and Ben.

'STEVE,' Lance shouted, 'we need to move.'

Stephen moved to his left just as he saw a dozen guards and twenty prisoners thundering out of the kitchen door, colliding in the atrium like lions in battle.

51

Stephen shook himself back into the room. His eyes widened as he saw the guards and inmates hitting each other, some falling limp to the floor as others swung wildly hoping to hit a target. The guards were starting to win the battle as they showered down on inmates with batons and liquid, which was sprayed into the inmate's faces; pepper spray.

Stephen and Lance turned the corner and attempted to run as they carried Ben, who was gently putting full weight onto his own two legs. As the corridor got narrower, they knew they were approaching the bottleneck, getting closer to the outside door. They stopped suddenly on the spot as they saw a man almost as big as Roger or Phil standing by the door pushing it back and forth. Next to him was the warden's assistant, who looked fearful and nervous.

'Too late,' Matthew said, 'we've locked it.'

Stephen could just about make out screams from behind him coming from the atrium either from the inmates or from the guards, who were showing no remorse.

'Unlock it then,' Stephen said.

'Says the guy with no weapons, carrying a little weed,' Matthew replied. 'Doesn't matter now about you getting outside, you can't get out of here and the armed police will arrive soon. You'll be back in your cell soon with another thirty years.' He continued smiling menacingly as he unclipped his baton from the side of his waist belt.

'Open the door or we will put you down,' Lance said.

Matthew began to laugh, and Stephen stood there thinking. Ben was leaning more onto his shoulder and Stephen sensed Lance was gently letting him go. 'Face it,' Matthew said, 'after tonight, you'll be somewhere far worse than here.'

Stephen was about to react as he knew they were running out of time. He let go of Ben about to move forward, but he was instead frozen as he saw Lance fly forward, landing a hard right to Matthew's cheek. Stephen heard Lilian scream as he pulled Ben to one side and leant him against the wall, where he swayed slightly, but remained standing. Stephen turned around and saw Lance fly across the room as Matthew dropped the baton.

Matthew had hit him back and the mass difference had shown. Lance fell backwards but got straight back up, with his cheek immediately looking swollen. Stephen run forward, his shoulder still thumping beneath the roar of the alarm and he grabbed Matthew's upper arm trying to swing him around. Stephen threw a hard right, which caught Matthew in the mouth.

Stephen pulled his fist away and tensed his jaw. He looked at his right- hand knuckles and saw a blood stain. He wasn't sure if it was this Matthew's or his own. Stephen had to be quick now and he knew if Lance was able to help him, they may have a chance. Stephen tried to throw another punch, but Matthew saw it coming and he moved his head, returning with his own body shot, which winded Stephen, making him breathe desperately.

Lance was rushing back at Matthew, but he saw him coming. Lance got onto the balls of his feet and struck a boxing pose. Lance threw a dummy right but instead he kicked Matthew in the middle of his lower leg, taking him off balance. Matthew ran forward and speared Lance, picking him up, running him into the wall. Stephen heard Lance shriek under the force and Stephen's eyes focused on the baton.

Stephen knelt forward and picked the baton up. He tried to wipe the pain from his shoulder and stomach from his mind. He got within a metre of Matthew and with all his might and force; Stephen hit him on the back. Stephen was sure a normal sized person would have collapsed but Matthew stayed on his feet and released Lance, who fell to the floor.

Matthew turned on the spot, with his arm swinging and his elbow caught Stephen just below the eye. Stephen just fell into a seated position and brought his hands up to his face, as if trying to heal the pain he was feeling. He knew the blow had cut him. He could feel hot liquid running down his face and he could feel the vision in his right eye become distorted as blood went into his eyes where he had rubbed the wound. Looking out of his left eye, he saw Matthew smiling, but then he saw Lance standing again. He hit Matthew hard across the side of the head.

Matthew's smile was wiped from his face as he fell sideways onto the floor and lay motionless next to Stephen. Stephen looked at Lance who was holding the baton, whilst looking tired and deflated. Lance was looking down at Matthew, who was now bleeding from the back of his head. Stephen flicked between the pair as he tried to move onto his own two feet.

Matthew stirred seconds later, and he then returned to being immobile. Stephen imagined he wasn't getting up for a long time. 'You ok?' Stephen said, 'thank you.'

'I'm fine, you're cut, though? We need to move,' Lance replied. 'Grab him and get out those doors.'

Stephen stood upwards and looked at Ben, whose face was looking a little more colourful and his eyes were widening. The blood on his face had dried but the gash above his eyebrow was still weeping, looking sore. Stephen grabbed his arm but now Ben supported himself more than he had in the previous hour.

Stephen looked back to the doors and at the lady called Lilian. She was stood with her hands over her mouth and she looked frozen. 'Are you ok?' Stephen shouted.

'I can't get out. I'm scared,' she replied.

Stephen took deep breaths and started to think. If he left her, she could die, and he would never forgive himself. She couldn't defend herself. He looked at her bright, blue eyes and he could feel his head screaming at him to move. What would Stacey have done? 'Come with us, we know another way out.'

She looked at him dubiously and they stared at each other. 'You won't hurt me?'

'No, now come on,' Stephen said, and Lilian ran across the floor.

'Stephen, I need to talk to you,' Ben said sounding more animated in his voice.

'Later, we need to move,' Stephen replied.

Ahead of Stephen, Lance had swapped places with Lilian at the yard door and was kicking at the base repeatedly, but the door wasn't moving. It bounced against its hinges and moved back into its normal position. Lance was grabbing the handle trying to move it back and forth, but the door wouldn't budge, 'it's definitely shut,' Lance said with panic written across his face, 'we're locked in.'

'Smash the glass,' Ben said loudly, his voice becoming urgent.

'It's tempered, not even bullets can break it,' Lance replied.

'Back that way,' Stephen said throwing his head backwards.

The four of them walked back into the atrium of the prison and Stephen could see guards and prisoners battling still, their weapons laid across the floor with no advantage to either side. Stephen saw the prisoners trying force the guards back into the kitchen, but they were being pushed back every second. The guards outnumbered the prisoners. A couple of guards looked over in their direction and their mouths moved at one another, as they cradled a small baton each. The guards broke into a speed between jogging and walking as they both started to move towards the four of them.

Stephen, was ready to battle again, he knew time was running out and he knew he didn't have any other choice; the guards weren't taking it easy now. Stephen's shoulder ached and his cheek was still bleeding. Stephen could see blood drops covering his orange top and he could feel additional weight in his cheek. The vision in his right eye was slowly reverting to normal.

Just as Stephen came to within around ten metres from the two guards, he saw an inmate knock down a guard and the scream echoed against the atrium walls. The guards, who were facing Stephen, both turned and Stephen and Lance ran past them. The two guards chose not to follow and instead returned to the battle behind them. Batons whipped through the air along with the hanging smell of pepper spray.

The sheer aggression of the inmates pushed the guards away from the kitchen, making space for the four of them to enter. Stephen, pushed Lilian against the wall and they stood still watching as prisoners and guards fell to the floor and got back to their feet, trying to stay in the fight.

Stephen waited for what felt like an hour before Lance grabbed him and Stephen then grabbed Ben and Lilian. They stood by the side of kitchen entrance and Stephen saw Lance peer around the corner, 'the kitchen drain, we need to move for it.'

Stephen didn't reply but he nodded to himself and pushed off the wall, running into the empty kitchen. The benches were littered in orange clothing and food trays. Food was strewed across the floor and scattered against the white walls. Stephen's attention was diverted as he heard Lance gasp in front of him.

Stephen saw why seconds later as beside the entrance to the back of the kitchen where the staff usually worked, lay a man bleeding from the back of his head, limp across the slabbed floor with his arm underneath his torso. His head was caved in at the back and his eyes had rolled up into his head. Stephen felt immediately sick and Lilian looked close to tears. Lance pinched Stephen's arm, 'keep moving.'

They turned the corner and ran for the drain. They both stopped and looked at the drain, which was wide open, the cover lying next to it. 'The freezer,' Stephen shouted knowing they had no time to lose. Lance moved quickly and opened the silver freezer. Lance opened each draw and emptied the contents onto the floor. Frozen vegetables and hard packets of poultry bounced off the floor, followed by each plastic draw.

Stephen was beginning to move towards Lance, when he heard the sound of a metal ping, against the floor.

Amongst the debris beneath them was a rusted hammer with a dented wooden handle. Stephen leant down to pick it up. It felt cold against his palm. Ben was standing now unsupported. 'Others have escaped this way,' Lance shouted.

'I thought they all went out the doors?' Stephen replied. 'No time, come on.'

Stephen looked down the drain hole and felt his breathing grow deeper and faster. His mouth was dry, and his body screamed in pain. Stephen sat down on the edge of the hole, still holding the hammer, ready to jump. Stephen wasn't the first person to be passing through this corridor tonight.

52

Roy's eyes focused on Stephen and Lance as they supported the bloody Ben. The guards were unable to contain the inmates. Roy looked down at the man he had hit, who lay still on the cold floor below. Roy didn't need to hit him again; he wanted to save his energy. Roy rocked on his heel ready to walk over to Stephen. Roy knew he had a prime opportunity.

Roy's mind couldn't help but think about why Stephen had gone down to Ben's cell in solitary. Roy didn't understand. They weren't even close, were they? Then they were gone, they had run in the other direction. Roy knew what they were planning to do; escape. But Roy was confident Matthew had locked the prison down, Stephen had been too late.

Roy moved to the side of the room and watched the guards beating down the prisoners, but the prisoners weren't giving up easily. Roy tried to slide past them unnoticed and he came into the kitchen entrance and kept his back to the wall. He looked within the room and saw it was empty. Roy could smell the night's food moving through the air.

Roy hid behind the kitchen wall, and he watched the fighters brawl before him. Roy had an urge to join in and smash every prisoner down to the floor. He didn't for three reasons. Firstly, energy preservation, secondly, he didn't want *any* prisoner, he wanted Stephen and Ben and thirdly, he knew he couldn't do it. His arms felt tired and his chest ached. He was worried his body was failing him at the last hurdle. Nonsense, he thought, you're a new man.

Roy tried to think of what Stephen would when they realised the outside doors were sealed. Roy couldn't think of where else they could escape from, unless they went through the staff quarters. Impossible. There were so many doors and codes and they would have no sense of direction. Even if they did get that far, the police would have arrived, and it would be over.

Then he stopped. Would they be able to escape once Matthew had finished with them? Three against one, no problem Roy thought. But, it wasn't really though was it? It was maybe two and a half vs one, even better. Roy didn't care what way it was looked at. He now started to hope Matthew wouldn't harm or cause damage to Stephen.

Then Stephen came into view. He had blood across his face. They had no Matthew with them either. But what they did have, made Roy's blood boil; Lilian. She was stood adjoined to Stephen's hip and she looked terrified. Roy thought, at first she may have been a hostage, but not now; she was willingly, standing next to Stephen.

Two guards approached Stephen brandishing their batons. Roy moved further into the kitchen, trying to keep his focus on Stephen. The alarm was ringing throughout the prison, but Roy could still make out the sounds of a scream in the centre of the atrium as a guard fell, his arms clutching his head. Stephen began running in Roy's direction. Roy made a dart for the back of the kitchen, limping as his breathing became harder.

Roy came to the small gap by the glass counter and the wall, which led to the store cupboards and fridges, when a man in an orange jumpsuit ran from behind the worktop and started swinging at Roy with a wooden stick. Roy leant back on his bad knee and he felt it give way under his weight, but Roy's mind didn't falter. He felt the breeze from the stick as it brushed past his nose. Roy saw as the stick came swinging backwards, ready to come forward at him again and Roy moved backwards once again.

The prisoner looked possessed. He had been hidden all this and Roy felt the hatred rise within his body. Before the prisoner had a chance to swing again, Roy pulled out his metal pole and swung it hard through the air. It hit the back of the prisoner's head and blood splattered against Roy's face.

Roy stepped over the guard, weary and aching but close to his goal. Roy crept round the back of the kitchen and he waited for the right moment to leave hiding. Roy could hear Stephen now. He returned to his position behind the wall, when in the room, he heard the words "kitchen", "drain", "exit and move" and now Roy understood where they were headed.

Roy quickly darted towards the back of the kitchen, where the old entrance door was shut. He looked for a place to hide. Then he arrived at something, which made his eyes narrow and his mouth curve; a drain, which looked loose. Now Roy knew where they were truly headed. He willed for his mind to think quick and he knew he had seconds left.

He bent over, trying to resist the urge to bend his knees and he picked the drain by the centre point with both hands. The drain bolts came out of the ground effortlessly as Roy hoisted it up and rested it gently next to the hole. Roy quickly, lowered himself to a seated positon, and plunged down the hole, which he knew wasn't deep.

He landed awkwardly and groaned as his knee buckled and his chest tensed and roared. The room was dark, but the light from the kitchen allowed him to see forward. The old air vent was no longer there, and Roy saw the hole he could walk through, just as above him he heard Stephen and Lance's voice.

Roy moved forward and approached the revolving door. It swung through as he heard sounds behind him. The next room was pitch black but, he knew where the light switch was, and he begged for it to work. He blindly felt around the wall around half- way up and found the small plastic square. He flicked the switch down and the room lit up with a weak, golden light. Roy gained his bearings and stood to one side, gripping the bloodied, metal pole. He slid the gun out of his pocket and waited for Stephen and Ben to arrive as he thought about his wife.

53

Stephen sat on the edge of the drain staring down below. This was not the first time tonight that he had felt nervous and tense. Had someone been down there already? Was someone down there now? Had someone escaped this way? 'I'll jump down, you pass Lilian and Ben and then follow,' Stephen said continuing to look below him. Stephen pushed himself off the edge and landed softly with his knees bent.

Stephen checked the room quickly, trying to listen for movement. It was lighter down here than before due to the drain being open. Stephen looked up and saw Lilian lowering herself down the hole, with the help of Lance. As she landed, her foot slipped, and she fell forward into Stephen's arms. They looked at each other and Stephen's mind became adrift and his eyes lost in hers.

They let go of one another as Ben then fell through the air and Stephen caught him underneath the arms, holding him upright. Lance took slightly longer to come down the hole and as Stephen stared upwards, he could see why. Lance was positioning the drain back on top of the hole. Stephen heard the drain bolts hit the floor beside him. Lance was aiming to hide the fact they had escaped this way. Stephen could sense Ben's shallow breathing behind him.

Lance jumped and the drain made a small ping as it recovered the hole. 'Maybe someone has already escaped?' Lance said as he looked at Stephen, who could just make out his face.

Stephen looked to the vacant area the air vent had left and tried to make out anyone ahead of him. He didn't agree, with Lance, he just didn't feel right. Keith had only told a few people about the old kitchen route and Stephen had gone further into the corridor than anyone else. Or was it further than anyone he was aware of? 'We need to move now,' Stephen said. 'I've lost track of time, but police will be here soon. We need to move to now.'

'Let's go,' Lance said.

The four of them moved slowly through the room and over the threshold. The noises of the siren slowly quietened as they looked down the corridor. They were submerged into almost pure darkness and Stephen felt his eyes adjusting to the blackness. Stephen tried blinking several times, urging his eyes to tune themselves to the low lighting conditions. Stephen kept walking ahead towards the revolving door.

As they moved away from the air vent, Stephen looked at the others. Lance looked tired but eager to move. Ben looked confused and weary. Lilian looked traumatised. Stephen rubbed his hand across his cheek and looked at his palm. Even though it was darker than before, Stephen was able to make out dried blood across the tips of his fingers and he could see fresh blood on the inside of his hands. Stephen had no way to stop the bleeding on his face, but he had more pressing issues now; how comes he could see his hands clearly?

'It's lighter than before,' Stephen said.

'What?' Lance replied.

'When I came down here, both times, this corridor was

pitch black. Now I can see you clearly.' Lance didn't reply and Stephen continued, 'up here, there's a revolving door. It opens both ways. We get through there and keep walking until we come to the final corner and then we'll reach the door. The door must be open if someone has been down here before us.'

'Then what happens when we're through?'

'We run,' Stephen said. 'Ben, we got you out of here as we promised we would.'

Stephen didn't see the whole of Ben's expression as he flicked between him and the door. When Ben didn't reply, Stephen started walking, hearing the others following him closely behind. The darkness seemed to be replaced by light as they walked further into the corridor and Stephen was able to make out the room. The room was mouldy, and damp was etched across the walls and the ceiling.

Stephen felt more nervous than ever as they approached the revolving door. He tried to block everything else from his mind, but for the noises in the tunnel.

'Come on, let's go,' Lance shouted, loudly, and Stephen sensed him striding past him.

Stephen followed next to Lilian with Ben metres behind. Stephen strode across the rock floor, his shoulder pounding. Stephen could feel his cheek swelling but his desire grew stronger. He felt as if the end was in sight, as long, as they made it through the next two doors. He didn't want to think of the aftermath of escaping. Would he be looking over his shoulder every day?

He wiped the thought from his mind and again began to wonder if whoever had opened the drain before them would have remembered to shut the door leading to the car park. If not, what if the prison officers spotted the door wide open? They'd be sitting ducks.

They reached the wooden, revolving door and Stephen bumped into Lance. 'This the revolving door?' Lance said.

Stephen now could make out Lance's face beside the door. It looked blackened and tired. Stephen didn't want to know what he looked like. 'This is it,' Stephen replied, and Ben was now next to them. 'Go,' Stephen finished. Stephen swung the door open and walked in a metre as the other two followed. Stephen looked ahead of him as he stopped suddenly on the spot; the light above them was on.

'You sure it was dark?' Lance said.

'It was?' Stephen replied, 'I'm sure it was.' The door swung gently behind them and as Stephen attempted to move forward with Lance to his right, out of the corner of his eye, he saw an object speeding towards him and as he felt his knees go and he was surrounded by darkness once more.

54

Stephen was sat on the floor with his head resting against the wall. He felt a new, fresh pain in his forehead and his headache had worsened, sending pain down his neck and into his eyes as if they were popping out. Stephen opened his eyes slightly, seeing light before him. Stephen didn't know what had hit him and he didn't know where the others were either. Stephen placed both his hands on the floor preparing to stand.

'Ah, here he is, awake at last,' Stephen heard from somewhere in the room. The voice sounded excited. Stephen tried to heave himself up and as he did the voice spoke again. 'Get up, Stephen, now.' Stephen opened his eyes fully and he felt the urge to scream as his head begun to thump harder.

Stephen pushed his back hard up against the wall, using his knees to slide himself upwards. Stephen could feel blood running down his face and as he got half- way up the wall, Stephen saw where the voice had come from. Stephen's eyes took a moment to adjust to the man before him.

'Welcome back,' Roy said. 'You've been out for a few minutes.' Stephen attempted to move towards Roy who was sneering. As soon as he moved, he saw Roy raise his right hand, which was gripping a black handgun. 'Like my little weapon?' Roy said.

Roy had a smile curving out of the corner of his mouth. Stephen glanced at Ben who was stood up against a wall with hands resting by his side looking worried and tired. Next to him was Lilian who had her hands around her neck. Stephen looked to his other side and saw Lance lying against the wall with his head leaning back and his eyes closed. Stephen moved to kneel- down next to him. 'Lance,' Stephen screamed.

'Don't move,' Roy shouted back, his arm straight still holding the gun. 'Back away from him and stand next to, Ben, now,' Stephen could see the wooden hammer lying next to Roy's feet.

Stephen could see blood across Lance's neck. If he touched him, he feared he could be shot. Stephen took two sideward steps closer to Ben who was stood there anxiously. Stephen tried to think but he couldn't. It was like his mind was blank and his energy drained. 'He's not dead,' Roy said. 'I saw him breathing. It was this I managed to catch you both with,' Roy continued pulling out his black pole, 'where's Matthew?'

'He's upstairs out cold,' Stephen said. Roy didn't reply, 'why are you here? How?' Stephen asked.

'Why am I down here?' Roy replied. 'Isn't it obvious? I'm here to stop you of course, to stop the pair of you.'

'People are escaping upstairs,' Stephen replied.

'I don't care about anyone else, Stephen, I never have.' Stephen looked at him puzzled and alarmingly. 'You look confused? It's always been my intention to stand here pointing a loaded gun at you. But since about an hour ago, both of you have been my target and I've got you both now. Don't be surprised, it will all make sense very soon,' Roy finished moving backwards, to lean against the wall.

'Roy,' Lilian said for the first time in a while.

'Lilian, I didn't expect you to be down here. Why are you accompanying inmates during a potential escape?'

'They saved me. I couldn't get out. The fire was growing.'

Stephen felt hot, his shoulder and cheek ached uncontrollably, and his headache was pulsating through his weak body. Stephen looked left at Ben who was looking dead ahead at Roy frozen. Stephen sensed Roy wasn't one hundred percent mentally or physically. Every few seconds, Roy kept gripping his chest and fingers were tightening across his sternum as if they were sinking through his top and into his skin.

Stephen started to panic. He knew the moment when the fire crew arrived could have been anytime now and then the police were soon after that. Stephen pictured Keith and the others running into the distance, fugitives on the run with the only care they had being to find shelter and to become invisible to the outside world.

Stephen had so many questions he wanted to ask. So many things he wanted to know. There were only two things that he thought Roy may be able to answer; Bertie and Oliver. Stephen wanted to pick his moment, but was there a good time to ask when someone was aiming a gun at you? Stephen closed his eyes thinking of how to escape and if Lance was ok.

'Stephen,' Stephen heard opposite him. 'Look at me.'

Stephen raised his head slightly to look at Roy. Roy was no longer smiling, but instead he looked angry and contemptuous towards him. His left hand was still gripping his chest and his right arm was still held outright. Stephen glanced down at Lance and he saw that his eyes were now open and that he was breathing. His face was bloodied worse than what Stephen had thought previously.

Stephen gulped once and looked back at Roy, 'what happened to Bertie?'

'What?' Roy replied.

'Bertie, you know the laundry guy. He died in here not so long ago.

'I guess it doesn't matter now does it?' Roy said. 'This story will never pass outside of these walls will it?' Roy looked at them both and smiled; his teeth visible beneath the sneer. His hair looked scruffy and wavy. 'Bertie was a pure inconvenience. He got nosy. He started to somehow source information on me from outside, something I had hidden very well, well enough I thought.'

'But in the end, I knew that it was too dangerous to have him in here, spreading stories of my life. I went to see him, I was going to attack him,' Roy said now laughing, his laugh cold and evil, echoing off the walls, 'but natural causes helped me. I was in front of him and he keeled over and collapsed. I could have saved him, no question, but why would I? I laughed at him and let him suffer.'

'You disgusting immoral person -' Stephen said, but he stopped midsentence as Roy raised his gun to Stephen's eye level.

'Keep going,' Roy said. 'You'll understand, Stephen soon enough. We do things to people, that are not very nice. Surely, you would have known that, after all these, years? Ben certainly did,' Roy said nodding at Ben who was now breathing more frequently. 'Bertie was gone, and I was able to forget about him quite quickly, one less criminal.'

Lance's chest was rising and falling every second. Stephen hoped he was recovering and that he was listening. 'That what

303

you thought of Oli too?'

Roy stopped smiling for a moment and looked at Stephen angrily. 'Oli, Oli, Oli, yes he was a stupid boy. Cigarettes eh? They'll kill you in the end.'

'You killed him,' Stephen replied.

'Indeed, well in a way, but Ben helped me.'

'Me?' Ben said speaking for the first time since reaching the abandoned corridor.

'Yes, you told me about the plans, and I thought Oli might know something, but he kept his mouth was shut tight. So, I released the gas valves and boom, he was up in flames. Another one who fell by my order, you two will join that exclusive list soon.'

'You're sick,' Stephen said.

'*Ask yourself why,*' Roy shouted in the semi-darkness. The room seemed to have silenced the outside world, so that all could be heard was their conversation. 'I have been sick for a long time, more time than I ever knew imaginable, all because of you, Stephen, because of you.'

'Because of me?'

'What's wrong? You looked afraid,' Roy replied, his voice rasping in the silence.

'I only met you when I came in here.'

'O but your fate of meeting me was planned years before this, believe me. We will get to that part though, trust me. We have time; I assumed you shut the drain entrance? You wouldn't have wanted people knowing how you tried to escape would you?'

Stephen nodded as his reply.

'So, no-one other than us four, well five if you include

sicknote down there, knows we're down here. The fire won't get this far. But firstly, let's start from the very beginning. Ben, you've been lying to me all this time, haven't you?'

'No,' Ben replied sheepishly.

'Lying to me all this time,' Roy repeated holding the gun straight. 'I have read your diary tonight, Ben.' Ben looked a mixture of angry and upset, as he fidgeted with his top, looking at Roy, swallowing and blinking repeatedly.

'You read them?'

'Not word for word, but most of them, yes. Interesting read you little maggot,' Roy said scornfully. 'I found out about your formative years, Ben. You were a labourer, weren't you?' Roy watched Ben's expression change to a glare, and he continued, 'you went to church a lot too I read, very religious wasn't she your mother?'

'Enough about her,' Ben said angrily.

'No Ben, not enough about her. Now we're going to go back to the night of your mother's death. If you stop, I will shoot you and I will tell it for myself, but Stephen should hear it from your lips. You're close after all aren't you, Ben? It didn't strike me initially about why you dropped Stephen's name to me all that time ago, but a certain chapter told me everything I needed to know.'

'What's he talking about?' Stephen said looking at Ben.

'I'm sorry,' Ben replied.

'Sorry? Ben, I don't think sorry will cut it. You're the reason Stephen is in here.'

'Ben, what's he talking about?' Stephen said concerned.

'Ben,' Roy said, 'tell him the whole story, now.'

Ben looked at the floor, continuing to play with his bloodied top. 'I lived at home with my mother, who was ill. I lived with her all my life and she brought me up. She was lying in bed and we got talking about her life.' Stephen felt himself become transported into the room with them and he listened to the conversation.

'You've always been a good boy to me, Benjamin,' the old lady in the bed said. She was wrapped up in thick sheets and had three pillows resting behind her head. She was grey and she looked thin and undernourished.

'You'll be ok mum,' a younger Ben said. The younger Ben was just a younger looking, care- free boy, still with the skin pigmentation on his chin. He was smiling; something Stephen hadn't seen him do once. He was wearing over baggy clothes, which didn't fit, and his hair was messy. He looked tall and gangly.

There was silence in the room as the pair looked at each other smiling serenely. The lady then spoke after a few minutes and her voice sounded more powerful and determined than before. 'You know I've always loved you don't you, Benjamin?' she said.

'I know mum,' Ben replied.

'You know your father always loved you too, Ben. He always did.'

'Why did he go?'

She tried to push herself up the bed. 'He left on his own free will, but he didn't want too, he loved you'

'I've never met him.'

'No, but he met you and he loved you straight away, that I swear. He couldn't stay with us.'

'Why?'

'He couldn't settle down. I thought he could, but God had

given him another path to follow and I respected that.'

'Sorry, mum,' Ben replied smiling shyly.

'No, no don't be, we had a few wonderful years together. We were married soon after we met in a lovely little ceremony. He was kind, romantic and energetic. He said he had no family and it was just us and my best friend. He had no friends either, which was sad at the time, but I thought it would bring us closer.'

'Where did he come from?'

'He told me he was from a town a long way from here. He never went back, even though he sometimes mentioned it. I found out why later in life.'

'Why couldn't I talk about him?'

'Because I didn't want you to get upset about him, he was a good man.'

'I feel you're about to tell me something mum,' Ben said laughing.

'I am Benjamin; I'm just catching my breath. Your father made a grave mistake. His name was Ronald. I loved him from the word go, but he left suddenly, and I never saw him again, until a few years ago that was, and all for the wrong reasons.'

'Mum?'

'There was an accident in the village we lived in. We didn't live far from where it happened, but we moved away straight after. A man killed a woman in a hit and run accident and he died soon after. The village was in uproar and it upset everyone, especially me. I read the reports and I knew the man who had killed her. That man was your father,' she finished looking at Ben without any expression.

Ben remained silent for a moment and he just stared back

at her, looking unsure on what to say, 'dad killed someone?'

'He didn't mean too, I'm sure of it, Benjamin, believe me.'

'He killed someone, and you've kept it from me all these years?'

'To protect you.'

'We moved away from the village and everything, I knew no one. I've always been a no one.'

'To protect you.'

'How could you hide this from me?'

'To protect you.'

'This woman, who was she?'

'An innocent woman, she didn't suffer.'

'How do you know?' Ben screamed.

'There's more, you need to know this.'

'How could you?'

Ben's mother just continued to talk ignoring Ben's previous comment. 'It's about your surname, Benjamin. I changed it for you, just after he moved away. I wanted to remember your father as he was a fantastic person. He had his reasons why he left us, but I never forgot him. Your surname, Durant, is another word for enduring and my love believe me has and always will be for your father. I changed your surname to protect you. Your middle name is your father's surname; Chester.'

Ben got up and walked around the room scratching his head furiously. He looked angry and upset, but he looked annoyed more than anything. He looked annoyed that the truth had been thrown in his face after all this time. 'You've named me after a killer, a murderer.'

'That's your father, Benjamin, don't be rude.'

'He killed someone, and you stood by him.'

'One more thing that you should know, Benjamin, before I go.'

'Can it be any worse?'

'Your father admitted a few things to me the night he left. A few things I never knew about. When we met, he said he had been in a previous relationship. I never knew what happened to the lady and Ronald didn't want to discuss her, but he said he had never married her, and he left her one day, without even as much as a goodbye.'

'And you took him in still? Ben said, 'even though he had left another woman?'

'He told me that his previous relationship wasn't right for him. It didn't have any impact on me. Something else did matter though.'

'What else matters?'

'Well, he then told me that he had a son. He's a few years older than you. He's called Stephen.'

Ben began to scream at her, and he began to throw things around the room, as vases smashed onto the carpet and pills spilled out across the bed. The lady just looked at him with her head slightly lowered. She looked sad and embarrassed about what she had just told Ben, but she looked happier than she had minutes before. Ben was striding around the room looking the complete opposite. 'I have a brother and you never told me about him?'

'I was loyal to your father. He didn't want us to know so I respected that. Chapter three, verse three to four says; n*ever let go of loyalty and faithfulness. Tie them around your neck; write them on your heart. If you do this, both god and people will be pleased for you.*

Ben ran at her in anger and picked up the pillow lying beside the bed and he shoved it over her face. Her wrists rose slightly but she didn't fight back, she just held onto Ben's wrists. Then they fell to the bed and Stephen opened his eyes.

'Wonderful,' Roy said.

Stephen looked to his side at Ben and he couldn't believe what he had heard coming out of Ben's mouth. Stephen was shocked and speechless and angry. Part of him wanted to attack Ben. The other part of Stephen wanted to run at Roy for putting Ben through the story.

Stephen knew the truth about parts of his life he would never have dared imagine or believe unless he hadn't heard it for himself. He now knew about his father. The so- called *kind, romantic and energetic* man was nothing but a deserter and a murderer. Stephen hated his father. Only from his minor years did he have the odd recollection of a man scooping him up and throwing him in the air.

Stephen pictured his mother being distraught when his father left without saying a word. Stephen felt repulsed by him. Stephen was positively sure that his father never paid a penny for his upkeep nor did he support his mother in any way. Stephen was glad he was dead. Stephen was only pleased not for himself but for his mother and for the pain that she must have gone through.

But Stephen also felt a sense of questions bubbling from his stomach, working their way up to his throat. Stephen couldn't help but think his father was a murderer, but was there more? The word murderer kept swimming around his dazed head. Stephen couldn't remove it. It was the same word he had been called on countless occasions and he gritted his teeth and shook his head violently. 'I don't get it, you're my brother?' Stephen said.

'I'm sorry,' Ben said staring down at the floor.

Roy spoke again, 'I bet you're thinking about your life, Stephen? About what could have been had your father not left your mother? Whether you would have turned out differently? Whether you'd be in here?'

'My father had nothing to do with this or my life. I'm glad he's gone for what he did.'

'Maybe you should know something else, Stephen,' Roy said with a sadistic grin.

'How would you know anything about me?' Stephen said.

'I know too much, that's your problem, well, both of your problems now in fact.'

Ben had been looking down at the floor when he raised his head and looked at Stephen with his eyes now wide open and alert, 'he killed your wife' he said pointing at Roy.

Stephen digested what he had heard and looked at Ben for a few seconds before he looked at Roy and saw the old man before him, smiling from ear to ear. Stephen felt dizzy and sick and confused and desperate for answers, 'killed my wife?'

Roy raised the gun a little higher and pointed it at Stephen's face. He was still smiling, but his face looked more concentrated and prepared. 'Ben, Ben, you ruined my surprise.'

'You are sick,' Ben said.

'Tell me what you are talking about,' Stephen said ignoring Ben.

'Shall I tell you another story then?' Roy began to nod his head and he continued, 'I didn't kill your Stacey. But I know who did,' Roy said staring at Stephen.

Stephen kept his eyes concentrating on Roy. Ben looked scared. Stephen had no pain in his body now. His shoulder and head pain had been replaced by the feeling of losing his wife all over again and he had someone telling him the answers he had been asking himself for what felt like so long, 'you're lying.'

'Stacey Farley. She lived at Southdown Avenue, which was down a cul-de-sac and had a side gate leading to a little alley? Stacey was lawyer, no?' Roy said. Stephen looked back at him non-despondent. Stephen clenched his fists and remained silent. 'I had her killed by a man. You're here because of me and Ben. We worked together to get you in here.'

Stephen felt the urge to hit Ben hard on the nose, but he wanted to know more first.

Ben said, 'I didn't know, I didn't think about it.'

'That's your problem, Ben, you don't think, do you? It came to me earlier today about why you wanted to tell me that story about your father. You wanted me to look for Stephen. You knew Stephen was your brother and you for some reason had a problem with him, am I right so far? Then your wish came true; I got him in here. Is that correct?'

Ben didn't answer; instead he began to relook at floor. Stephen was still staring at Roy firmly and aggressively.

'Is that correct, Ben?' Roy repeated. And then Stephen's heart skipped a beat. Roy flicked a small part of his gun and it clicked loudly in the room. Stephen watched Roy grip the gun, his white knuckles visible in the glow and now Stephen knew they were in trouble. Stephen glanced right at Lance who was still lying against the wall.

'IS THAT CORRECT?' Roy screamed.

'YES,' Ben shouted back, and Stephen could make out

tears from the corner of Ben's eyes. Stephen looked back at Roy and saw he had clenched his chest again and his face slightly grimaced.

'Tell me what happened to her,' Stephen said, 'and why.'

'Isn't this nice? We have you two brothers and me before you; judge, jury and executioner. Well let me tell you how it started. I found out you existed, and I couldn't have it. From the word go, it ate away at me like a bug infested cesspit. So, I set away ready to have your normal life deleted.

'I hired a man who was once a prisoner here and he watched your movement for several weeks, every day and every hour. You went to the gym that day she was killed, yes?' Roy asked smiling at Stephen who was taken aback and stunned.

'Keep going,' Stephen replied pleading to hear the rest of the story. Above them, there were two large bangs, but Stephen didn't avert his eyes, he was only focusing on the man in front of him who had changed his life.

'Xavier went to your house after you'd left, and he killed her. He said he used a rod on her, twice actually. He said she screamed. Then he left out the side gate and you walked into the crime. There was only ever going to be one outcome; you were coming in here with me.'

'Why not do it yourself?' Ben said quietly.

'Why would I need to? I could have done it myself, yes. I wouldn't have needed to wait a few weeks to survey your life. I would have walked straight into your door and shot you both, game over. But that was too easy, far too easy. I wanted you to lose someone you cared for and then be locked away for it, never knowing exactly why this had all happened.'

Stephen took a step forward and Roy pointed the gun at

313

Stephen's chest now. 'Don't move, Stephen. I've got a bigger margin to aim for with your chest. A fragment of your sternum may hit Ben in the face, knock and bit of sense into him. So that's the story of your life. I've been trying to get close to you for months, long, hard months of anger and frustration. Ben was meant to get close to you and then he suddenly lost his bottle, the useless worm.'

'I didn't lose my bottle,' Ben said.

'Why did you stop watching Stephen then?' Roy replied bluntly.

Stephen saw Ben turn to face him, his brother in the flesh next to him, wounded and different but the same in blood. Ben looked embarrassed and he turned away from Stephen with his eyes semi closed, 'I wanted Stephen yes. I blamed him for sending my mother over the edge. I was trying to blame someone. I couldn't blame my father, even though he was the only one I should have ever blamed. So, my mind told me someone else had to pay.'

'Go on,' Roy said urging him to carry on.

'I tried to find Stephen to tell him, but I didn't know who he was and where he lived, but I had one bigger problem than that; I was locked inside. The hate for you, Stephen almost killed me and then when I met you in here, part of me realised, it was never your fault. It was my father I should have been angry with. So I decided to try to get to know you, but I couldn't. You were too heavily involved with the shifters.'

'This is lovely, Ben,' Roy said sneering and with his left hand he raised it to brush his hair back slightly and then he quickly brought it back down to his chest as Stephen saw his teeth were ground together.

'Then my mind understood something. My mother never did anything to hurt me and neither did Stephen. I pushed two people away from my life and the first one, I'd never have been here if I'd realised that all those years ago. I'm sorry, Stephen,' Ben said. 'Roy, I have nothing to lose now. Kill me if that's what it takes.'

'Why did you set out to get us like this, we'd never met you?' Stephen asked ready to pounce when he saw Roy grimace again.

'No, you're right, we'd never met, but your father did something I could never forgive any of you for.'

Stephen looked back into the green eyes of the old, sturdy man, and felt hatred like never before. Stephen started to ponder on what Roy had just said. What had his absent father done? Then it came to his mind like a flash of lighting; bright and sudden. 'Who was the woman that Ronald killed in that hit and run accident?'

Roy's eyes narrowed and he looked at Stephen menacingly as he slowly rubbed his tongue across his upper lip from left to right, 'he killed my Linda, my wife.'

55

Stephen felt locked inside someone else's body for all that he had heard tonight couldn't have been true. This pain couldn't be real could it? He imagined the police and ambulance sirens would be lighting up the grounds of the prison as they spoke, just before the armed police circled the vicinity. Stephen's mind whirred back what felt like hours ago to when he first came through the revolving door and he went over what he had heard once more.

Roy had been the central piece to the downturn of events in his life. Stephen knew the man before him had pushed the first domino, which spiralled Stephen's life out of control. Stephen knew he had to try and hate someone, but he couldn't, he knew he didn't have it in him. He felt anger and revulsion for Roy for what he had done to his wife, but he knew he had lost someone, and Stephen knew his father was the only one to blame for all of this.

'You won't get away with this,' Stephen said moving inches away from Ben who remained rigid and still.

'I will and you know it. I'll shoot you both in a moment and then I'll be gone. I will have fulfilled my duties once I know you're both gone; the last known relatives of a murderer.'

'You won't,' Lilian said. Roy looked bewildered. He didn't want to kill one of his own. 'I have worked here for weeks and

I've been noting down your moves,' Lilian continued, patting her trouser pocket. 'I am a detective inspector, transferred here from an anti-corruption unit in London. They told me suspicions and you've admitted to every single crime.'

'O, Lilian. What a disappointment.'

'My real name is Kirsty. You need to come with me, sir.'

'A snake amongst us,' Roy sneered. 'It matters not. You're not needed here' and Roy raised his gun pointing it at Kirsty who gasped.

'Tell me about your wife,' Stephen said, and he saw Ben turn his body abruptly.

Roy's, reaction, was similar, to Ben's. He became still suddenly and his mouth dropped half an inch and his eyes looked between Stephen's eyes to his mouth, repeating the words he had just heard. His left hand was still holding onto his chest and the gun was slowly falling lower. 'You think I'm going to stand here and tell you all about her?'

'Why not?' Stephen said. 'We had nothing to do with her death. That was our father. But you've had everything to do with my wife's death. So, I think I should know.' Stephen had to do something to stall Roy.

'She was lovely, heart of gold. She went out and never came back. I went out looking for her, but instead I found a crime scene. Luckily for him, your father died at the scene. The drunken fool veered off into a wall after he hit my wife. I got to see her body; bloodied and bruised.'

Stephen looked ahead and at the two o'clock position on a clock face, he saw Lance still stirring but his left hand was moving across his chest and his right was covering his forehead, trying to stop the pain. 'Do you think this is what she would have wanted?' Stephen said.

Roy looked back at Stephen with venom in his eyes and he raised the gun slightly, but Stephen could see Roy wasn't holding it as firmly and it looked as if he was shaking slightly. Stephen watched Roy's left- hand knuckles turn whiter and whiter and Stephen pushed his left heel back into the ground, ready and waiting.

'Don't you dare,' Roy shouted, 'don't you dare. She doesn't have a choice in the matter, but she will be smiling upon me as I wipe your father's seed from the earth once and for all.'

Stephen saw the events unfolding a moment before they did. Lance was starting to move more, and Stephen knew Roy would see him any moment and that meant Lance was in more danger. Stephen looked left at Ben who had tears in his eyes and his face looked blotchy. Stephen was sure he could still hear the siren above them from the fire and he pictured the fire blaring across the ceiling.

Stephen looked back at Roy who was smiling, and he saw him raise the gun a further inch and grip the butt of the gun steadier. 'Lance,' he shouted.

As soon as he spoke, Roy turned his body to look at Lance and Stephen pounced, running at Roy, just as he saw the flash of a muzzle, followed by the sound of the gun fire echoing across the room.

56

Stephen ran into Roy, who went flying back against the room, dropping the gun, which scattered a metre away from them all. Stephen stopped for a moment and looked into Roy's eyes, which were gazing back with excitement yet anxiousness having lost his primary weapon. Stephen thought he should be in pain, but he felt none. He looked down at his body and he saw no blood.

Stephen turned around and saw why. Ben was hunched over clutching at his stomach and he was looking up at Stephen with a look of shock. His mouth looked as if it was trying to speak, to plea with Stephen for help, but he remained unmoving and motionless. Stephen looked at the gangly Ben, his brother and for so long an outsider and he knew he couldn't help him.

Stephen turned around and saw Roy swinging a small black object through the air, curving at a downwards angle, due to hit Stephen hard across the temple at any second. Stephen ached more than he had ever done before, but he knew he needed to keep working and he tried to draw every inch of energy back to his body.

Stephen ducked under the pole and he sensed it swerve above him, missing his hair by inches. Stephen pushed Roy hard in the chest. Roy hit the wall and looked back at Stephen alarmed. Roy's mouth was twitching and his eyes were flickering from side to side. Stephen felt more nervous than ever and he moved left slightly to be closer to the unoccupied gun.

Roy didn't move; he just watched Stephen inch away from him towards the gun and all he could do was remain rigid. Then Stephen knew there was a reason why. Roy pulled his left hand up his chest and Stephen saw him cling onto his breastbone like his life depended on it, which it probably did. Stephen jogged back to Ben who was still hunched over with Kirsty's hand on his back.

Stephen held his shoulders and said, 'sit down.' Ben fell backwards with Stephen having to bear his weight. Stephen rested Ben down and walked back to Roy who was sliding slowly down the wall, still gripping his chest with one hand and with the other he was holding his upper arm. Stephen knew it was a heart attack and that it had been pending very early in the night. Roy's face was etched with disbelief that this was happening

Then Roy's mouth started to move, and his body became inflexible as he started to writhe in agony, falling into a seated position. Stephen watched his hands cling on to his body, trying to prevent the pain from spreading but it seemed to grow more ferocious with every second. Roy fell and lay at an angle, his legs no longer moving. The power in his lower body had gone and it was as if a disease was working its way up his body.

Roy shook his body one last time and the last thing he would have seen was Stephen staring down at him unwilling to help and unforgiving. Stephen had a sense of guilt even though deep down, he knew Roy deserved it. Stephen ran to Ben and as he reached him, he looked at Lance who was on his knees, coughing trying to regain his breath.

Stephen and Bens eyes met. Stephen looked into Ben's dark brown eyes and he knew the eyes were like his own. 'Ben, come on, you're going to be ok.'

Ben didn't reply, but he instead smiled back at Stephen and kept gazing back, trying to take deep breaths, whilst trying not to move. Stephen watched Ben remove his hand from his stomach and Stephen saw a circle of blood across his orange jumpsuit. The top was now dark orange, especially in the artificial light and Stephen pushed his hand back. 'I won't make it,' Ben said.

'No, you will. Keep your hand there and apply pressure.'

'I'm sorry.'

'Don't,' Stephen said maintaining eye contact. Stephen heard a footstep behind him and saw Lance was on his feet, staggering over with blood on his face, holding the two saws in either hand. Stephen twisted a little more and he saw Roy lying there still and silent.

'Are you ok?' Kirsty said, but Lance didn't reply.

'I'm sorry,' Ben repeated as Lance stood looking over them.

'Don't,' Stephen said again.

'No, this is my entire fault, you, being in here, your wife, tonight.'

Stephen couldn't help but agree. It was all Ben's fault, but he knew his brother was dying before him and he didn't want him feeling any guilt. 'No, it's Ronald's. He was no father to us, and he made all of this, not you.'

Ben tried to laugh but he grimaced as his body shook slightly. 'Shall we move?' Lance said wearily.

'He can't,' Stephen replied.

'Go without me. I'm not leaving you,' Stephen replied,

'Lance, Lil-Kirsty, you go on.' Stephen looked around the room for the hammer and he saw it now lying by the revolving door.

'Not without you,' Lance said.

Stephen tried to smile at Lance, to show some gratitude, but he couldn't. His body didn't have emotions left; instead his wife's death and Ben's pain replaced everything else. Ben shook in his seated position and he moved both arms slowly into the air and rested his bloody palms onto Stephen's shoulders. Stephen didn't stop him nor did he speak.

'Get out of here now, if you don't, what a waste of your whole plan. Before you go though, please just do me one thing, Stephen; forgive me,' Ben said and he rested his head against the dark, cold wall. Stephen felt the grasp of Ben's hands on his shoulder loosen and Stephen glanced at Lance, pleading for help.

Stephen knew that Ben felt just like him. They were boys with no father, raised by a single parent who only ever did her best. A boy who became a man, never knowing the truth, protected by their mother's, who only ever had the best intentions. But were they any different after that? Stephen had a good job, a wife a home. Stephen didn't know anything about Ben. He didn't think anyone did.

'I forgive you,' Stephen said, and he saw a tear trickle from Ben's eyes and Stephen felt himself fighting back the tears. Ben's arms released their grip and they slid down the front of Stephen's top, landing in his lap. He took one more look at Stephen and he smiled wearily just before his dark eyes rolled up into his head and Ben was no more.

57

Stephen closed Ben's eye lids and raised himself. He felt nothing. He felt no guilt, nor did he feel sad. He just looked down at the man who was, supposedly, his brother and he thought about why he was in here. Stephen started to breathe in and out heavily, trying to get the feelings back to his body. Seconds later he felt the pain from his shoulder and his head.

'We need to go,' Lance said with a little more animation and urgency in his voice. Stephen looked at him and saw the cut on his head, along with partially dried blood across his neck. He looked aged from the blow. Kirsty's face was covered in soot, but her eyes still looked vibrant.

'Do we leave him?'

'We can't take him. We'd be spotted a mile off.'

Stephen agreed and nodded with his eyes closed. Stephen attempted to walk away at a pace, but his body wouldn't allow it. He felt incapable of running or even speaking, his whole body ached, and Stacey circled his blurred mind.

Stephen was ten metres away from Ben, approaching the corner towards the final door and hopefully freedom. Stephen knew that the outside of the prison was probably in chaos and that attempting to escape now could be fatal, but they had come this far and learnt so much, that Stephen felt there was nothing to lose.

There was a sudden roar across the room, which made Stephen stop dead on his feet, looking at his own shadow on the floor beneath him. Stephen swallowed two or three times and felt his heart pumping blood around his body. Stephen's mouth went suddenly dry and all he could picture was his wife walking gracefully down the carpeted stairs, her radiant smile lighting up the room. Behind her was the final door to the exit, and then he saw the door being dragged away.

Stephen's eyes looked down at his blood sodden top and he gently placed his hand over the fresh wound below his rib cage. Stephen then felt his adrenaline draining and he felt his temperature drop within a second. Stephen felt his knees buckle slightly and he looked right at Lance who was staring at him with his mouth wide open and his hands supporting his red chin.

Stephen twisted, trying with all his energy to keep his feet on the ground and his balance straight. He saw Roy lying there on his chest facing them with his arms outstretched holding the gun. Stephen breathed in quickly. The pain tore at his body and he tried to swallow. He saw Roy drop the gun, hearing the metal hit the flooring, giving off a small reverberation around the room, as Roy's head fell in between his arms and he was still once more.

58

Roy felt numb and in shock. He had probably deleted one of Ronald's children from the world but the other one, the primary target, was still free and alive. Months and months of planning was all to be ruined by a pain in his chest. He remembered standing there; pulling the trigger as he watched the muzzle flash and the bullet hit Ben forcefully in the stomach.

Roy had tried to hit Stephen, but he knew he was in trouble. His chest pounded and roared as his blood supply began to stop and he felt the tingling down his arms like he was plugged into electricity. He wanted his body to fall so he could grasp the gun, but his legs were standing strong, trying to remain loyal.

Roy gripped his chest and crossed his arms and he started to slide down the wall, trying to spot the gun. Stephen was now standing over him and Roy knew he was too late, Stephen had won. Roy knew he was dying, and he started to shake as his body started to shut down. Roy felt himself sitting and he tried to hold his chest to stop the pain spreading.

Roy fell forward at an angle deliberately and his hip shook with agony as he looked upwards at Stephen and he closed his eyes trying to relax. Roy lay there begging for his heart to keep pumping blood, but he knew his heart had caved. His wife came swimming into his mind and he smiled from the floor, knowing he was coming for her soon.

He heard Stephen and Ben talking about how Ben would survive. Ben asked for forgiveness. Roy heard footsteps, which sounded further away with every step. Roy opened his eyes and twisted slightly on the floor. He saw the gun and he used what felt like his remaining bit of energy to grab it, turning it thrice in his almost numb hands, so it was pointing at the two people sluggishly walking away.

Roy held the gun between both hands and pointed it at Stephen's legs knowing his hand would fly into the air from the pressure. He put all his might into the grasping the gun and he pulled the trigger gently feeling it ease backwards and the gun fired. Roy looked over the gun and saw Stephen standing in the same spot, static and shocked, with blood emerging through his top.

Roy saw Stephen turn around inwards little by little. Roy dropped the gun to the floor and felt his heart give one last pump before it ceased working. Roy didn't get to see Stephen's face, but Roy couldn't do anything now but hope Stephen was suffering. Roy could feel his neck muscles wilting under the pressure of his head and he fell to the floor as he closed his eyes knowing his wife was waiting for him.

59

Stephen was pushed around the corner of the room quickly by Lance who was looking at Stephen in disbelief and horror. Even though they had turned the corner in essentially the same room, it was considerably darker and cooler. Stephen could just about make out Lance's facial expression, which looked panicky and anxious. Kirsty just stared in disbelief.

'Steve, you'll be ok, come on,' he said rubbing Stephen's shoulder.

Stephen could feel the pressure of Lance's palms stroking the lower part of his neck all the way down to his triceps. Stephen could taste blood as he swallowed and he could feel his body screaming at him to sit down and relax, but his mind was prioritising the escape first. Stephen wondered whether Roy was dead, or whether he was about to come thundering around the corner, waving his gun in his face ready to shoot again.

Stephen's arms felt tired and his legs felt exhausted. He felt as if he was almost dead, but Lance's hand seemed to keep the blood flowing around his body, every single movement driving life into his soul. Stephen took a step forward towards the door at the far end of the tunnel and he was just about able to make out a small inch of light through the crack in the door. Stephen tried to keep his focus on the gap, like a fly to a light.

Stephen walked past the rooms either side of the corridor

and the further he approached the door, the darker it became. Stephen was confident that there was a light switch somewhere this end of the room, just like before, but he knew they couldn't afford to waste any more time and that they had to get to the exit. Stephen came to the table, which he had placed days there before, pushed tight up against the door.

Lance ran forward and threw the table over, Stephen feeling a light breeze as the cloth flew through the musty air, followed by the clatter of the table skidding across the floor. Stephen saw Lance take a step back and with all his effort, his kicked the door with his right foot, central of the door and it flew open, fresh air engulfing them. 'You ok?' Lance said.

'Yes,' Stephen replied quietly, 'I'll be fine, I am fine.' He could sense Kirsty bent over next to him.

Stephen's head nodded forward and he struggled to keep his eyes open. He yearned for a five- minute sleep, just to keep going, but he knew that to keep going, he really couldn't afford to sleep. After a minute, Stephen walked forward with Lance, holding him by the elbow. 'You're going to be ok,' Lance said encouragingly, 'you'll be fine.' Stephen didn't reply.

Stephen was dazed and he looked ahead through the door. The fresh, cold air was beautiful. It felt different to the air in the yard. It smelt like freedom. Stephen looked slowly up at the stars as he took a deep breath. His body screamed at him and he closed his eyes, just as he felt Lance pull him by the elbow.

Stephen could hear sirens and to his left, he could see red and blue flashing lights. Stephen tried to gently breathe in the fresh air, which became harder with every inhalation. Stephen felt as if every breath was helping the small amount of energy he had left, leave his fatigued body. He looked to his right and saw Lance next to him clearly in the new light and he felt his arm being pulled as he was heaved further into the car park.

Stephen saw what was in front of him. They were stood in the small car park, which was almost unoccupied other than for two cars. Stephen looked at the parked cars as he felt his chest tighten slightly. He saw the cars were a blue Mondeo and white Polo. Stephen stared around the car park, making out the large metal fences protecting the perimeter, but for the first time in months, Stephen felt free.

Stephen looked up at the sky again, which was dotted with bright stars and he could feel himself smiling. He knew that they'd made it and he knew they were closer to being free than ever before. Stephen pictured his wife and mother staring down at him. He wondered if they were proud of him and whether Stacey had forgiven him for that final argument. Stephen wanted nothing more than to rewind the clock and stay in the house with her, ready to protect her.

Based in the middle of the car park, were three evenly spaced tall lamp posts, which were lighting up the ground below in wide spheres. Stephen saw a gate beyond the lights, which led to the outside world of freedom. Stephen could make out the sirens in the distance, which were loud and constant. Stephen tried to move and hide.

Stephen aimed for the lofty lamp post as his next checkpoint and he kept his breathing at the same pace. Stephen heard Lance move and break into a gentle jog. Stephen trudged across the yard, until he was metres away from the post listening to new sounds of shouting in background. Stephen placed his hand around the post and Kirsty spoke, 'keep going, we're almost there.'

'I'm almost there,' Stephen replied. Stephen wouldn't have believed he had said it if he hadn't felt his mouth moving as he uttered the syllables.

'You're not going to stop us?' Lance said at Kirsty.

Kirtsy, didn't reply but just stared at them unable to speak.

'Steve, come on,' Lance retorted but Stephen heard panic in his voice along with apprehension.

Stephen took a step forward, his mind urging him to continue his journey, but his legs wouldn't, they refused to move, and they forced him to remain stationary. Then Stephen went to a place he had never visited before. It was peaceful and calm, and he felt no more pain. Stephen looked at the gates and tried to determine how far away they were and how long it would take them to get there, when Lance came into his vision holding Stephen by the shoulders.

Stephen smiled at his closest friend and fell to his knees. As he hit the floor, his kneecaps bounced off the ground and Lance leant down beside him, trying to pick him back up; Stephen knew he was a dead weight. 'Steve, please, don't do this,' Lance shouted.

'Lance, I won't make it. Give me five minutes, please and I'll catch up with you.'

'Steve, no, we're in this together. Get up, come on, please.'

Stephen, placed his hands across his chest and stomach, and he felt the hot liquid running across his top along with flaky, dried blood sticking to his trousers. Stephen once again looked up at the stars and smiled feeling himself being transported to a different place; a beautiful type of place, which was free.

Stephen saw his wife again before him and she looked like she had done on the first night he met her. Her blonde hair was waving across her face and her smile lit up the room along with her piercing blue eyes. Stephen couldn't ever bring her back and he knew why she had been taken away. She had been taken away from his life for something his father had done and for something he never knew existed.

Stephen had a brother who knew the whole truth and had played a part in getting him framed for the murder in one way or another. Ben had begun working with the warden, but Stephen didn't know for how long. Stephen knew his brother was free now, but he knew his father had caused him just as much pain.

Lance came back into his vision and Stephen looked into his worried eyes. Stephen lifted his right hand and cupped it around the back of Lance's shaven head. Lance looked back into Stephen's eyes and didn't blink underneath the bright lights, 'don't leave me,' Lance said.

'Lance, do me something.'

'What is it?' Lance replied.

'Go.' Stephen kept his eyes on Lance, who looked back startled. Lance looked more fearful than before and he took a moment to reply.

'I can't.'

'You can, please,' Stephen said. 'I'm staying here. If you don't go, you'll go back inside, I won't be.' Stephen said in a factual manner as if he knew Lance couldn't retort. Lance's eyes moved across his body, looking at obvious marks across his face and then down to his torso, which was covered in red. Stephen didn't take his eyes off Lance's face.

Lance's eyes connected with Kirsty's and she cried, 'go.'

Lance smiled and looked back at Stephen, 'you will be fine.'

Stephen fell backwards against the lamp post and rested his spine against the metal, which was painted white. Stephen imagined the post was ice cold, but he felt nothing now. He continued to look at Lance and he swallowed as his head rocked backwards so he was looking up at an angle. 'Lance, you've been great to me, always have been. But now, it's your time to go. If you don't go now, you'll get caught. Give yourself a chance.'

Stephen watched Lance's eyes and he saw the eyes moving underneath his eyelids. Stephen could see a layer of tears building up around the bottom of his eyelid and when Lance blinked, a single tear run down the curves of his face. Lance didn't reply, but he placed both of his hands, which were bloody onto Stephen's shoulders and Stephen looked back at his closest friend.

'Go, Lance, go,' Stephen said pleading.

Lance stood up breathing heavily, his face stricken with fear. Stephen was staring at him from an angle and he was trying to move his neck so he could see Lance's whole body. 'I love you,' Lance said, and he turned on the spot, Stephen could hear him running away from him towards the gate.

Stephen felt at peace and he could sense Kirsty kneeling-down next to him. Sirens resonated around them and he could see the flashing in the sky and on the floor before him. Stephen tried to slide his legs backwards, but he couldn't, his energy had gone. He could feel a small quiver underneath his skin, as his heart rate dropped. Stephen knew that by his heart doing the job it was meant to do, it was ultimately killing him.

Stephen knew his conscience was completely clear. He, hadn't killed his wife, he hadn't killed Roy; his weak heart had done that. Stephen knew he hadn't killed any of the guards he'd met during their escape. Stephen felt completely free and he knew that wherever he was going, was going to be much better than this place. Stephen wanted to rest here quietly, and with nothing but positive thoughts.

With his left hand, he felt around his body for the open wound. He found it in the area between his back and the side of his body and he could feel hot blood seeping from the wound. Stephen knew nothing he could do would matter now. He pictured his wife and knew he would do anything just to see her one more time.

Stephen became delirious and he stared at the woman in front of him. His white lips were turning blue. Kirsty's face came closer and he whispered, 'Stacey, I love you.'

'I love you too,' he heard in reply.

Stephen grimaced once more, and he felt a shock drive through his body. Stephen knew his heart was ceasing and he felt his body draining. Stephen couldn't feel his toes, or his legs and he felt his torso go completely numb as he lay motionless against the post as if anaesthetised. Stephen felt his right hand drop beside him and land harshly on the cold concrete. He couldn't raise it anymore and he resisted trying.

Stephen felt his eyes become heavy and just as he shut them, he heard the gate near him burst open, followed by flashing lights and loud sirens and he closed his eyes for last time, thinking of freedom and Stacey.

60

One Month Later

Lance stood in a graveyard in his orange overalls, with his hands cuffed together by a metal chain, which connected his hands to his ankles. Lance was listening to a priest and he was joined by several other inmates which he knew from his first sentence. He was looking upwards at the clear blue sky and he was thinking about his mistakes, which had come back to haunt him and his friends.

Lance kept thinking of the mistakes he had made; the first one being leaving Stephen too late. Lance kept seeing Stephen in his mind and he remembered Stephen telling him to leave. Lance had ignored it, which was a mistake as it hadn't gotten him very far, but it was also something Lance was proud of; either way he couldn't have won. Lance had gotten over the gate, with four long climbing strides and he had headed straight for the nearby woods.

Once in the woods, he traced round the outskirts of the woods trying to creep at a pace, but he came to water and he knew the only way to move forward was to walk on the road. He threw his orange top onto the moist ground and he begun to run along the dark road. He stopped when he saw sirens heading in his direction and he threw himself to the floor, attempting to hide.

He heard the police car stop for a moment and then he heard the engine roar and the car thundered forward onwards to the prison. Lance leant on one knee and watched the car travel further away from him. Lance remembered seeing the two towers in the background and they were silhouetted in the sky. Then Lance took a hard blow to the head and the next thing he remembered was being in a hospital bed.

The police car had dropped two police officers off to search the woods and Lance hadn't heard them approaching him on foot. They hit him with presumably a baton and caught him completely unaware. He knew when he woke up, that being caught meant it was the end. Lance was resentenced and an additional eight years were added to his already long sentence. Lance's main worry wasn't the prison term, it was more to do with another punishment; the loss of friends.

Lance looked down at the grave in front of him and then at the dozen people around him. There were around four people there who were also inmates including himself. The other three inmates were James, Lee and Johnny, all of who looked ten years older since Lance had last met them. They were all to be separated into different prisons and Lance knew they would never meet again. He was surprised that they had been allowed to attend this funeral.

There was an elderly couple stood opposite the prisoners. There was a bald man, who looked tired around the eyes. He was a short man and he looked distraught before them. The lady was crying into her husband's chest, and his arm's embraced her, as he in turn tried to fight the tears. She was just as tall as him, but her hair had a small black bow tied to the top of her head.

There were two men who were wearing smart suits, with waistcoats and a fabric type tie. They were cleanly shaven, and they looked sullen and full of guilt. Lance imagined they were previous colleagues and once friends. They had come to pay their final respects, but Lance couldn't help but feel being here today wouldn't wipe clean their guilty conscience.

The other people there were actual prison and police officials. Some had badges pinned to their chest, others stood in full uniform. Lance looked at them one by one and recognised none of them. He had seen some people enter and leave the prison before, on their way to meeting the warden, but none of these stood out. He knew they were here doing their bit to hide the scandal.

The priest at the head of the grave was around forty and he stood talking in monotone voice, showing his lack of care for the victim below him. Lance would have loved to have run at him, only to make him show some respect, but by the time he moved his first leg he would be down on the floor, another year heavier on his sentence.

The prison fire had spread considerably up into the ceilings and into the first- floor cells and it had taken over ten hours for the emergency services to control the situation and eradicate the flames. A handful of innocent people had died during the escape. Several other people had been injured and the whole event was still under investigation. The prison was still closed and was under rebuild, which meant every inmate was being kept at maximum security.

Lance had two guards behind him and there were four guards

spread evenly around the other three inmates. Lance turned his head down to the grave and he smiled a little. He knew the grave would hold someone he had always liked and someone who was completely innocent. He looked down at Stephen's wooden coffin and he thought about the car park again.

So much had happened since that fateful night and everything had been in favour of Stephen himself. Lance had talked about the events in the basement as soon as he was caught. He told them word for word what he had heard whilst he lay on the ground as Roy held a gun to their faces. How Ben found out about his childhood. How Roy had wormed the story from him. How Roy had employed a man called Xavier to take Stacey's life and how Stephen had taken the rap.

The police at first completely disregarded the story. That was until Kirsty Martin, who had been working under the alias of Lilian, stepped in and confirmed the story. The chief superintendent stepped in and reopened the case at the same time after spending time with Clifford Lovell. To Lance's relief, the fire hadn't spread to the guard's quarters and Ben's diaries had remained undamaged.

The police read the diary page by page; it took over two days to fully read the contents and make their anecdotal notes. After the second day, the police commissioner investigated Roy's entire life including his phone bill and his bank statements. They found over a dozen calls to a certain number around the time of Stacey's death and a sum of £50000 withdrawn within a short space of time before and after her death.

This led them to a man called Xavier. They questioned him aggressively. The police struck a deal with Xavier; the truth for immunity and witness protection. Apparently, Xavier had committed several murders for different people. He gave the names of the people he had helped and confessed to his part in Stacey's death, telling them the story of his and Roy's conversations.

The police were unable to convict Roy around the death of Bertie and Oliver, as they only had Lance and Kirsty's word. Lance grew to appreciate the work the police were doing. They had followed on with their investigation and taking all facts into consideration, they concluded Roy was behind the deaths of Stacey, Ben and Stephen.

Shortly after, the police apologised for the original trial. They opened proceedings on the officials involved with Stephen's sentence. The prosecutors were under investigation and some were suspended until further notice. A man called Frederick McManus and even his superior, were put on immediate leave and were under investigation too.

According to what Lance had heard, Frederick had been involved in a lot of insider dealing and had been completing tax fraud successfully every year. The prison was unable to hide the scandal and it seemed the jobs belonging to anyone who had ever met Stephen, were now up for debate. Lance was pleased that this had happened. Stephen deserved it and if it ever happened again, then Lance was sure the trial would be fairer.

Lance looked around the graveyard and he thought about the people that should have been here. Lance had heard about the main antagonists of the plan from James and Lee, who had almost escaped themselves, but fell at the final hurdle. They had been free for over four days and had spent the whole time with Keith and the other shifters. That was who Lance first started to think about.

James and Lee had said that Keith and the shifters had gone underground. James and Lee were due to meet them, but were captured in their hostel, after the owner had suspected they were dealing drugs. James and Lee were resentenced but hadn't been sent to a definitive prison. Keith and the other four shifters were still wanted, but Lance knew they'd only be found if they wanted to be found.

Lance imagined Keith going abroad with the nurse. He imagined him starting up a company listed in the Cayman Islands and he could see him sharing the profits with the other shifters. Lance knew Tony and Laurence would stick together, but he didn't know what Karl and Peter would do. Lance didn't even know if they would be ok on their own.

Roger and Phil were both captured during the tower fight. They had made a break to escape but along with half a dozen of their mates who had attacked the towers, they were captured by armed forces and were currently in the maximum facility. They weren't bothered about being captured and according to other inmates; they had already had four fights since.

Roger and Phil were facing life behind bars now after being convicted of manslaughter during the tower attack. Once they had infiltrated the tower, they had made their way to the top and taken control of the guns. They threw a single guard off the balcony and he fell just below the prison fence. Neither one of them admitted to doing it themselves, but they both said that they knew who had done it.

The rumour was that the towers would never open again. The new prison chief had made safety his number one priority and he said if you were to have a tower within the prison, it should only be occupied within the prison walls. Lance knew there was so much work for the authorities to do, and that his life wouldn't be settled for a while yet.

Lance looked at the priest, who threw a handful of mud into the grave. Lance had heard things about Malcolm spreading through the prison. Malcolm had apparently already changed his identity and was waiting for the dust to settle before he returned into the open. Lance never got to know Malcolm well, but he was a solitary figure and he wasn't surprised by the rumours.

Lance had found out what happened to Bernard. Bernard had after all cut open the fence and this had been talked about by inmates throughout the prison. Bernard hadn't been able to attend the funeral as he was still in maximum security. The prison was unable to convict Bernard of cutting the fence.

Lance watched another handful of mud bounce off the coffin below him. Lance wondered where they had buried Ben. He had heard rumours that he was buried near his mother, but Lance didn't think this was true as after all, he was one who killed his mother. Ben had admitted to it eventually. Lance kept thinking about how Ben had managed to keep his secret for so long and how he managed to help capture Stephen.

Lance didn't like that idea, but the one thing he took on a positive note was that Ben had worked hard at the end, trying to bring Roy down and trying to help his brother, who never knew about him. Lance couldn't understand the thinking behind Ben; why did he have such an issue with Stephen? Stephen seemed to be at fault for everything. It should have stopped with their father, but neither Ben, or, Roy agreed with that.

Lance tried to think about whether Ben would have been welcomed into the escaping group had he just told everyone he was Stephen's brother. Lance didn't understand why he hadn't before, but he guessed it was because he had no way to prove it. Lance also guessed he was scared to approach the group through fear of being attacked by Roger or Phil. Ben's last wish had been for Stephen to forgive him, but Lance doubted Stephen ever could.

Lance had heard rumours about Kirsty and how she was set for a promotion in her anti-corruption team. She had remained anonymous during her investigation on the prison and Roy. She had spoken freely about what she had heard, and she lied to her superior about how Lance escaped. Lance appreciated it, even though he hadn't got very far.

Lance looked at the police officials and he tried to count the badges pinned to their chests. Lance was still outraged like most of the inmates and their families that Roy had been allowed to work at the prison for so long and that he had been behind several deaths. They claimed the health and safety aspect was unacceptable and they said things had to change.

Lance hadn't slept properly since Stephen's death without waking up raging, his body covered and plastered in sweat, as he turned and faced Roy, whose eyes looked menacingly at him as he pulled the trigger and Stephen was gone. Lance didn't think he would ever get over Stephen's death. Lance watched as the vicar finished his service and made a short prayer. Stephen had been caught up in a complete storm, but this storm had brought them close together.

Stephen had got involved with the escape plans straight away. He gave it his all and he died trying. Lance knew he was just a fatality, just a statistic, but to him and everyone else inside, he was a hero. He was part of a group of individuals who had attempted to escape and made their break for freedom. Lance had heard the police were searching for only eleven people who had escaped, and he knew who at least six of them were. Lance wished he and Stephen were the twelfth and thirteenth.

Lance watched as the vicar walked away from the head of the grave and behind him, two young men appeared holding large shovels and they headed straight for the mound of wet dirt. Lance watched as the police officers turned their backs on the grave and headed for the car park. James, Lee and Johnny were staring at Lance and Lance nodded once to them; his way of saying goodbye.

The elderly couple stood looking down solemnly at their graves before them. Lance could tie the description Stephen had given him of Stacey's father to the man before him and Lance was pleased that they had closure. Lance just wished it hadn't come to this. Lance felt his cuffs tighten in front of him and he felt one of the guards grab his elbow.

Lance looked to the right of Stephen's grave and looked at the headstone belonging to Stacey Farley. He read her birth date along with her date of death. Lance read the message below the inscribed dates, reading aloud, *loved by all, always and forever.* Lance knew Stephen's would have the same message. Lance smiled to himself as he was led away; he knew Stephen would be happy now.

THE END

ACKNOWLEDGEMENTS

I'd like to thank my family; Mum, Kirsty, Nan Rena and Grandad Cliff for all the help and patience you've given me along the way as well as all the encouragement you've shown me. I am forever grateful.

My thanks also to my publisher James Essinger of The Conrad Press, my editor Francesca Garratt and to Charlotte Mouncey of Bookstyle for designing the cover.